THE GUILTY DIE TWICE

THE GUILTY DIE TWICE

DON HARTSHORN

Sign up for Don Hartshorn's newsletter at
www.donhartshorn.com/free

Published by TCK Publishing
www.TCKpublishing.com

Get discounts and special deals on books at
www.TCKpublishing.com/bookdeals

Check out additional discounts for bulk orders at
www.TCKpublishing.com/bulk-book-orders

1

T HE HIGHWAY POINTED ARROW-STRAIGHT TO the horizon, leading Travis Lynch to very last place in the world he wanted to be. The state of Texas intended to put a man to death, and Travis had agreed to serve witness.

Two hundred miles in a car with no air conditioning. In the middle of a Texas summer. Fitting penance, Travis thought. A salty trickle rolled down his angled cheek, and his eyes wandered to the dashboard clock, one of the few amenities in his auto that still worked. Travis did the math in his head. Less than three hours left, a little over one-hundred-twenty miles to go.

Time enough.

He steered off the highway, following the signs that had been counting backwards for half an hour. "30 miles to Byrd's" had steadily become "1 Mile to Byrd's" and then "Exit Now for Byrd's" and Travis followed. His car rolled to a stop in the gravel parking lot of a gas station that had seen its better days half a century before. But there was shade under a huge live oak and signs for cold drinks, and it looked like the gas pumps were a few decades newer than the front door. Travis unfolded himself from behind the wheel; the seat adjustment was another thing his car had given up on, and the driver's seat was stuck halfway between too far up for him and too far back for his wife.

"You're open, right?" Travis called to the thin older man standing in the dim recesses under the overhang. The man wore a dark uniform that blended in with the shadows so well it seemed he was nothing more than a pale, suspicious face and gnarled hands clutching a red shop rag. The man nodded slowly, once.

"I like to keep it local when I can," Travis continued as he pumped his own gas. "No sense putting another buck in a big corporation's pocket."

The man stepped to the edge of the shade, the tips of his shoes just sticking out into the sunlight. A shiver ran up Travis's spine as the man stared at him, silently accusing him.

"How long has this place been here?" Travis asked, nerves making his voice a touch too loud.

"Quite a while," the man said, his words colored by an East Texas twang. He kept his chin raised as if he were waiting for Travis to try something underhanded. "We got cold water inside, looks like you could use some."

"Definitely," Travis sighed, slapping his hand on his car's griddle-hot roof, "I picked the wrong day to be out in this piece of junk."

The man stepped off the porch and out from under the overhang, squinting in the bright sunlight. His black work shirt and black slacks perfectly matched his shoes, and his black cap kept his face in the shade. He continued to wipe his hands with the red shop rag, though Travis couldn't see a spot of grease.

"Car can't be much older than you," the man said. His chin lowered just a touch.

Travis flashed a friendly grin and shook his head. "My parents got this for me when I graduated high school. Brand new. I'm the only owner. Trying to be frugal, you know?"

The old man's chin raised again and his eyes narrowed. "You look familiar."

Travis's heart dropped into his stomach but his smile didn't waver. "Never been here before."

Strong, gnarled hands kneaded the red shop rag as the old man held Travis transfixed in his thoughtful gaze. "Been on the TV?"

Travis glanced away, telegraphing the lie. "Nope."

The old man glared suspiciously and stood his ground as if he were guarding the worn-out building from burglars. As the pump trickled gas into the tank, Travis could feel the man's eyes on him. Judging him.

"Where you coming from?"

A lump formed in Travis's throat and he coughed self-consciously. "Austin."

The old man jammed the red rag into his back pocket, suddenly done with fidgeting.

"Where you going?" The words were a condemnation.

"East." How slow could this gas pump be?

"There's a whole lot of Texas east of here."

"Huntsville." Travis didn't look up.

The numbers ticked over on the pump and the hot breeze brushed Travis's cheek. His eyes flicked to his black suit draped carefully across the back seat, laid out and pressed, not soaked with perspiration. He'd change when he got there.

"I know where I seen you," the old man said. "You're one of those Lynch boys. Jake?"

Drops of sweat falling from his forehead spattered Travis's hands. "Jake's my brother. I'm the other one."

The old man folded his hands across his chest. He'd made up his mind about Travis years ago. "How long until the execution?"

"Three hours." Travis's face burned hot but it had nothing to do with the weather.

"Take you almost that long to get the rest of the way," the old man snarled. "Probably wouldn't be a good idea for you to hang around after you're done paying for your gas."

"Probably not," Travis agreed.

Tension hung in the District Attorney's office like a poison fog: thick, heavy, and deadly. Staff kept their conversations quiet, supervisors closed their usually-open doors, and anyone who could come up with an excuse to get away had fled hours ago. The DA, Jake Lynch, was having an extremely bad day, and he was eager to share it with anyone who crossed his path.

Jake leaned back in his chair, his eyes flicking toward the clock on the wall, which hadn't budged since the last time he checked. He sighed and ran a hand across what was left of his blonde hair, feeling the heat radiating from his scalp. He didn't need a mirror to know that the first pink blush of frustration that typically showed on his cheeks now had to be a red-hot angry beacon from his neck to the top of his head. Jake's body had always betrayed his moods.

His fingers curled around the file in his hand, threatening to crumple it. If the day wasn't already difficult enough, he had to deal with this garbage. Unacceptable. Like they were trying to make him angry.

"Susan?" Jake called from his chair, knowing his voice carried through the entire office. The desk in front of Jake's door sat conspicuously empty, his assistant nowhere in sight.

Jake's teeth ground together, but he took five deep breaths before he got to his feet. Just like he'd promised his wife Rita he would.

"Susan?" Despite his best efforts to stay calm his voice came out dramatically louder. And angrier. "Susan, get in here."

His assistant didn't answer. Jake kicked his chair back and stood, determined to collect himself, to still his roiling temper. For a brief instant it felt like his anger might have found a release, like it might have been melting away. Then his eyes caught the clock again and his shoulders tightened painfully. His feet practically stomping holes in the floor, he stalked out of his office.

Jake cut an imposing figure, not because he was tall (nature dealt his younger brother Travis that card) but because he radiated a muscular anger, a violent energy that would either spark a similar fire in others or burn them down. In court, this aura had won Jake dozens of cases; in the office, it won him nothing but fear.

Jake's broad shoulders and thick neck came from his college football days, his thinning blonde hair and flushed face came from his mother's side of the family, and the early wrinkles around his eyes were a legacy from his father's father. The misdirected fury was all his.

"Goddamn it!" he yelled as he surveyed his assistant's vacant desk. "Anybody know where she went?"

Silence answered him. All his attorneys, all his paralegals, all the assistants and secretaries and computer guys found somewhere else to look, something else to occupy them. No one dared to speak for fear of attracting Jake's attention and becoming the surrogate for his rage.

"Velasquez," Jake growled, his gaze settling on a tall, slender man with a thousand-dollar suit and a politician's salt-and-pepper haircut. "In my office. Now."

For the briefest moment, Bobby Velasquez's mouth popped open like a suffocating goldfish's, but he regained his composure in an instant. He paused to tug at his tie, adjust his cuffs, and flash a too-white smile before he headed straight for his boss.

Jake felt the tension release like a needle jabbing an overinflated balloon. Normally loathed in the office, at that moment Velasquez could have been elected President; he was taking the bullet for everyone else.

"Today, Bobby," Jake growled as he disappeared behind his big oak door.

Jake was already in his chair when Velasquez eased in, his brash charm outside the boss's office turning into timid apology once he crossed the threshold.

"I've been going over the upcoming docket," Jake said quietly, tapping the file in front of him, "and imagine my surprise when I looked at the Baker case."

He didn't ask Velasquez to sit, leaving his subordinate standing awkwardly at the corner of his desk.

"I assigned that case to Doyle," Jake said slowly, carefully, even though he could feel his face getting hotter.

"Doyle had too much on his plate," Velasquez explained hastily. "I offered to help."

"Since when are case assignments your call?" Jake growled. "You get what you get and you make the best of it."

"I did that, Jake," Velasquez said, deciding to take a seat uninvited. He leaned eagerly onto Jake's desk, as if he were arguing in court. "Made the best of it. Baker's in the bag."

Jake raised an eyebrow, glaring. "Oh?"

"They want to plead," Velasquez continued, practically gushing, "and I think it's a good deal."

For a very long time Jake said nothing. He leaned back in his chair as Velasquez waited, his expression hopeful but guarded. Once again the DA's eyes wandered to the clock, with hands that moved on a geologic time scale.

"No way," Jake barked, glad to see Velasquez's expression collapse to confused disappointment. "I need a conviction, not a plea."

"What do you mean?" Velasquez stammered, his face turning red as he stifled his outrage. "It's solid. His attorney's behind the deal."

"The deal's solid?" Rising, Jake felt completely in control, more than he had for the past several days. "That case is open and shut. I could empanel a jury of nuns and they'd hang him."

For a moment, one instant, Velasquez seemed about to object, about to give Jake a piece of his mind, but he swallowed his outrage.

"All right," Velasquez said finally. "No deal. I'll inform opposing counsel."

"You mean Doyle is going to inform them," Jake corrected.

Defeated, Velasquez nodded. "You think if we go to trial we're getting a conviction?"

"Doyle will," Jake responded. Yet again his gaze wandered back to the clock, but he forced himself to focus on the issue in front of him. Velasquez. Anxious, enthusiastic, impatient, hungry Velasquez.

"I guess I can see your point," Velasquez said, rising timidly. "As far as the public is concerned a conviction's better than a plea. And next year's …"

"… an election year," Jake interrupted. He refused to look at the clock just over Velasquez's shoulder. "Yes, I know. Go tell Doyle he's got Baker again."

His back stiff, Velasquez retreated. As much as he disliked being reversed, he disliked being replaced even more—it showed in his expression. Jake knew the look well, he'd worn one exactly like it many times after encounters with his old boss, the previous DA.

Velasquez stopped at the threshold and turned, obviously working up to something. Jake waited patiently, making it no easier.

The junior DA licked his lips and swallowed. "Jake, I know there's no delicate way to put this, so I'm going to come right out and say it."

"You're wondering who's going to replace Rosenbaum?" Jake asked. He was glad to see surprise flash across Velasquez's face—as if he weren't as easy to read as a children's book.

"Well, he was your second," Velasquez said. "You need a number two. Seriously. There's a lot of work backing up that no one tells you about."

"I know everything that goes on in this office," Jake growled.

"With all due respect—" Velasquez began.

"You want the job?" Jake interrupted.

"Are you offering it to me?" Velasquez knew his boss too well to give in to hope, but it was there, buried under the smarmy political exterior.

"No," Jake snapped. The last thing he needed was to give authority to the office backstabber. Velasquez didn't move, and Jake's temper rose again. "Anything else?"

"Aren't you going home?"

"It's not quitting time, Bobby," Jake said, turning his attention to the stacks of paper on his desk. "You got something to do that you need me out of the office?"

"No, no," Velasquez protested. "It's just ... it's tonight."

"What is?"

"Reilly Sutton," Velasquez answered. "His execution. Six p.m."

"Oh?" Jake said nonchalantly, his eyes drawn back to the slowly-advancing hands of the clock on the wall. "Yeah, I guess it is."

"What do you owe this guy?"

Travis could still hear his wife's words echo in his ears even though he'd left her back in Austin. Shirley Rojas—she hadn't taken his last name—had stared up at him, her green eyes blazing, boring into Travis's own.

"You were done with him years ago, why do you want to revisit the past? What does that case mean to you?"

Everything, Travis thought, but the word wouldn't come out. Couldn't come out. He hadn't anticipated his wife's objection, and it made him wonder how much she knew.

"How do you know they're even going to let you in?" his wife had demanded, putting herself between him and the front door.

Travis explained it all—again—and worked his way around her and out the door. Shirley was furious, as mad as he'd ever seen her, but she let him go. When she got on her tiptoes to kiss him goodbye, the tears on her face mixed with his own.

He put his hand to his cheek, feeling the tracks that had dried two hundred miles ago. She didn't want him to go, almost demanded he stay, and now that he had arrived, Travis was perfectly willing to admit his wife had been right. His hands shook as he shrugged on the black jacket and fumbled with the black necktie. The sun beating on his back was another penance, righteous judgement for what he'd done. For what he'd allowed to happen.

He slipped his car keys in his pocket and tossed his sweaty, wrinkled shorts into the back seat. He was now dressed in his courtroom finest after changing in the parking lot like he'd been at the beach. Despite the itchy black wool suit, it still wasn't too late, he could just get in his car and drive off and no one would ever know that he had been here. But a coward avoided pain; a real man drove into the wasteland of his soul, head held high.

Travis locked his car and glanced at the protestors across the street from the Huntsville Unit, waiting for one of them to recognize him, but none of them did. He tugged at his jacket and took a few deep breaths. This was going to happen, and he was going to be there for it. He walked up the steps and through the gate.

His passage to the viewing chamber was a blur of forms, instructions, metal detectors, and stern guards. They took his cell phone and inspected his shoes for contraband. Travis allowed himself to be led, threatened, lectured, and finally escorted to the viewing room.

Tiny, not more than fifteen feet across, the chamber held two rows of chairs. Travis counted ten people, including the corrections officers. No one sat. Through a wall of glass, Travis saw the place where Reilly Sutton would at last face his Maker. The table was smaller than

Travis thought it would be, nothing more than a modified hospital gurney, with straps to tie the offender in a position suited for …

Travis blinked and looked away. Bile rose to the back of his throat, and his stomach wrapped itself into a painful, nauseous ball. As difficult as he imagined this would be, it was already ten times harder—and Sutton hadn't even been led in yet.

"It's never a pleasant sight," a woman said softly over his right shoulder, "and I've been to a few of these."

He knew the husky, smoky voice. Christine Morton, political reporter for television, newspaper, and Internet, stood at his side.

"Been a while, hasn't it, Travis?" she said, holding her hand out.

He hadn't seen her in person in years, and he was surprised to see her aged very little. A few extra lines around the eyes, any gray hair hidden under the salon blonde, but nothing dramatic, nothing out of place. She seemed nearly the same as the pretty, driven, iconoclast reporter he had encountered years ago at the beginning of the Sutton trial. Time had been kind to the one person Travis hoped would endure every cruelty.

Travis felt his face getting hot as he tried to ignore her. The only other thing to see, however, was the terrible, empty table on the other side of the glass. After a moment, Travis looked at his shoes, feeling like a child shamed into acting properly.

"These are the press seats," Morton said, gesturing at two metal chairs in the back row.

"I'm with the family," Travis mumbled. "Or I would be, if they were coming."

Morton's eyebrows raised but she just pointed at an empty row of chairs on the glass, a sad testament to Sutton's character, another tragic note in the awful symphony of his life.

"Would you like to make a statement?" Morton asked. Even here, on this day, she displayed no sense of propriety.

"This isn't about me," Travis hissed. His mouth was dry, and his forehead had broken out in a cold sweat. Why did he think he had to be here?

Morton took out a small pad and a pencil. "Is there any reason your brother didn't come?"

"You'd have to ask him yourself," Travis replied curtly.

The officers stirred, and on the other side of the glass a door opened and a gang of guards escorted Reilly Wayne Sutton into the chamber. He had lost weight on death row, his thick neck now shrunken, his once-powerful arms now thin sticks in his white prison uniform. His brown hair was cut short, making his bald spot even more prominent, and his dark, sunken eyes contrasted with his pallid skin.

He shuffled between the guards who towered over him, his haunted face catching sight of the table. Sutton pulled back, instinct telling him to try one last time to avoid the inevitable. The guards dragged him forward, lifting him onto the table as if he were a child. Sutton struggled for a moment, then lost all fight as the first of the restraints closed over his ankle. The guard on his right arm pulled the sleeve up, exposing the soft spot at the crook of the elbow, the place where the needle would go. As Sutton surrendered to the process, he turned his head to look through the glass, his pathetic gaze catching Travis's eye and freezing Travis's soul.

"So you don't have anything to say?" Morton pressed.

"Show some respect," Travis spat as he glanced away. He swallowed, his lips pressed tight, as his stomach threatened to rebel. His breath came shallow and fast, close to hyperventilating. He lowered himself into one of the empty chairs and Morton sat directly behind him.

On Travis's side of the glass, a man in a neat suit cleared his throat. It took Travis a moment to recognize the warden, who reached for the switch on an ancient intercom.

"Reilly Sutton," he said, formally and with ceremony, "do you have any last words?" Travis expected someone in that position to approach his job with a cold distance, but the warden's voice caught. His fingers trembled just like Travis's and his eyes glistened with unshed tears.

Sutton had been paying attention to the doctor inserting the needle into his arm, but he turned his head away to look out through the glass. Travis had expected Sutton to deliver his last words standing up, but that final dignity was denied him, he had to make his statement on his back, strapped to the instrument of his death.

"I didn't live a good life," Sutton said, and the familiar Central Texas drawl took Travis back years in an instant. "I could have done better. Should have. I know that now."

Sutton glanced from the warden to the guards. "I did a lot of bad things. I hurt a lot of people. But what you're doing ain't right. It ain't ever gonna be right, no matter how you try to justify it."

Travis's heart leapt into his throat as Sutton looked directly at him again. Tears welled in Travis's eyes. Why in God's name did he think he had to be here?

Sutton broke the gaze, glanced at the needle in his arm, then nodded once.

The doctor slowly injected a solution into Sutton's arm.

"That's sodium thiopental," Morton whispered. "It's a sedative."

Travis nodded; he'd read up on the procedure. But that didn't make witnessing it easier. He leaned forward, trying to take deeper breaths, trying not to fall over or pass out. Morton slapped a small waxed paper sack into his hand and pressed it there until he took it. She never shifted her gaze from the scene on the other side of the glass.

In less than a minute Sutton's eyes fluttered, and his body relaxed as if he had just fallen asleep. The doctor injected a second solution into Sutton's arm.

"Pancuronium bromide," Morton said softly. "Stops breathing."

Travis knew he should have been angry with her for talking during this moment, but now he needed something, even Christine Morton's words, to put limits on this experience. He hadn't been in the vet's office when they put down family pets, but he was here now. He was watching a man die.

Sutton's chest stopped moving. The doctor injected a third solution.

"Potassium chloride," Morton said, and Travis was surprised to hear her voice quiver. "Stops the heart."

On the table, Sutton didn't change. He didn't jerk, didn't convulse, didn't cry out. The doctor checked his heartbeat, did the various tests to make certain a person was dead, and began filling out a form on a clipboard.

"Reilly Wayne Sutton expired at 6:09 p.m.," the warden said.

Morton diligently jotted the information down. She was trying to project a calm, professional attitude, but her hand shook as she absently twirled her hair around her finger. She rose, putting her things into her purse with a deliberate rhythm, a slow-motion repetition of her regular habit, as if she didn't trust herself to move too fast.

Travis tried to stand, he tried to do like Morton did and pretend this was routine. But his legs refused to obey him. He tried to push up with his arms but they fell limp and his hands shook uncontrollably.

The doctor and the guards began preparing Sutton's body to make the journey to wherever it was bound. Travis heard the others filing out, and he knew the guards waited for him, but he couldn't stand, not just yet. It was difficult to wrap his mind around: five minutes ago Sutton had been alive, speaking, thinking, breathing, and now he wasn't any of those things. He made the transition silently, and, Travis hoped, painlessly.

"We should go," Morton said gently.

Nodding, Travis tried to stand again. He made it halfway to his feet before his legs gave out and he collapsed back into the chair. His vision blurred as nausea overcame him. Someone grabbed his head and pushed it forward between his knees.

Travis coughed and gasped and vomited what little was in his stomach into the paper sack Morton had given him. Then he retched again. And again. He heaved and choked until there was nothing left, until his stomach muscles cramped and tears streamed down his face.

"And that's that," Morton said, her hand on Travis's shoulder.

When he looked up, the execution chamber was vacant. Sutton was gone.

2

THE SUN HAD GONE DOWN hours before, yet the hot, moist air was still a stifling curtain that inflamed tempers and put the restless on the move. In a quiet neighborhood north of the university, on a quaint street where students lived side-by-side with hard-working folks, three young men pretended they belonged where they didn't.

Sam Park paced nervously in front of Roger Laubach's twenty-year-old piece-of-crap car, a white econo-box that hadn't been cool even when it was brand new. Roger sat in the driver's seat facing straight ahead, his fingers tight on the steering wheel, his fat, olive-skinned face all scrunched and worried. Such a pussy—if Roger hadn't been the only one with a car, Sam would have let him stay home to jerk off to Japanese porn. As he walked the length of the car and back again Sam stared at his cell phone, eager for the text message he was expecting.

"They punked out, didn't they?" Mark Kidd called out from the back seat. He sat with his hands across his narrow chest, sullen and angry, his eyes nothing but black pits beneath his thick brows.

"It's not time yet," Sam snapped, even though he was thinking the same thing. "Besides, they better not leave us hanging."

"Or else what?" Mark sulked, stroking the scraggly, wispy excuse for a beard that clung to his sharp chin like Spanish moss hanging off an oak tree.

"Keep it down, dipshit," Sam muttered.

"Weren't they supposed to be here half an hour ago?"

Sam slapped the roof of Roger's car sharply. "I mean it: Just shut up. It'll happen, okay?"

"It better happen soon," Mark groused. "I'm getting hungry, and it's hot and Goddamn Roger won't turn on the AC."

"It uses too much gas," Roger protested weakly.

Sam's phone buzzed, startling him so badly he nearly dropped it. Roger's eyes grew wide, but he kept his hands glued to the wheel as Sam read the message.

"They're on the way," Sam said. His phone buzzed again, another message. "Crap. They changed it. They want to meet at some construction site. Off Mopac."

Mark grumbled from the back seat, and even in the darkness Sam could see him roll his eyes. "Don't want to keep those assholes waiting, do we?"

"Listen, you'd better be on board," Sam said, talking past Roger who tapped furiously on his cell phone. "We can't have someone who's only in halfway."

Mark frowned and turned his head, concealing his face in the midnight shadows.

"Dammit, we all have to be together on this," Sam said. "Otherwise we might as well forget the whole thing."

Sam wanted to punch somebody, kick something. They'd been planning this for so long, they'd been so careful and tried to think of every angle. Tonight was the big score, only some of them—fucking Mark—were getting cold feet. And stupid fat bastard Roger was so hyped up and nervous he looked guilty without even doing anything. It was all falling apart.

"There are two constructions sites on Mopac," Roger said, his voice cracking. He held up his phone which showed a grid of Austin streets and a bright blue line for driving directions. "Which one are they at?"

"Are you fucking kidding me?" Sam snapped. "You're mapping it on your cell phone? Jesus!"

"You're the one texting." Mark's voice was a sullen drone from the darkness.

"Yeah, but I got … I got a plan for that … " Sam said, realizing Mark was right. Texting. Like the cops weren't going to look for that. "I'm gonna … when we get … "

"Shut the fuck up and get in the car," Mark snapped. "Let's get this over with."

"You're not even gonna do it," Sam said, too loudly.

"I'm the one in the car," Mark said. "You're the one walking around outside like a pussy."

"Can we count on you?" Sam asked, catching sight of his straight black hair and unmistakably Asian features in the rear window. Christ, he looked like his father.

"To do what?" Mark asked. "Beat up some rich fucks? Hell, yeah. To be your bitch? No way."

"This isn't just me," Sam said. "This is for all of us."

"Whatever," Mark said, looking at his watch. "In five minutes, I'm walking."

Frustrated almost to tears, Sam paced back and forth beside the car. He knew he could count on Roger, the kid probably would have asked permission to breathe if his body didn't do it for him. But Mark was a problem: He was too independent, too much his own man.

"All right," Sam said after a moment's consideration, "but you better stick to the plan. No cowboy shit, understand?"

"Don't you worry about me," Mark said. "I know what I'm doing."

"You'd better," Sam said, crossing in front of the car as Roger cranked the engine. "We're the Three Musketeers."

"If they were poor," Mark muttered.

"This car smells like your dad, man."

Three boys, Peter Carlisle, Kenny Galipo, and Shane Ablin sat in Peter's father's BMW, adrenaline pumping and blood boiling. New high school seniors, all three stood over six feet tall, all three lettered in multiple sports, and all three knew that tonight, they were fucking invincible.

"Shut up, Kenny," Peter snapped. Sometimes Kenny just didn't get it. When you were going to make a deal like this, you had to keep cool, you couldn't let yourself get distracted.

Peter squinted out the window, scanning for headlights on the road leading into the dark and lonely construction area. What had once been rolling hills with scrub grass and mesquite trees had been scraped down to dirt and rocks, space for a new housing development. Dots of streetlights were the only illumination, in a neighborhood a few hundred yards away.

"You think they're gonna show?" Shane asked from the back seat. He looked around at the deserted darkness of the construction site, wondering which shadow their contacts lurked behind.

"Definitely," Peter said. "They're counting on making five thousand bucks tonight. If they can even count that high."

The others laughed, but it came out forced, awkward, like strangers in a crowded elevator.

"What if they bring more than three guys?" Shane asked.

"Shut up," Peter said. He looked in the rearview mirror as a car drove past in the inky darkness. The vehicle didn't even slow. That wasn't their contact, and it wasn't the cops. He nervously rubbed his misshapen nose, broken three times over the years in basketball games. "Things are going to go just like they're supposed to."

"No, Shane's got a point," Kenny said. "What if they bring four guys?"

"You're the one on the wrestling team," Peter snapped, unwilling to be questioned. "You're such a badass, *you* take care of the extra one."

Kenny didn't respond. He sucked on his teeth like an old man, a habit from when he wore a retainer. The sound drove Peter insane, but he ignored it for now.

"Nothing's gonna happen," Peter said casually, confidently. "And if something does, so what? We can handle it."

"Like you've done this before," Shane said

"At least I'm taking it seriously," Peter said, drumming his knuckles nervously against the window.

"And I'm not?" Shane said. "If it wasn't for me you wouldn't even know where to go."

"Yeah, you're an original gangsta," Peter snarled.

"Hey, is that them?" Kenny said, looking out the rear window.

Roger braked to a squealing stop on a graveled stretch of roughly-graded road. The car's headlights shone on the rear bumper of a sleek new car just ahead.

"Is that them?" Roger whispered.

"Yeah, I recognize the Beemer," Sam said. He squinted through the rear window of the car in front of them, trying to count silhouettes.

"You sure?" Roger asked, his voice quavering. "They could be someone else."

"I see three guys," Sam replied with more confidence than he felt. "Besides, who else could it be?"

Roger, Sam, and Mark stayed in the car, their breathing heavy, their hands shaking. A few yards away the kids in the BMW did the same. Nobody moved.

"Are we going to sit here all night?" Mark asked.

"I'm doing the talking," Sam ordered. "You two just wait for me to give the signal."

"What's the signal?" Roger asked, and Sam just sighed. Clueless. Utterly fucking clueless.

"You'll know," Sam replied, cracking his knuckles. "What kind of high school kid drives a Beemer anyway? Coming out here like they own the place. Bastards."

"Dude, what did they ever do to you?" Mark said.

"Don't call me 'dude,'" Sam snapped. "It makes you sound like them. Stupid rich kids. Do you want to be like them?"

"If I could drive a car like that," Roger mumbled.

"I swear to God, I'm going to punch you in the throat," Sam snapped, seething. He was working himself up, making himself angrier and angrier.

"You think they're just going to hand it over?" Mark asked.

"They will if they know what's good for them," Sam muttered.

"Not if you don't have any leverage," Mark muttered. "Something they can't ignore."

"What?" Sam replied.

"They're all big, aren't they?" Roger interrupted. "I remember that black guy Shane had big shoulders."

"Don't worry," Sam said. "I …"

"Dude, don't say 'I got it all covered,'" Mark snapped, "because you don't."

Sam fumed, barely holding back his temper. Even his own people refused to give him the respect he was due. If he had any idea at all how to launder five thousand dollars, he would just as soon have left Mark home. But people asked questions when a poor kid showed up with brand new clothes or shiny new rims, and if anyone knew how to spread five thousand around with no one noticing, Mark was the one.

"I have it covered," Sam finished. "I thought of everything. Trust me."

"What's the deal?" Shane said anxiously. "Who goes first? Didn't you figure that out?"

"It's them," Peter said, surprised at how confident he could sound when he had absolutely no idea what he was talking about. "I'm pretty sure. No. Yeah, it's them. They're supposed to come to us."

The sound of creaking doors echoed across the construction site, and the three inside the BMW tensed up as shadows interrupted the other car's headlights.

"I see one, two," Peter counted in the mirror as the other kids emerged from their car, "and three. Unless they got someone lying on the floorboards, there's only three. Just like we agreed."

"At least they can follow directions," Kenny said, cracking his knuckles. "If the fat one runs, I get him, okay?"

"Just be cool," Peter said, rubbing his finger nervously underneath his nose.

"I'm cool," Kenny said. He took a deep breath and unbuckled his seatbelt. He pressed against the passenger door and grabbed the handle. Peter shook his head. Not yet.

In the back seat, Shane turned around and squinted into the darkness behind them. "What are they doing?"

Peter craned his neck. One of the shadowy figures lifted the trunk of their pathetic beater, another creak sounding through the night air.

"I don't know," Peter said, feeling a tingling at the back of his neck. Something wasn't right. It wasn't supposed to go this way. "Getting the stuff, I guess."

"Should we get out?" Shane asked.

"I don't know what …" Peter stuttered, his heart pounding in his ears as he stared into the rearview mirror. Something wasn't right. It almost looked like the other three were arguing? This wasn't the way things were supposed to go at all.

"This is gonna be so cool," Shane said. "Think of all the money we're gonna make. Who needs an allowance, right?

"We haven't made the deal yet," Kenny said.

"Yeah, but when we do," Shane said, "we're gonna be kings."

Peter shifted nervously in his seat. Just yards behind the car the scruffy kids from the wrong side of Austin closed the trunk and turned his way.

"Guys, I don't like this," Peter said, reaching for the ignition.

On the scraped earth that would one day be a pleasant boulevard, three figures stepped in front of the headlights of the white car, their voices low and fast as they gestured sharply, still arguing.

The BMW roared to life. Behind it, one of the shadow-cloaked figures stepped forward and raised a gun, while the other two stepped back in shock and surprise.

Inside the BMW, the first shot took Peter Carlisle in the back of the head, spattering blood and gray matter forward across the windshield, killing him instantly. The next two shots hit him in the neck, making his lifeless form jerk and jump.

The next five shots hit Shane Ablin in the back, perforating his aorta and severing his spinal column, making him slump forward against the front passenger seat even as foamy blood poured from his mouth. Shane's agony lasted long seconds until most of his blood left his body. He died with his eyes open.

The crack of gunfire, the splintering of auto glass, the dull thud of bullets hitting bodies, his friends' death rattles: These were the sounds of Kenny Galipo's world coming to an end. Fire burned along his right arm, and he saw his own blood flowing dark and glistening in the scarce light. He knew what had happened, he'd seen the truth on Peter's face, but it was too late. Reality spattered across his face as Peter fell forward from that one perfect, terrible shot.

Kenny reached for the door, but something was wrong. His fingers curled awkwardly, and all the blood made it hard to grip the handle. He twisted and pulled, filled with an animal instinct to run as far and as fast as possible. But he couldn't feel his legs.

Sam stared at the gun on the ground as if it were a rabid animal.

"What the fuck just happened?" he whispered.

"Shut up, shut up, shut up …" Mark wrung his hands, flapping them like they'd been burned. He pushed past Sam and headed for Roger's car.

Sam looked to Roger, who blinked, slack-jawed, in the headlights. Useless.

The BMW's tires crunched across the gravel and over shards of shattered safety glass as the car rolled slowly down the slight grade, only to jolt to a stop less than fifty feet away on a mound of banked earth, the engine still idling, three bodies slumped in their seats.

"Wait … you can't just …" Sam sputtered, turning to follow Mark.

"I told you to *shut up*," Mark spat as he paced back and forth in front of Roger's car. "I knew it was a stupid idea. I knew it."

Sam looked back at the BMW, still idling, its passenger door yawning open. A flicker beyond caught his attention. There were houses on the other side of the construction area, less than a quarter mile away. Lights blinked on and dogs barked.

"People heard us," Sam hissed.

Roger was already at the BMW, peering into it as he waved a flashlight around. He retched and coughed and cleared his throat. "I'm pretty sure the guy driving is dead. I think they all are."

"Fuck," Sam muttered. He looked to Mark, whose jaw dropped. "What do we do?"

"No, wait," Roger called out. He shone the flashlight into the open passenger door. "I think this one's still alive."

Sam stepped toward the BMW, accidentally kicking the pistol, which skidded across the packed gravel. There was an odd scent on the air: kind of burned, kind of sweet, kind of metallic, like nothing Sam had encountered before. Was that what gunpowder smelled like?

He turned back toward the car, but Mark was nowhere to be seen. He'd become one of the shadows, leaving Sam and Roger alone.

"Son of a bitch," Sam spat. "We need to go."

"I don't think they brought the five thousand dollars," Roger called out. He leaned inside the car, his flashlight catching the bright red spatters on the shattered windows.

"Fuck me," Sam whispered. How had this all gone so wrong so fast? Fucking Mark. "We need to go *now*."

Roger's voice echoed from inside the car. "Shouldn't we at least take their wallets?"

Sam hesitated, then he reached down and picked up the pistol with two fingers. The warm metal was heavy, the balance unfamiliar. This was all Mark's fault. And he wasn't going to get away with it.

"You're right. We need to get something out of this."

3

CONSCIOUSNESS BROKE OVER JAKE IN small, painful waves, each ripple nudging him that much closer to waking. As he surfaced, he felt a dull ache spreading across his shoulders and running up his neck, terminating in his right temple, where his pulse beat an agonizing rhythm against the inside of his skull. His body felt twisted and cramped, contorted unnaturally as if he'd fallen half out of bed. He lifted his head, only to find it weighed three times what it should have.

He stirred, pushing himself upright and regretfully coming to. He turned toward warmth, and sunlight pierced his eyes, a white-hot torment that sent his pulse throbbing so hard he hoped his head might burst.

For a moment, Jake didn't know where he was; he felt like he was wrapped in gauze, all his senses dulled. Then his vision cleared and he found himself in his office, teetering in the chair behind his desk where he had been slumped over. His bleary eyes focused on a nearly-empty bottle of Jim Beam and an upended shot glass that glittered like a diamond in the light streaming through the window.

It was morning. He'd been here all night.

Rita. Jake clamped his hands to his throbbing temples as the thought of what his wife was going to do made his head spin into new spasms of agony. He needed to call her. He felt for the spot on his belt where his cell phone should be, but his belt was gone and the cell phone with it.

He reached for the desk phone and stopped halfway. Not only was that phone also missing, his desk and office had become a miserable shambles; an avalanche of scattered files and papers littered every flat surface and the floor from wall to wall. What had previously been an ordered system now was the ragged aftermath of a tornado. And there was the desk phone, upside-down and unplugged, resting on the file cabinet.

His tongue was a fur-coated lump, and every time he blinked, it felt like his lids scraped sandpaper across his eyes. Hobbling on unsteady legs, Jake went to his window where the sun beat down at him with unblinking severity. With a sharp tug on the blinds, he sent his office into darkness, hiding himself from the judgement of the heavens. He looked at the wall where the clock was supposed to be, finding only a blank space. A vague recollection floated through Jake's mind—of him furious with the clock, seeing an enemy in its circular face.

"Susan?" Jake squeaked, his voice a coarse, feeble whisper. "I need you to call …" He broke off, rubbing his aching throat.

Jake leaned back against the desk, needing something solid beneath him. His eyes went back to the bottle of bourbon. And to the file underneath it. It was an old file, the DA's office hadn't used that kind in years, and Jake squinted as he tried to read the hand-written label, red ink scribbled across the tab.

Sutton.

The previous night's events dribbled back to him in still-life memories, sepia-toned moments frozen in time.

Cracking open the bourbon at five-forty-five p.m. to salute Reilly Wayne Sutton and the bitter end he'd demanded.

Pouring himself another three fingers at quarter after six when the warden called to let him know Sutton had gone.

Feeling an inexplicable tear roll down his cheek at five after eight and reaching for the bottle again.

Throwing the desk phone across the room at nine-thirty after the sixth reporter called to ask him how he felt about the execution.

Yanking the clock from the wall at midnight, convinced it would run backwards and Sutton would rise from the grave.

With shaking fingers, Jake picked up the file. He didn't remember trashing his office, but he must have been looking for this.

He'd so carefully misplaced it that he'd legitimately forgotten where he'd hidden it, but in his bourbon fog he'd found it—God only knows where it had been—and used it for a pillow. His first real success, his last dismal failure.

A low hum finally penetrated the cotton in his head, and Jake looked around his office, searching for the source. At first he thought it was his lost cellphone, but, no—the noise wasn't electronic. It sounded more like … people.

The realization hit Jake like a slap to the face. It was a week day. A work day. The District Attorney was still in business, and it sounded like something big was happening just beyond his locked door. Jake stumbled across the wasteland his office had become, and after a moment's fumbling, his fingers thick sausages that barely obeyed him, he threw the door wide.

The DA's office buzzed like a stirred-up hornet's nest. People darted back and forth, yelled at one another across the room, everyone on the knife-edge of panic. When Jake emerged from his office a wave of shocked silence radiated from his door across the room, calming ripples in a turbulent pond. One by one, heads turned his way.

"Holy crap, you're here?" Susan snapped.

Mid-fifties, matronly, and tougher than a Green Beret, Susan had been Jake's office admin since he was elected DA the first time. Nothing could surprise her—except the sight of her boss coming out of an office she assumed was empty.

"What's up?" Jake croaked.

Susan took a breath, hesitating. This was bad news. She never hesitated, ever. Despite his efforts to remain calm, Jake felt his heart begin to race.

"Thank God you showed up," Velasquez called from across the room. He hurried over to Jake, letting a relieved young clerk get back to her work.

"I never left," Jake said, closing his door behind him, hiding the disaster area.

"Let's go in your office," Velasquez said, advancing like he was going to take a beachhead. He'd obviously put himself in charge when they thought Jake was out, and he had the entire staff in a blind panic.

If he wanted to be second-in-command of the office, he wasn't making a very good show of it.

"Just fucking tell me," Jake said, his skull throbbing with his heartbeat.

"Two kids shot dead last night, one survivor wounded at least twice. He might not make it," Velasquez reported, puffing up as if he already had a conviction.

"So?" Jake replied. "Why is everyone panicked? What's the big deal?"

"The newspaper reporters have been lined up outside since before the sun came up," Susan said.

"What *for*?" Jake loudly demanded as the last remnants of his patience shredded into tiny bits. "Who got shot? Little kids or punks who should know better?"

"This is a big deal, Jake," Velasquez said, leaning in confidentially, as if no one else in the office knew what was sending them all into a tailspin.

"Goddamn it, Bobby ... " Jake said, his face growing redder by the moment.

"One of the dead kids is Dave Carlisle's boy," Susan said plainly, just as Velasquez opened his mouth.

"Carlisle?" Jake could feel the heat rising from his chin and over the top of his head. "Are you sure?"

"Positive ID, confirmed by the medical examiner," Susan said.

"Son of a bitch." In an instant, the morning Jake thought couldn't get any worse, did.

Much, much worse.

In a quiet corner of Austin's west side, a small, neat house stood under a giant, spreading ash tree, one of many similar dwellings built after the Korean War but before Vietnam. Its thin walls left the interior hot in summer and cold in winter, but the roof was watertight and the doors locked. The front porch was wide enough to receive guests or leave a package, and the back porch was big enough to have a few friends over to grill burgers. In its time, the house had served as home to students, teachers, businessmen, and dreamers, been the site of many minor injuries, some major accidents, two births, and one death. Now it was the home and office for Travis Lynch, Esq. and his wife.

Travis wiped a bead of sweat from his forehead as he listened to the clicking, sputtering window-unit air conditioner. That was not a good noise: the sound of a machine about to fail. Another expense he didn't need.

"Excuse me?" the woman sitting on his couch prompted, a touch timidly. "Mr. Lynch? You were going to say something?"

He stifled the urge to flinch. He'd actually forgotten his client, who was sitting two feet from him. Just zoned out, listening to the air conditioner, his mind four hundred miles east. He smiled at the lady, a thin, sad-looking woman who looked to be in her late forties but was actually—according to her driver's license—in her early thirties. He hesitated before he spoke. What was her name?

"I'm sorry, Mrs. Steenman," he said, her name rolling off his tongue as if it lived there. "I have a lot on my mind."

"Oh, I can imagine," she replied politely. "I saw the news. Terrible, terrible thing. That poor man."

Travis's throat tightened and his stomach spasmed. He bit the inside of his cheek, forcing the emotion back, shoving it down inside where it wouldn't get loose again. "Well, thank you, but that's no excuse for not giving you my complete attention."

He cleared his throat and busied himself organizing long pages dense with legalese. He placed a stack on the coffee table and handed his client a pen. "If you initial on the X and then put your signature at the bottom, this will all be wrapped up."

Mrs. Steenman hesitated, the pen in her hand shaking slightly. "Are you sure?"

Travis smiled reassuringly. "Positive. We'll file this with the county, and you'll get a letter in a few weeks. Then it's done. They'll leave you alone.

She lowered the pen but stopped short of putting it to paper. She looked up at him, her eyes wary as a cornered possum's. "What about, you know … paying you?"

The smile froze on Travis's face. He and Shirley had had a "discussion" about finances early this morning as they were brushing their teeth. Things were tight this month—just like every month—and Travis was awash in pro bono work. They just couldn't afford to keep helping people who couldn't pay.

But one look at Mrs. Steenman's haunted, desperate expression drove all thoughts of money out of Travis's mind. She needed help, and he was the only person who could help her.

"We'll figure something out," Travis said reassuringly.

"I don't see how," Mrs. Steenman sighed. She put the pen down and started to sniffle, tears welling in her eyes. "I have just enough each month to cover rent and food. I can't even afford new shoes for the kids."

Travis wrapped an arm around her shoulder. "Then save up for shoes, and worry about paying me later."

"Really?" Mrs. Steenman asked, hopeful but still guarded. "Like layaway?"

"In reverse, sure," Travis replied. He pressed her hand to the page.

As soon as she finished signing, Mrs. Steenman exhaled heavily, as if she'd just come to the end of a particularly grueling race. "I never thought I'd see this day. Thank you, Mr. Lynch."

Travis stood, shaking her grateful hand. "Glad to help. I'll have Shirley call you next week, to work out payments or something."

Mrs. Steenman practically ran for the door. "Thank you, again. So much."

The door closed behind her, a waft of hot from outside air billowing into the barely-less-hot inside. Travis watched as Mrs. Steenman fled down the walk and down the street, headed for the bus stop down the hill. Feeling his heart swell with pride, he turned back to the living room/office, only to find his wife standing by the couch, arms folded over her just-showing pregnant belly.

"'Work out payments or something'?" Shirley repeated, one eyebrow raised, her beautiful green eyes glaring. Standing barely five-foot-three, his wife seemed to occupy far more space when she was angry. And she'd been angry a lot lately.

"Maybe she can come in a few days a week to help file?" Travis offered.

"You know she's not going to answer when I call." Shirley pushed her dark hair back over her ears, the way she always did when she was upset.

Travis slumped onto the couch. "What was I supposed to do? Turn her away? They were going to take her kids, Shirley."

His wife's warm hands kneaded his tense shoulders. "I love your compassion, I really do. But we need paying clients, and not tomorrow. We need them today, right now."

"We needed them yesterday," Travis muttered.

Shirley continued to massage him, and, ever-so-slowly, Travis relaxed. "I really think you should go talk to Claire."

Travis shook his head but didn't respond. He wasn't going to have this conversation.

"How about your father?" Shirley said. "I know he doesn't really run things any longer, but Claire will listen to him."

"These people need help." Travis retreated into the kitchen, pretending to search for something to drink while visions of Reilly Wayne Sutton filled his mind.

"Why do you think you have to be the one to help them all?" Shirley demanded.

"Who else will?" Travis said angrily. He saw Sutton strapped to the table, looked into his desperate, pleading eyes. He heard Sutton's words: *This ain't right …*

Travis took a plastic cup and filled it with tap water, his hands shaking with emotion.

"This afternoon, I have to decide whether to pay the electric bill or the phone bill," Shirley said. "Maybe you want to make that decision? Or should we let the people getting your services for free do that?"

Travis slammed the cup into the sink, where it clattered and rattled loudly. "You don't understand."

Shirley followed him as he stalked out of the kitchen. "No, I don't," she said, as furious as her husband. "Why do these people mean more to you than I do?"

He stopped cold. "Did you think it would be like this?" Travis said softly.

"What do you mean?" Shirley asked.

"When you married me," Travis said, reaching out to take her hand. "Did you think it would be like this? You married into the Lynch family, after all."

"Travis …"

"It's okay, really," Travis said, squeezing her hand. "I know you wanted something more. When you talk to Claire or Mom, or even Rita, I can tell you're uncomfortable."

"That's because I don't like Rita," Shirley said. "Too much hair spray."

"Don't try to—" Travis broke off, his words failing. "You married the one Lynch with a conscience."

"Well," Shirley said, pursing her lips, "I can't say that I understood why you wanted to do this." She gestured at their small home, their nearly-bankrupt law practice. "But I didn't marry your family. I married you. And I'm with you, for better or for worse."

"Which part is this?" Travis asked.

Shirley smiled and shrugged, turning toward the kitchen. Travis sank onto the couch and put his hands to his face. He could still smell the execution room, the antiseptic aromas that reminded him so much of a funeral home. He could still hear the squeak of the metal chair under him. He could still feel his heart pounding as they injected the third drug into Sutton's arm.

Shirley's hands rested on his shoulders again, startling him out of his reverie. Travis had no idea how long he'd been zoned out this time, but it was long enough for his wife to make him a sandwich.

"He was there," Travis said without preamble. "Then a moment later he was gone. You could tell. There was something missing. I never … never watched someone …"

Shirley clutched him fiercely, holding him close.

The interior of the coffee shop was cool, a pleasant contrast to the summer heat just outside the door. The dark corner where Sam lurked suited him. He sat with his back to the wall, leaving no way to approach the table except directly from the front. He learned this trick from a movie when he was little, some Western with bad guys and a dusty saloon, and doing the same thing made him feel like a serious badass.

He'd nursed his drink for two hours now, while he waited for Mark to show up for work. Other green-aproned drones came and went, back and forth like happy worker bees, but Mark never showed. And Sam silently seethed.

Mark was gone. Disappeared. He wasn't at his job, his jerkoff friends hadn't seen him, he wasn't anywhere a complete tool like Mark hung out. He'd gone off the grid. Like an idiot. Might as well have signed a confession.

Sam took a tiny sip of his iced latte that was now mostly water and stared at the coffee shop door through his sunglasses. Roger was late too—he'd been out looking for Mark.

The odd odor from last night still lingered in Sam's mind, but this morning he'd finally placed it. Fireworks. The smoke smelled like the inside of that convenience store on the Indian reservation where they sold Chinese bottle rockets and Roman candles year-round. He remembered his brother Charlie coming home with a cardboard box full of fireworks; they'd spent the entire night launching them off a few at a time, then running like hell from the police. They'd gotten away with it, too.

"Oh, hey, I didn't recognize you," a cheerful voice said, too loud. Roger had made his entrance while Sam was preoccupied. "Why are you wearing sunglasses inside?"

"Sit the fuck down," Sam snapped.

Roger, the stupid fat bastard, picked the seat directly across from him, blocking his clear line of sight to the door. Sam just shook his head; there was no use trying to explain anything, Roger wouldn't understand it anyway.

"He wasn't at his house," Roger said, taking a big sip of whatever whipped-cream abomination he'd bought himself, "but his dad was."

The hair on the back of Sam's neck went up. "Wait a minute. Did you talk to his old man?"

"Yeah, it's cool though," Roger replied easily, "me and Mark had the same econ class last semester, the one I failed. I told his father I wanted to borrow the notes. He asked me where Mark was. He's not here, is he?"

"Does it *look* like motherfucking Mark is here?" Sam hissed.

Clueless, Roger took a moment to scan the room. "No. Are you sure he was clear on the plan?"

"It was his idea where to meet," Sam seethed. "Remember? 'Keep it normal.' Like he was some mastermind. 'Do what we always do. Go to work, play ball, whatever.' And then the fucker disappears."

Roger nodded absently, but Sam could see the implications slowly work through his thick skull. For a white guy, Roger could be so dense. After some consideration, Roger's expression turned indignant. "Yeah. He must have told me five times: 'Meet at the coffee shop.' Over and over and over. Like I'm stupid or something."

"I've been here all day and he hasn't shown." Sam waved his hand at the dolts surrounding him. "Tons of people, but no Mark. You know what that means."

"Fuck him," Roger said.

"Goddamn right," Sam said. He reached into his pocket, taking out a wad of twenty-dollar bills. "You got your share?"

Roger produced a few bills from his wallet, a thin stack, barely more than two hundred dollars' worth. "It's all there."

"I trust you," Sam replied, even as he quickly counted the cash. "Those BMW fucks sure aren't going to miss it."

Sam joined the two stacks of bills, counting them out. "Four-hundred-thirty-seven dollars." Sam frowned up at Roger. "All there?"

"I needed gas," Roger said apologetically. "And breakfast."

"Forget about it," Sam said. Twenty bucks wasn't going to make a difference, not when they had expected so much more.

He counted out two piles of bills, keeping a few twenties in reserve. He handed one pile to Roger. "Half for me, half for you. Mark can suck it."

"What about the extra?" Roger asked. He glanced nervously at the other customers in the coffee shop, but no one seemed to pay him and Sam any mind.

"This is the expense fund," Sam held the third stack out to Roger, who eyed it suspiciously. "It's for what needs to be done."

Roger blinked, uncomprehending. "What needs to be done?"

Sam glanced at a red-and-blue athletic bag on the floor by his feet. "It's in there."

"What is?"

Sam slid the bag over to Roger with his foot. "The thing you're going to hide in Mark's room."

"Me?" Roger asked warily.

"His father doesn't like me," Sam replied. "Maybe it's because I'm not in school like you guys."

His expression doubtful, Roger picked up the bag, testing its heft, shaking it from side to side like a Christmas present. He glanced inside, and his face went white. He froze, stuck there looking into the bag like he was staring into a crystal ball. The same smell of fireworks from last night drifted out of the bag.

"You can get in there again," Sam pressed. "Tell his father you really need those notes. It'll take two seconds to stash the gun."

"I don't know…. What if I get pulled over?" Roger was waffling. He didn't have the guts to do this alone.

"Then don't get pulled over. Just do what you always do," Sam replied. "Besides, he's the one who ran off. I'm not getting stuck holding it."

Roger's spine went straight and outrage twisted his features. He grabbed the cash from Sam's hand. "Yeah. He ran off. Left this with you and me. That son of a bitch."

"Calm down," Sam urged, motioning Roger to keep quiet. "We're taking care of it, aren't we?"

Roger nodded. "He's the one who left us. It's his fault."

"Goddamn right," Sam grumbled. "Make it look like he tried to hide it. Back of his closet or something."

Nodding, Roger rose and headed for the door. He proved surprisingly collected, just another douchebag leaving a coffee shop with a drink and a gym bag.

Sam eased back into his dark corner, watching the other patrons from behind his sunglasses. They were so clueless, all of them. Ignoring him like he was just some anonymous Asian face in the crowd. If they knew what had happened last night, they'd show him more respect.

TEN YEARS AGO.

Jake sat at his desk, head in his hands, as details of the trial ran through his mind. Where had things gone so wrong? He'd planned for everything, each contingency meticulously mapped out.

Except for one. Failure. Spectacular failure. Unanimous jury verdict failure.

His hands shook, and he thought he might throw up. He'd never felt like this before, so helpless, so out of control. He'd always had a clear path and he'd reached every goal he'd set for himself. But here, now, his fate was no longer his own and his careful plans had fallen apart.

"Tough break," Travis said, striding through the office as if this catastrophe were nothing unusual, just another day. Jake had questioned the wisdom of hiring his brother as his law clerk, but Mama insisted, and "no" wasn't an answer you gave to Mae Lynch. "You need a beer and I'm buying."

Jake shook his head. "Not tonight," Jake said, "I have to provide a debriefing. Try to explain … "

"Lynch!" a booming voice cut through the nearly-vacant DA's office. A short, stocky man barreled across the office. Matthew Caroll, the DA—and Jake's boss.

Jake's heart sank. He knew there'd be hell to pay, he just hoped to put it off a few hours.

"'Slam-dunk,' Lynch? Isn't that what you told me an hour ago?" Bloodshot eyes glared at Jake through thick lenses. "I expected the deputies to drag Sutton out of there in handcuffs. Instead he's giving me the finger as he walks out the door."

"I'm sorry, Matt," Jake stuttered. He glanced at Travis who took the hint and beat a hasty retreat. "The jury didn't return the verdict I expected."

"Because you didn't convince them," Caroll said, stabbing a thick finger into Jake's chest with each word. "My Assistant DAs secure convictions. It's your Goddamned job."

"I'm sorry—"

"That son of a bitch Sutton is back out on the street. Because of you." Caroll brushed his dark hair from his eyes. "What are you going to tell the next person he robs? 'Sorry, I thought it was a slam dunk?'"

"Look, Matt, the guy is a total recidivist," Jake replied, feeling like he was begging for his job. "He's gonna try to hold up another store, and I'll ... "

He trailed off, his face flushing with red-hot embarrassment.

"This isn't some exercise in class," Caroll said quietly. "This is the real fucking deal. You need to step it up, Lynch. And you need to remember that whatever Sutton does next, it's all because of you."

Jake squinted as the lights from the TV cameras shone full-on into his face. Like it wasn't hot enough in the tiny press room already without thousands of watts of illumination adding to the swelter. Trickles of sweat rolled down the back of his neck and it wasn't just from the heat and the lights. He hated doing press conferences. He hated answering stupid questions, and he hated being forced to be polite to people he would rather toss out on the sidewalk. He hated the way he looked on camera, heavy and plodding like a past-his-prime boxer. And today, of all days, his head throbbed and his swollen hands refused to grip anything reliably and loud noises—like a small room packed with people—pierced his brain, spoiling his concentration.

The bourbon had definitely been a very poor choice.

It had all been one slow-moving train wreck from the moment he came to, and the day wasn't getting the slightest bit better as he stood at the podium facing silhouetted reporters eager to ride this story like a stolen horse. These bandits of the Fourth Estate eyed him eagerly, willing to rob him of the tiniest bit of information for a screaming headline, even if they would compromise a witness or the entire investigation to do it. Each of them would ruin his efforts in a heartbeat if it meant more readers and viewers, but he had to pretend they were providing some kind of civic service, rather than chasing another dollar.

"I won't take questions," Jake began without preamble as the flashes from strobing cameras lit up the room, "I'm here to present the facts behind the shootings last night. Peter Brooks Carlisle, dead, multiple gunshot wounds. Shane Carlton Ablin, dead, multiple gunshot wounds. Kenneth Hamilton Galipo, critical condition and currently undergoing another surgery. All three of them seventeen years old, incoming high school seniors."

Jake paused, pretending to consult his notes but really just taking a moment to make sure his hands weren't shaking. The reporters grumbled, whispering to one another. What Jake had to say, they'd known for hours.

"Detectives have worked all day at the scene," Jake continued, "taking photographs, conducting interviews, doing their jobs so we in the DA's Office can do ours. Witnesses in the neighborhood can time the shots exactly: three-thirty in the morning. One of the neighbors even helped Kenneth Galipo, stopping the bleeding before the paramedics arrived."

Heads nodded and pencils scratched on notepads, the part about the neighbors helping the Galipo kid was new. Jake hoped it was enough.

"And that is where we stand," he concluded. "The investigation is ongoing, and so we can't comment further on the case."

Voices in the room rose, a small ripple of discontent becoming a giant wave of outrage before Jake could take two steps from the podium.

"Mr. Lynch!" Strident words rose above the others, setting Jake's teeth on edge. He knew the voice, and just hearing it made his blood boil.

Christine Morton elbowed her way to the front of the room, hand raised as if she were in school. "Jake! What about the shooters? The neighbors say there was more than one. What charges are you going to file?"

Jake mouthed "no comment" and turned away.

"Don't you think the families deserve some answers?" she pressed.

Jake walked for the door as the clamor from the media swelled louder.

"You're just going to ignore the grieving families, Jake?"

His hand on the doorknob, Jake stopped. Slowly he turned, looking back over his shoulder. There was Morton, front and center, her face set with its familiar smug, challenging expression, the queen bee of the local press. Jake was about to turn away but his eyes flicked past something familiar. No, *someone* familiar. Someone who shouldn't have been in the press room. A tall man, whose strong features and graying hair gave him an aura of dignity and importance.

"I'm sure Mr. Carlisle would appreciate details," Morton said. She laid one hand protectively on David Carlisle's shoulder and placed the other on a matronly black woman's arm. "So would Mrs. Ablin."

Jake's jaw clenched so hard he could hear the enamel grinding off his teeth. Morton, bitch that she was, had muscled the parents of two dead kids into the press room. Rage pure and raw flashed through Jake, and red tinged the edges of his vision. As if he didn't hate her enough already, Morton had just cemented her place at the very top of his enemies list.

Mrs. Ablin had obviously been sobbing; her red, swollen eyes searched Jake's face as he returned to the podium. Carlisle sniffed and swallowed and raised his chin as he fought back his grief. With two children of his own, Jake could easily imagine the agony they both felt—but when the victim was the son of one of the most powerful men in Austin, things were that much worse. Jake felt like he had been walking barefoot through broken glass all morning, every step taking him closer to this unwelcome encounter. He cleared his throat, all eyes and every camera in the room locked on him.

"Murder is a tragedy," Jake said carefully. "It's terrible to lose a life, especially such young men."

"That's not an answer, Jake," Morton said. She stood proudly, with her face turned in three-quarter profile so her cameraman could get her good side in the shot. "What charges are you going to bring?"

The room buzzed with a murmured consensus; they all wanted to know what Morton told them they wanted to know.

"It's barely been twelve hours, Christine," Jake snarled. "Back the fuck off."

Morton smiled, and Jake knew he'd given her the sound bite of the night. "I have a follow-up. Are you going to treat this case differently because all the victims are from well-to-do families in your own neighborhood?"

The room fell silent, but anticipation rang in the silence, like the pregnant suspense just before a thunderstorm broke. Carlisle did live on the same street—three houses down—and there was no reason to doubt Morton's assertion that the other two families lived nearby. Jake's face flushed hot, and he glared his rancor directly into her eyes.

"No—*you* are," Jake replied tersely. "Two men were murdered on the East side four days ago. Why don't I have to call a press conference for them? Because you don't care about them. I have the same number of DAs on that case as on this one. But your editors have assigned you bottom-feeders to make this senseless crime a twenty-four hour news event. And why? Because they're rich kids? How do you sleep at night, Christine?"

Morton just shrugged, pushing her blonde hair from her face to make sure her image was clear and bright as the cameras flashed. Her smug grin never faded as Jake allowed his staff to escort him from the room. Velasquez had gone white from head to toe, and the junior DAs were already discussing damage control. Jake didn't care: the truth was the truth, and he accepted the responsibility to speak it.

The conference room door closed behind him, and though Jake wanted to drop into a chair and sleep, he refused to show any weakness. He felt like he'd just been on a five-hour carnival ride, the sort of dangerous, rickety contraption run by gap-toothed yokels that was the wrong kind of scary—the fear-for-your-life kind.

"Pull her credentials," Jake barked, his words echoing in the hallway. None of his staff had to ask who he meant. "I don't want to see her face in there again."

The door to the press room swung wide and David Carlisle barged through, followed by Mrs. Ablin. Jake just caught a glimpse of Christine Morton's smarmy grin before the door closed again.

"I'm gonna get right to it," Carlisle said, his voice gravelly. His red rimmed eyes shone; his pale lips quivered. "When are you gonna get those bastards that killed my son?"

Beside him, Mrs. Ablin nodded her endorsement. Her hands wrung her scarf absently and tears rolled down her cheeks.

"The police are still in the earliest stages of their investigation," Jake said carefully. He waved off the junior DAs who tried to usher Carlisle and his guest away. "We don't have any concrete leads as to the culprits."

"Murderers," Carlisle said loudly. His eyes pierced Jake's, holding his attention like a mongoose staring down a cobra. "Tell it like it is. They killed my boy. And you're going to get them."

"You should take it easy—" Jake began.

"Find them," Carlisle demanded, stepping too close to Jake, invading his space, towering over him like a schoolyard bully. "I want their bastard heads."

Jake fought the urge to shove the man away. "Dave, before you go saying anything you're liable to regret, you might want to ask yourself what your boy was doing in an abandoned construction site at three in the morning."

A huge sob erupted from Mrs. Ablin and her hands flew to her face as emotion overcame her. Chagrined, Jake stood aside to let his staff escort the grieving mother to a chair.

"Damn you, Lynch," Carlisle hissed, still far too close. "My boy is dead, and you need to find the sons-of-bitches who did it. You got witnesses, descriptions. Get them and hang them from the nearest oak."

Taking Carlisle by the elbow, Jake tried to lead him down the hall. With a flourish, Carlisle pulled his arm free, glaring at Jake as if the DA had killed Peter himself.

"You can rest assured this office will pursue the case to its end," Jake said quietly, hoping Carlisle would take the hint, even if he didn't notice all the eyes turned their way. Downtown Austin was a rumor mill, and they'd already given the gossips far too much to talk about.

"Don't try to brush me off," Carlisle snarled. "I got you elected. I can get you un-elected, too."

Jake's heart skipped a beat; this was a threat Dave Carlisle could back up. Jake might have power in the DA's office, but even the DA owed others.

"Dave, you're understandably upset," Jake said, his voice almost a whisper.

"Goddamn right I'm upset," Carlisle said. "They put a bullet in the back of my boy's head! You find those bastards and you hang them. Or next election, you can get a new job." He poked his long finger square into Jake's face. "Do you read me, Lynch?"

"I'm sorry for your loss," Jake said softly, through clenched teeth, his temper a roaring lion he barely held back.

Carlisle hesitated. He'd obviously expected a fight; he'd done everything to provoke one, and now Jake refused to cooperate. The air went out of him, and the tall man shrank before Jake's eyes, shriveling as emotion overcame him at last. Jake took the grieving father under the arm and pulled him toward the DA's office. If nothing else, Carlisle could get a cup of black coffee and a comfortable chair for a while.

"Who would do something like that, Lynch?" Carlisle mumbled, close to sobbing incoherently. "What kind of monster would do that to another human being?"

Sam slammed the car door and slapped the roof, waving curtly to Roger, who nodded back. A bead of sweat rolled down Sam's cheek, one to match the others rolling down his neck and back. Stupid Roger still wouldn't turn on the air conditioning, so Sam had been hanging his head out the window all the way back from the mall, hoping for some relief from the heat. Roger's car wheezed and rattled as it pulled into traffic and tried to come to speed, like an old man with a walker trying to run. Sam glanced out of the corner of his eye, wondering if anyone in the neighborhood saw him get out of that ancient white piece of crap; Roger didn't know enough to be embarrassed, so Sam had to be embarrassed for him.

Pushing his shoulders back, letting his knees loosen, Sam sauntered down the sidewalk easily, proudly. He had a ways to go, and he wanted to look good getting there. Roger dropped him off at the corner, eight houses away from Sam's place, because Sam's mother didn't like Roger. She called him "shifty." Actually, she used the Korean word that also meant *sneaky and clever*, which Roger absolutely was not. Sam tried to defend Roger time and again, but his mother wouldn't hear it, so Roger just stopped coming by the house. It was easier than an argument every time Sam needed a ride somewhere.

The old man who was always out watering his lawn stood there now with the hose, giving Sam the stink eye. Sam held the man's gaze as he ambled past, flaunting the brand new, blinding white sneakers fresh from the most expensive shoe store in the mall. The old man sneered and shook his head, the same thing he always did, but instead of saying anything he turned away.

Sam stood a little straighter. It was about time he got more respect. And all it took was some new kicks, a creased pair of jeans and a shirt so starched it crackled.

He caught a few more eyes from both sides of the street, none of them admiring glances, but none of them dismissive either, not like they would have been two days ago. His neighbors saw the change in him, the change Sam felt deep in his bones. He used to be nobody, just another poor face on Austin's east side. Not anymore.

He pushed open the front door to find his mother sitting in a chair at the entrance, an envelope resting in her lap. She'd been waiting for him.

"Hey, Mom," Sam said in English as he headed for his room.

"Soon? What is this?" his mother, Min, asked in Korean, using his Korean name and brandishing the envelope as she leapt to her feet to intercept him, faster than her short, heavy frame suggested she could move. She looked more tired than usual, and Sam noticed the spots on the back of her hand as she nervously brushed back her gray-streaked black hair.

"Jeez, it's rent," Sam replied, still in English. He hated when his parents expected him to speak Korean, he spoke it like a five-year-old. "You're always after me to chip in, and when I do you get all freaked out about it."

His mother reached for his face, but her hand ended up behind his ear, rubbing the back of his head. "You got a haircut."

"I wanted it short, because it's too damn hot," Sam mumbled, gently pushing her away.

Min shoved the envelope in his face and Sam stared at the floor, unable to meet her gaze. "Where did you get this money?"

"I did some work," Sam muttered, the words thick in his mouth, as if they resisted being spoken.

"Good work?" Min asked, putting a hand under his chin and searching his face, "or the kind of work Chol did?"

Sam groaned painfully. She was like a scratched CD, saying the same thing over and over and over again. "Leave Charlie alone. At least he tried to make something of himself."

Min tugged at his brand-new pants and kicked his new shiny white shoes. "Did you work for these too?"

"Yeah," Sam grumbled. "It all came from the same job. But they didn't pay as much as I thought they would. Bastards."

Tears welled up in Min's eyes. "Chol talked like that before he got in trouble. I don't want you in trouble."

"I'm all right," Sam mumbled. He hated talking about his brother. His entire life he'd never really been Sam, he'd always been "Charlie's brother." It was time people knew him for himself.

"Soon, promise me you won't do what Chol did," Min said. She faced him directly now, searching his face, his eyes, trying to get inside his head. Sam squirmed uncomfortably, feeling pinned like one of those butterflies he saw in the museum.

"I'm not in trouble," he said, his voice cracking.

"Then tell me where you got the money for all these things," his mother said softly, sadly. As if she knew the truth.

"Some stuff I got going on, all right?" Sam exploded. "That's all you need to know!"

"What kind of work pays you this much money?" his mother demanded, waving the envelope in his face.

Sam pressed past his mother and stormed down the short hallway. He slammed the door to his room hard enough to shake the house to its rafters. Unbelievable. He kicked his bed, feeling like he could spit nails. With a single swipe, he shoved everything on his desk to the floor in a shower of spare change and an avalanche of paper. He raised his hand to punch the wall but stopped just short of actually letting loose.

What was her problem? She wanted him to get a job, to bring some money into the house, but when he did she turned into an FBI agent, full of questions.

A soft knock sounded at his door.

"Go away!" Sam yelled, fully expecting his mother to ignore his demands and barge in like she always did.

Nothing happened.

Sam watched the doorknob, waiting for it to turn, the announcement that his mother intended to continue the discussion. Nothing. He heard a noise from the hallway—it might have been a sigh, it might have been a sob—and the door rattled.

Without a word his mother pushed the envelope with the rent money under his door.

The stillness inside the intensive care unit took on a life of its own, a presence as real as any person, with its own demands and expectations. Normal speaking voices seemed too loud, brassy intrusions on the hushed environment, so nurses and physicians spoke only when absolutely necessary, using low, calm tones, huddling together for consultation, their only accompaniment the muted beeping of monitoring devices.

Kenny Galipo lay in the bed nearest the nurse's station, the spot reserved for the most desperate of cases. His skin ashen, his eyes closed and sunken, he looked half a corpse already, his breathing so shallow his chest scarcely moved. His parents had come and gone, allowed a visit but not allowed to stay, his mother touching his cheek with trembling fingers, her tears falling to the blanket that covered his body.

It was against hospital regulations for armed officers to be in the intensive care unit, but one stood in the hall just outside the door, his hand never very far from his sidearm. Nurse Hutchinson passed the officer with a curt nod and a barely-disguised sneer; it wasn't as if Kenny were going make a run for it, the neurologists said the kid was likely paralyzed from the waist down.

She took immediate charge of the unit, getting her updates from the duty nurses in short order. She scraped a foot across the linoleum, wondering what piece of equipment had scuffed the floor, when a one-note change in the monitors made her head snap around, calling her to immediate action. Something was going on in the number one bay.

The duty nurse beat her to the station, barely, checking the monitor first, then the patient. With a groan, Kenny Galipo struggled back to consciousness.

"Didn't they know this kid was an athlete?" Nurse Hutchinson said. "He's going to need more sedatives to keep him down."

"I'm taking care of it," the duty nurse said. Kenny's eyes went wide and he tried to talk, though nothing came out but gurgles and sputters.

"I know it hurts, son," Nurse Hutchinson said, patting Kenny on the forehead. "We're going to put you to sleep."

Shaking his head, Kenny tried to raise his hands to his face, grasping feebly at the tube down his throat.

"Help me here," Nurse Hutchinson said, grabbing Kenny's hand while the duty nurse grabbed the other. "We're going to have to tie him down."

Mustering as much strength as he could, Kenny wrenched his hand free, touching his right forefinger to his thumb and making round, fluid motions with his hand. Nurse Hutchinson paused, looking into his eyes, seeing the pleading, frantic need to communicate. Taking her pen from around her neck, Nurse Hutchinson handed it over with the pad from her pocket. With trembling fingers, Kenny Galipo scratched two words on the paper in spidery, wounded, yet determined strokes. When he finished, he let his hands fall, returning to a state of almost-consciousness.

Nurse Hutchinson read what Kenny wrote and sighed; she'd have to speak with the police officer outside. The two words Kenny scratched were a name.

Sam Park.

5

HE DIDN'T WANT THEIR SYMPATHY. Things were embarrassing enough already as they were.

Jake sat in the lunch room, doing penance by eating his terrible sandwich alone. The other Assistant DAs shook their heads sadly and left without looking back. Jake knew he was being difficult, he might even be acting out, but he just didn't feel like being around other people. Not while Sutton was a free man. Because of him.

Other people in the office had failed, of course they had. Probably even the old man, Matthew Caroll. The DA's office didn't have a one-hundred percent conviction rate: That was impossible. But failure was new to Jake. It left a bitter taste, like biting into a rotten apple, and even made him consider—for a brief moment—whether he might be better suited to a different career.

But lawyering was what the Lynches did, what they had always done and probably always would do. Working in the DA's office was the first step in the Lynch cursus honorum, and Jake wasn't about to disappoint his family by abandoning the calling. Besides, he had no idea what else he could possibly do.

The lunch room door burst open and Travis rushed in, flushed and gasping as if he'd just run ten miles. He grabbed a chair and practically sat on Jake, getting close as if he were sharing a secret in a crowd instead of an empty room.

"They arrested him again," Travis whispered, his breath still coming in bursts. "Sutton. He's out two days and the scumbag beat up his girlfriend. We can get him, Jake. We can make this one right."

A jolt of electricity flashed down Jake's spine. This was it. Redemption. The way to put his career back on track. The way to prove he belonged in the DA's office.

"We have to pull strings, twist arms, kiss ass," Jake instructed his little brother. "Do what you have to, promise anything, but I need that case."

A huge grin split Travis's face from ear to ear. "I already called in the big guns."

Travis pulled Jake to his feet and dragged him out of the lunch room. Across the office, at the big double doors leading to the DA's chambers, Jake saw a tall, thin, familiar figure. His father.

"Oh, Trav, tell me you didn't."

"I had to," Travis replied. "The case was on Rosenbaum's docket and Mr. Caroll wasn't about to give it to you."

Jake's father laughed and clapped Caroll on the shoulder like an old friend.

"Getting Dad to fight my battles … " Jake sighed.

"Look at it this way," Travis replied. "At least I didn't have to bring in Mama."

Travis raised his hand to shield his face from the sun, squinting as he stared at his house. It wasn't exactly a showplace: It was a little run-down if truth were told, the brown yard more weeds than grass and every tree in need of a careful pruning, not just the big one near the driveway. The siding was worn, the paint slightly too eclectic with its many hues. But the place did fit the neighborhood, right down to the rusted low chain-link fence around the front yard and the crazy quilt of a sidewalk bent and cracked into odd angles and thrusts.

Ten years ago, Travis would have driven past this neighborhood as he headed for one of the new malls in the suburbs. This side of Austin didn't really exist for him then. But now he understood that people needed a place like this, somewhere not so fancy, not so intimidating, somewhere the little guy could approach and know he belonged. Somewhere the poor could get help.

A gust of cold air hit him hard, and Travis raised his face to the sky. He turned around, chin thrust upward, looking for the rain he could taste in the atmosphere. Clouds rolled across the sun and the temperature dropped noticeably. Looking west, Travis finally saw the line of storms moving in, a dark band stretching north to south across the horizon. This was going to be a good one.

The labored sputtering of his car caught Travis's attention as Shirley piloted the ancient vehicle into the narrow driveway. With eyes like a hawk's, she spotted the large, flat boxes on the front porch before she'd brought the car to a complete stop. She frowned at her husband.

"How'd the checkup go?" Travis asked as he opened the driver's door for her.

"She says my blood pressure is getting a little high," Shirley replied, almost ignoring him as her green eyes glared at the boxes. "I need to watch the salt. What are those?"

"You remember Allen, don't you?" Travis prompted. "Unpaid taxes?"

Shirley sighed as she clambered out of the car, refusing to be hindered by her pregnant belly. "Allen Duron? With the mustache? He never paid *us*, either."

"He brought shingles a foreman let him have," Travis said. "For the roof. Working off his bill."

Shirley looked up at her husband, amusement mixing with disbelief on her face. "Barter? Trav, we can't pay the mortgage by bartering."

"And Allen Duron can't pay our invoice with cash," Travis replied, annoyed. "This is a win-win. All I need to do is find where the leak is coming from ..."

"Absolutely not," Shirley barked as the wind from the approaching storm whipped her hair. "You are not getting on that roof."

"What? Why?"

His wife sighed dramatically, shaking her head. "I'm a few months away from delivering your first child. You are not going up there just so you can fall off and break your neck and leave me all alone."

The cool wind blew faster, and Travis hung his head. "But you wouldn't be alone. You've got your family in Houston. And I guess there's always my family. Mom and Dad could help, and Claire …"

Travis trailed off as his wife glared at him, fuming.

"Seriously, Trav? You're telling me who can help with the baby when you die?"

Travis shook his head as Shirley stomped up the front steps, turning her nose up at the stack of brand new shingles.

The first fat drops fell as Travis stood on the sidewalk, wracking his brain to remember which of his clients knew anything about roofing. Before he could make it the last fifteen feet to the safety of the porch, thunder rolled and the heavens opened up. The blast of rain drenched him instantly. He ran inside, letting the wind slam the front door behind him.

Even though he was squarely in the doghouse, one look at his wife made Travis forget about the rain and the shingles and the leaky roof. She was beautiful on her worst day, but since she'd been pregnant she seemed to get prettier every hour. It was true what people said: Women carrying children glowed.

"You want some lemonade?" Shirley called from the kitchen as Travis heard her taking glasses from the cupboard. A peace offering, more or less.

"I can make us some sandwiches," Travis said as he eased through the doorway.

Shirley glanced up at him, one hand held protectively over her belly. "How did you get so wet?"

"Listen, I'm sorry—"

A knock sounded at the front door and both he and his wife turned toward it.

"You expecting someone?" Travis asked.

"No appointments today," Shirley replied. The floor creaked as she went to the front door.

Who would be out in the thunderstorm? Travis dropped ice into the glasses, determined to get back on his wife's good side.

Shirley reappeared in the kitchen, leaning against the doorway. Travis caught a look in her eye, an odd, stern expression.

"You have visitors," she said flatly. "Potential clients."

"What are you waiting for? Send them in."

Sighing, Shirley came to Travis's side, leaning in closely, casting a glance back into the office. "It's the Parks."

"Charlie and Sam's parents?" Travis said, trying to see around his wife.

Shirley nodded, her eyes locked to Travis's. "No more pro bono: We need people who can afford to pay."

"Shirley …"

Grabbing his face with her hand, Shirley squeezed hard. "Travis, we're barely keeping the lights on right now. If you keep helping deadbeats …"

Travis gently pulled his wife's hand away, giving it a furtive kiss he hoped would defuse the argument. "They're not deadbeats. They just don't have enough money to fight for themselves. They need an advocate."

Shirley cast an angry glance back into the living room, where the Parks waited. She flinched as a lightning flash strobed the house.

"What did they promise us for defending Charlie?" she asked.

"That's not the point," Travis hissed, turning away and shaking his head. This wasn't a discussion he wanted to have at all, let alone with the Parks not fifteen feet away.

"It is the point, Trav," Shirley said. "We can't run a law office on good wishes and IOUs. They still owe us."

"We apologize. It is hard for us to pay."

Travis and Shirley turned to find Min Park and her husband Bae standing in the doorway, rain dripping from their soaked clothes. Min stood with her eyes downcast, Bae stared defiantly ahead.

"I am so sorry, Mr. Park," Travis said. He chanced a stern look at Shirley, only to see her, angry and intractable, staring Bae down as surely as a junkyard dog cowed her rivals.

"We will pay," Bae said, appealing to Travis. "We can make arrangements."

Before Travis could respond, Shirley jumped in. "You made arrangements last time, and you still haven't paid a dime. We're not running a charity."

"Soon is in trouble," Min said, her dark, pleading eyes tugging at Travis's heart. "He won't say what happens, but he has money and no job. New clothes, new shoes, but he won't say what he does for them. This is just like Chol."

"But Sam's smart enough not to get caught," Shirley said. Outside, bright lightning flashed, but she didn't move a muscle, standing straight and tall as a bronze statue, staring down the Parks. Thunder rumbled close by and she didn't seem to notice.

"We need someone to help him," Bae said, "someone to stop him before he goes too far. You helped our family before. You helped Chol."

"I did my best," Travis said. "What did Sam do?"

Bae and Min paused, looking at one another. "We do not know. But it is not good."

"When was he arrested?" Travis said.

"He has not been arrested," Min replied.

Helpless, Travis glanced from his wife back to the Parks. He shrugged. "Unless he's been charged with something ..."

"You are a good man, Mr. Lynch," Bae said. He paused and looked pointedly at Shirley.

Shirley took the insult gracefully, though Travis could practically feel the waves of hot anger radiate off her. "I won't put you out in the rain," she said tersely, "but as soon as it stops, I want you to go."

Withdrawing slowly, almost regally, Shirley retreated up the back stairs, leaving the Parks with Travis. For only the second time in his life, Travis was at a complete loss for words. He had never seen his wife act like that. Somewhere, at some time, she had become as hard-nosed a businesswoman as his own mother. Not that he would ever tell Shirley that.

"My son, he is in very much trouble ..." Min said softly.

Bae spoke to her sharply in Korean. Travis didn't understand the words, but he knew the conversation, he'd seen it often in his practice, desperate parents trying to win the battle between their pride and their means. Min and Bae argued back and forth, until Min finally choked back a sob and nodded.

"Mr. Lynch," Bae said, "we are sorry for interrupting you. We are not wanted here, so we will leave."

"Tell your wife we are sorry," Min said, glancing at the ceiling. "Perhaps if we had more money, she would be nicer to us."

Her words were a knife to Travis's heart, and he prayed that Shirley could hear from upstairs.

"Maybe if you had more details," Travis said. "I know all kinds of social services, people Sam can talk to. But I can't really help you unless—"

"Unless we pay," Bae interrupted.

Travis shook his head. "Unless he's charged with a crime. I appreciate you coming to me, but I'm an attorney, not a social worker. I hope you understand."

"We will leave," Bae said, turning his wife toward the door.

"At least stay until it stops raining," Travis said, following them.

Lightning flashed and thunder cracked, but Bae shook his head, stubbornly proud as he reached for the door. "Rain will only get us wet."

The Parks left without lingering on the porch, marching from Travis's office into the rain. Travis watched them go, two small, frightened figures hurrying into the driving storm. He expected them to get into a car but there wasn't one outside, and it was only when they turned down the street that Travis realized they had taken the bus all the way here and they'd have to wait in the rain for the bus back.

Miserable, he collapsed onto the couch, mountains of paperwork still towering on the coffee table. Upstairs, he heard Shirley moving away from the window where she'd obviously been watching the Parks leave.

Travis picked up the nearest file and leafed through it, but his mind stayed on Bae and Min Park. He had no doubt that if Sam was anything like Charlie, the boy was up to something. But whatever trouble Sam was in, for the Parks' sake Travis hoped it was like the thunderstorm outside and would blow over soon.

6

TRAVIS HAD NEVER FELT MORE *like a little brother than now, sitting beside Jake with his hands folded carefully across his note pad, trying not to make eye contact across the table. Reilly Sutton sat two feet away, shackled into near-immobility. A tall man with a linebacker's build and a tuft of dark brown hair standing up on his balding head, Sutton's pale skin grew pink in the cheeks and ears as his temper flared. His nervous legs bobbed underneath the table, and every so often Sutton's dark eyes would meet Travis's own, an animal connection that let Travis know Sutton would just as soon gut him as look at him.*

"Jake, this is harassment," Sutton's attorney said. Ken Blevins was a Lynch family friend and a decent man. It must have hurt his soul to be assigned to defend Reilly Wayne Sutton.

"He beat his girlfriend and stole her car," Jake said. "The State is charging Mr. Sutton with those crimes. That's hardly harassment."

"Miss Grojean has already said she didn't want to press charges."

Sutton stirred, his handcuffs clanging loudly, but Blevins put his hand out, stilling the defendant.

"Only because she's afraid for her life," Jake replied. "We don't need her to press charges, the State does it for her. We have the photographs of the lacerations, x-rays of the broken bones, and we have Mr. Sutton's own admission to taking the car. Witnesses too, did I mention that? This is a slam dunk, Ken."

"Dammit!" Sutton exploded, slamming his hands on the table. Travis and Blevins jumped, but Jake remained rock-steady, his gaze locked to Sutton's, unwavering. "This is bullshit! You're out to get me!"

The uniformed officer advanced, hand on his Taser, and Sutton backed down immediately, still breathing hard and glaring with defiant eyes. Sutton was as dangerous a man as Travis had ever met; it would be better for everyone to have him back behind bars.

"All right, Jake," Blevins said, "I'll be plain. You didn't get a conviction before. My client's been out two days and all of a sudden he's back in, with the DA's office pressing charges that the supposed victim won't. You're not going to get this past a jury."

Jake shrugged expansively, nonchalantly. "I'm pretty sure I will. It's not murder, but it'll do."

Blevins said nothing, though concern furrowed his brow. He was a good attorney, waiting for the other side to reveal their cards first. Jake took his time searching his briefcase for some papers, flipping through the contents at a leisurely, almost carefree pace as the clock on the wall ticked the seconds by. Travis looked from his brother to Blevins and back again. One of them had to break first.

A small, short chuckle echoed in the small room. All eyes turned to Sutton, who wore a sinister, knowing grin.

"That's all you got, Lynch?" Sutton's deep voice dripped contempt. "Beating up some bitch who ain't even gonna testify?"

Blevins's hand landed on Sutton's. "Stop talking."

Travis's blood ran cold as Sutton's gaze met his, as the soulless glint in Sutton's eyes chilled him. Travis's lips quivered as he spoke. "What did you do?"

"I was playing pool all night, Junior," Sutton smirked.

"You're not conducting the interview, Travis," Jake growled.

"Jake, you can't let him get away with this!" Travis shouted as his brother pushed him out of the room. "He did something else!"

Jake entered the Lynch family law offices tentatively, almost furtively, like a supplicant instead of the first son. He waved sheepishly at the man behind the security desk in the lobby—Jake couldn't remember the man's name to save his life—and nodded politely to people who called him "Mr. Lynch." He didn't know if they recognized him from his press conferences or if they worked for Lynch and Brockhurst. There hadn't been a Brockhurst since Jake's grandfather's day, but for a law firm, name recognition was everything, so "Brockhurst" still hung in brass letters behind the receptionist's desk.

The receptionist was new, or at least she didn't look familiar, but before Jake could introduce himself two associates pounced on him, pumping his arm in fierce handshakes and trying to ask him about positions in the DA's office without seeming like they wanted to abandon the jobs they already had. Jake made his excuses and pushed past them and the people loitering in the surprisingly crowded lobby— were they all clients?—taking a right turn down a long, quiet, plushly carpeted hall toward his father's office.

With every step he took he felt like he should be glancing over his shoulder, waiting for Claire to challenge him. His little sister ran the family business now, moving their father into a well-deserved "advisory" role that left him with plenty of time to get in eighteen holes at the golf course several times a week.

The heavy door at the end of the hall hung slightly ajar, his father's signal that, yes, he was available, but you'd better have a good reason for bothering him. Through the opening, Jake could see the floor-to-ceiling bookshelves stacked with legal references, the old globe that still showed the USSR and Rhodesia, and the pistol in the glass case that had been there since before Jake was born. Time stood still for his father, evidently.

Jake stepped halfway through the doorway and knocked, drawing the attention of the gray-haired man with his ostrich-skin cowboy boots up on the desk. A thirty-years-older version of Jake's little brother Travis glanced up from his architectural digest, did a double-take, then grinned a charming and rakish smile.

"Look what the cat dragged in," Valentine Lynch said, coming around the desk with his hand outstretched. "What's it been, three years since you've been in here? Four?"

"Three," Jake replied, "since Claire took over."

"That's too damn long," Val said, pulling his son by the hand and practically shoving him into an overstuffed leather armchair. "Why don't you come around more?"

"Dad, we see each other almost every weekend," Jake replied, suddenly embarrassed. He had been avoiding setting foot in this office for a long time, avoiding even the mention of it.

"Sunday brunch isn't the family business," his father said. "But don't tell your mother I said that."

His father perched on the edge of his desk, an old oak monstrosity that had to weigh three hundred pounds. Jake had played under it when he was small, his father telling him eventually the desk would be his. Things hadn't worked out that way.

Val fixed Jake with that look he had, the one that said not only was he listening to everything you said, but he was just waiting for you to make a mistake. Sometimes when he talked to his father, Jake couldn't help but see Travis, the closest he'd come to his little brother in ten years. Both had angular faces, wise eyes, and ears that seemed just a touch too large for their heads, and both had a gentle manner that masked a rock-solid core. If he were to tell the truth, Jake envied Travis and how lucky he was to be so much like their father.

"Son, what the hell are you doing here?"

Jake fumbled, at a loss. "Do I have to have a reason?"

His father folded his hands across his chest and waited.

"It's been a miserable few days," Jake admitted, and even that tiny confession allowed him to relax a little bit. "This Carlisle case is something else."

"Tell me about it," Val said. "I've already had people calling me with questions."

Jake sighed. "Christine Morton?"

His father nodded. "One of these days you're going to have to tell me what happened between the two of you to make her hate you so much."

"She's a small part of it," Jake said. He took a deep breath, filling his nose with the familiar scents of his father's office. "I have to juggle the investigation, the press, the staff. The parents."

"Being the boss does suck sometimes," Val replied. "That's why I don't do it anymore."

Jake threw his hands up in frustration. "The media already labeled this the 'Rich Kid Murders.' Can you believe?"

Val waved a finger at his son. "That one's your fault, I saw the press conference."

"You did?"

"I watch 'em all," his father continued. "And you need to watch your temper. I swear, just like your mother … "

Jake stood and wandered to the bookcases, his fingers tracing the same lines across the wainscoting as they had in his childhood. "I loved coming in here when I was a kid. Did you know I used to rearrange these books? Did you ever notice?"

His father still sat on the edge of his desk, arms folded across his chest. The grin had disappeared though, replaced with an expression of resigned patience. "When you were a little boy it was kind of cute, watching you work your way around to the point. But you haven't been eight years old for a very long time, son."

As the heat spread up his face and across his head, Jake stared at the floor. By now he'd been an adult longer than he'd been a child, but his father could still make him feel like he was being scolded. "It's Carlisle. He's making demands."

"Oh, of course," his father sighed, clapping his hands softly, "I should have guessed. Been out of the game a little too long."

Valentine Lynch had run for governor twice, unsuccessfully. Jake had always gotten the impression that his father was relieved he hadn't won the nomination, that he was just going through the motions because that was what people expected him to do.

"Normally I can handle this sort of thing," Jake explained, his words coming a bit too fast, "I deal with bereaved families all the time. But this is different."

Already his father held his hand to his chin and stared up at the ceiling, his characteristic pose of contemplation. "It's not insurmountable. Carlisle's a vindictive bastard, though. Gotta walk softly around him. And, no offense, boy, but there's not a thing soft about you."

Jake sighed. "Thanks, Dad."

Val shook his head. "Don't thank me yet. This is about Carlisle's son. A man doesn't think straight when something happens to his family. I don't know what I would have done if that happened to one of you kids."

"I'll take any help you can give me."

Easing into his chair, Jake's father clomped his boots back onto his desk. "So why are you really here?"

Jake raised an eyebrow but didn't say anything.

"You could have told me about Carlisle over the phone," Val continued, gesturing with his architecture magazine, "or mentioned it Sunday over some eggs Benedict. Why did you come into this office after three years? Why now?"

Given their past interactions, Jake knew this was when he was supposed to take a seat. Instead, he wandered over to the pistol in the case and rested his eyes on the simple lines and gleaming nickel plating.

"Just the other day I was wondering if all this hassle was worth it." Jake stared at his reflection in the metal, not wanting to look his father in the eye. "I've been doing this for a while, and I wonder if I'm making a difference."

"Is that why you took the job?" his father asked.

Of course, were the words on his lips, but Jake didn't speak them. He thought for a moment, losing himself in the lines of the weapon in front of him.

"Not at first," he replied slowly. "It was more like something people expected me to do. I guess. And when I got elected, it just meant that I should be doing it. But it hasn't been fun for quite a while."

His father said nothing. Jake waited for condemnation, for the lecture about "that's why they call it work," and an admonition to get back to it. But the only sound in the room was the ticking of the wall clock, a slightly off-kilter masterpiece his father made with his own two hands.

"Believe it or not, I know exactly how you feel."

Jake dared to meet his father's gaze, only to find Val staring at the corner of his office, lost in a moment. "What do you mean?"

Val startled, and blinked, as if he only then realized where he was. "Nothing important. So let's get down to it. You've had a hard week at work, that prick Carlisle is getting under your skin, and you want to know if there's a spot for you at Lynch and Brockhurst."

"Um …" Jake cleared his throat, "is there?"

"Oh, Jake," his father said, a laugh in his voice, "absolutely not."

"What?" Jake looked for the joke in Val's eyes and found only sincerity.

His father shook his head. "You're the DA. The big cheese. If you came back here, what job would you want? Claire's? Well, Jacob Neill Lynch, your little sister is doing a bang-up job running this place, and I'm not about to ask her to stop just so you can have somewhere to hide."

Heat flushed his face and Jake looked away again. "I don't want her job."

"Come on, boy," Val said. "What other job would you be happy doing? You like being in charge. You're not used to asking anyone for anything. Do you think you're gonna kick me out of this office?"

Feeling just like a little kid again, Jake rubbed his toe at the carpet, as if he'd been caught stealing snacks from the big conference room. "I could do something else."

Val chuckled and shook his head.

A jarring vibration at his belt shook Jake from his petulant disappointment. He grabbed his phone and read quickly.

"Perfect," he said, more to himself than his father. "The Galipo kid gave us a name yesterday, and the Austin PD thinks they found the guy."

"You sure you want to give that up?" Val said. "Around here, there's a lot of asbestos, a lot of personal injury, mold, civil disputes. We don't really catch the bad guys. Not those kind of bad guys."

Jake's heart beat faster, and the flush he felt this time wasn't embarrassment, it was the thrill of the hunt. His father was right. Again. "Thanks, Dad. See you Sunday."

He was halfway out the door when his father's gentle cough stopped him.

"Somebody has to tell other people what to do, son," his father said gently. "Somebody has to make sure they do it. Somebody has to take responsibility for running a smooth operation, and somebody has to get the job done. That somebody's you, even if they hate you for it. That's what you signed up for."

Jake nodded. He did love being the DA—most of the time.

"We commend to Almighty God our brother Reilly Wayne Sutton, and we commit his body to the ground."

Travis expected he would feel something, but he was numb, watching with almost scientific detachment as the pastor scattered the coffin with crumbles of dirt in the shape of a cross.

"Earth to earth, ashes to ashes, dust to dust," the pastor continued as his words faded into the background.

The small cemetery occupied a few acres on the eastern outskirts of Austin, where the land flattened out somewhat and urban became rural. Tombstones tilted like jack-o-lantern teeth, and weeds and tall grass overran the ground. Today, five somber people gathered for a funeral led by a prison chaplain.

Travis lied to Shirley about where he was going; she wouldn't understand. So now, three days after he witnessed Sutton's demise, he stood beside a cool, dark hole in the ground and the simple pine coffin perched atop it. He didn't know himself why he was here, why he *had* to come, why he couldn't just let it go.

Stifled sobbing drew Travis's attention. A short, heavy woman dabbed at her smeared mascara, dribbled by her tears. She wore black denim and a black t-shirt, her harshly bleached hair tied back with a black ribbon; it was obviously as formal as she could manage. She glanced at Travis with red-rimmed eyes and smiled sadly.

" ... Kingdom and the power and the glory, for ever and ever. Amen." The pastor gently closed his liturgy, concluding the last gathering Reilly Sutton would ever be a part of.

Travis muttered "amen," the only sound he'd made since he'd trudged up the hill. The short woman and her three companions turned to him, and whatever resolve he had in reserve melted. He had walked into a private moment, forcing himself on the proceedings as if he had a right to attend.

"I didn't mean to intrude," Travis said, avoiding the woman's gaze. "I just wanted to pay my respects."

"That's all right, Mr. Lynch," she said, her voice low and gravelly from the cigarettes and beer that still lay on her breath. She extended her hand. "I'm Bubba's sister, Stephanie."

Travis could see the resemblance, Sutton and this woman in front of him. Same square face, same nose, same wary, probing eyes. Travis had seen that look before, not only on Sutton; it was the look of someone who'd been beaten, betrayed, and trodden on her entire life. The same look he saw on most of his clients.

"It's good that we could meet again," Travis said. He gestured at the near-derelict family plot. "Even if it had to be here."

"I should thank you for what you did for my brother," Stephanie replied, clutching his hand desperately before letting go.

Embarrassed, Travis couldn't meet her gaze. He stared instead at the casket still perched above the open grave, the final resting place for a terrible man. "That was ten years ago. I don't know that I actually made any kind of difference."

"Bubba made some bad choices," Stephanie said, dabbing at her eyes again. "Me and Mama, we just … after a while it kind of wears you down. You know? You want to be there for him, but when it's not doing nobody any good …"

She turned aside as the tears flowed again and sobs wracked her body. A whip-thin, angry-looking man gathered her in his arms and glared at Travis. Tattoos peeked out from the man's cuffs and collar, homemade work in ballpoint blue ink that testified to his time behind bars.

A stooped old woman tottered forward, steadied by the hand of a florid young man holding her by the elbow. She stared up at Travis through thick lenses, her rheumy blue eyes smearing and out of focus.

"I remember you from my son's last trial," the old woman muttered. "You're one of the Lynch boys."

"He's the good one, Mama," Stephanie called out loudly, her voice catching.

The old woman, Sutton's mother, laid a wrinkled, tiny hand on Travis's arm and held tight. "Was he saved, Mr. Lynch?"

"I'm sorry?" Travis sputtered, with another glance at the coffin. There had been no last-minute reprieve from the governor, no timely stay from any court. The needle had gone into Sutton's arm on schedule.

"Was he right with God?" the old woman pressed, pulling closer. Her lilac-scented perfume filled Travis's nostrils as she searched his face. "Reilly got kicked out of the church when he was younger than his nephew here. I never saw him take communion. I need to know, Mr. Lynch, did my boy find his salvation?"

She was drowning, a mother awash in unimaginable grief, flailing for the only rescue within reach. She wasn't crying, not in front of people—Travis recognized that from his own mother—but her nails dug into his arm.

"I don't think he talked to Bubba about that," Stephanie said, coming to her mother's side. She tried to pry her mother's hand off Travis's arm, but the old woman clung tight.

"Your son and I never really … " Travis sputtered. "What little interaction we had was ten years ago."

"You were there," Sutton's mother insisted, "at the last. That's what the warden said."

Travis wished he were anywhere else. "I was."

"The chaplain agreed to a proper Lutheran funeral," Sutton's mother said, her voice quavering, "but you tell me, Mr. Lynch. Did my boy know Jesus?"

Travis had no idea. None at all. But he swallowed painfully and looked Sutton's mother in the eye.

"Yes, ma'am, he did."

The old woman's lower lip trembled and she nodded to herself. She let go of Travis's arm and allowed her grandson to lead her slowly down the hill.

Stephanie sobbed anew, but she smiled at Travis and mouthed "thank you" before her husband took her by the hand to follow Sutton's mother. The pastor followed, offering condolences.

In a few moments, Travis stood alone beside the coffin that held all that remained of Reilly Sutton. By sundown, the box would be in the ground and the dirt beside the open grave would be mounded on top of it. The man was gone, but what he'd done still lived on, still had consequences that echoed now, ten years later. Travis didn't know whether to thank the memory of the man or damn him to hell forever for what he'd done.

After a moment's hesitation, Travis took a handful of dirt and sprinkled it on the coffin.

7

ALL CLEAR."

This time Sam didn't look around to make sure Roger knew what "all clear" meant. He sidled up to the car, slipped the slim jim between the window and its rubber seal and fished for the lever.

In less than five seconds, he had the car door open. Five seconds later, Roger leaned in and grabbed every loose item he could reach, tossing everything into a reusable grocery bag next to the car lockout kit. Five seconds after that, Sam had closed the door, and he and Roger walked off as if they were just crossing the parking lot on their way to somewhere else.

"This is so easy," Roger said, raising the bag so he could peer inside.

"Jesus, be cool," Sam snapped. He pushed the bag down and did a quick scan of the parking lot. No one seemed to have noticed them.

Roger let his arm drop and carried the bag stiffly at his side. He marched like a wind-up soldier, eyes straight ahead. He couldn't have looked guiltier if he'd been wearing a neon sign with an arrow pointing at him.

"I just wanted to see what we got," he whined.

"We're not trick-or-treating," Sam snapped. "It's not fucking Halloween. We'll sort it out when we're done."

Roger elbowed him in the ribs and nodded across the parking lot. A woman in office clothes slammed the door to an older mid-size import and stormed off toward the mall. She was angry, which meant she'd be careless, and she looked like the kind who left expensive things out in plain sight. She might have even forgotten to lock her car.

"What do you say?" Roger asked, his fat olive-skinned face brightening at the prospect of larceny. "One more?"

Sam took a breath, but before he could agree, a newer, dark-colored sedan rolled into the parking lot. There was nothing remarkable about the car, no markings, no lights, nothing special at all, but the hairs on the back of Sam's neck stood up.

Cops.

"I think we got enough for now," he said, looking away but keeping the car in sight. "No need to get greedy."

"Can you believe people just leave all this in their cars?" Roger said, following Sam like a dutiful pup. "I mean, these morons don't care."

"Shut up," Sam hissed. The dark sedan had rolled past them and the driver never looked back. But now a van with tinted windows followed the same line, creeping through the parking lot as slow as it could go without coming to a stop. A shudder crept up Sam's spine; he couldn't see into the van, but he could feel the eyes looking out. At him.

"I was just saying … " Roger muttered, hurt.

"Let's go this way," Sam said, turning Roger by the elbow and leading him back the way they had just come.

"My car's over there," Roger said, pointing over his shoulder, where the van had just turned around.

"Yeah, we need to be … I forgot something," Sam sputtered. It was impossible to tend to Roger and keep track of the two vehicles at the same time. No, not two. *Three.* A third carefully nondescript sedan rolled into the parking lot ahead of them.

One in front, two behind. Sam's heart beat faster. He had the distinct impression that he and Roger were being herded, pushed into a trap.

"Down here," Sam said, pulling Roger to the one part of the parking lot where there weren't any cars lurking.

"What the hell, man?" Roger protested. "Where are you going?"

"Just shut up and be cool," Sam muttered, even as his own cool was rapidly evaporating.

Four. A second van followed the second sedan, blocking off the far end of the parking lot. It was like a parade now, everyone following Sam and Roger.

"Drop the bag behind one of these cars," Sam said through clenched teeth.

Roger went white as a sheet. "Why? What's going on?"

Just then two clean-cut men stepped out of an SUV, each of them in plainclothes and flashing a badge.

"Sam Park?" the closest cop said, advancing quickly.

"Aw, crap …" Roger sighed.

"This will be a lot easier if you cooperate," the cop said.

"You got the wrong guy," Sam mumbled, backing away.

"I don't think so," the cop said. He grabbed for Sam's hand and the silvered glint of handcuffs flashed in the sunlight.

With a jerk and a twist, Sam pulled his fingers from the man's grasp and launched himself away, his legs pumping furiously. His heart threatened to burst from his chest, his only thought to get as far away as he could, as fast as he could. He caught one last glimpse of the look of betrayal on Roger's face before he ran for the low wall separating the parking lot from the street beyond.

They came out of nowhere, men in POLICE T-shirts converging on him with their badges dangling from their necks. At least six of them, big men, grim and determined. Sam cut left and dashed between two cars. If he could make it to the intersection, he just might have a chance …

Before he'd gone ten steps, Sam felt his legs kicked out from under him. His world spun and he hit the pavement hard. A heavy body landed on his back, knocking the air out of him. Hands grabbed his arms and his legs, and Sam couldn't even cry out in pain: He just winced as the tears filled his eyes.

The handcuffs were on before he could catch his breath, and a beefy, red-faced man tugged him roughly upright like he was a sack of potatoes.

"It wasn't my idea," Sam protested. "The other guy, Roger, he's the one carrying all the stuff. It's all his."

The officer rolled his eyes and shook his head. He marched Sam back to the SUV where the other officers waited, one of them holding Roger's grocery bag.

"You're a real piece of work, aren't you, Sam?" an older cop said. There was gray in his mustache; Sam guessed he was probably the boss. "Breaking into cars, too?"

Too?

"Hey, you know who this is, right?" the first cop, the one who'd tackled Sam, said. "This is Charlie Park's little brother."

The other officers nodded, as if that one bit of information answered all their questions and confirmed all their worst suspicions. A few of them were grinning, and soon all of them smirked and chuckled.

"What are you assholes laughing about?" Sam said. An odd, pungent odor wafted up his nose. Had he stepped in something?

A dark stain spread from the crotch of his brand new jeans down to his knees. He'd pissed himself when that buffalo of a cop jumped on his back.

The officer with the gray in his mustache stood over Sam, getting right in his face. Sam stared back at him with all the defiance he could muster while the other officers laughed at his urine-soaked pants.

"You're not such a tough guy without a gun, you piece of shit," the cop said with a satisfied grin. "Sam Park, you're under arrest for murder."

"S IT DOWN," JAKE COMMANDED AS he closed the door.

"You have to believe me," Travis insisted, walking to the window of the conference room, "he didn't just almost beat his girlfriend to death. Christ, listen to me ... 'Just' beat a woman half to death. Like that's normal ... "

"What's the deal when we're interviewing?" Jake growled. His face was bright red, shining like a stop light.

"You couldn't tell?" Travis blurted, incredulous. "One look at that piece of shit and you know he's been getting away with worse stuff for years."

"SIT. THE FUCK. DOWN!" Jake yelled, his voice rattling the walls.

For a moment, Travis froze, then he took a seat at the conference table. He stared at his brother, not saying a word.

"What did I tell you about interviews?" Jake barked.

"Don't say anything," Travis muttered.

"Not a peep," Jake replied. "You're like paint on the wall."

"I'm sorry," Travis said meekly. "It's just ... "

"That's my interview, not yours," Jake interrupted. "You have no idea what you screwed up."

Travis leaned forward, earnest and open. "But Jake, you saw Sutton, the way he was smiling. You heard him as clear as I did, can't you tell that he ... "

"We know."

Confused, Travis leaned back, blinking like an owl at noon. "Know what?"

Slowly, glacially, the red blush drained from Jake's face. He swept his hair out of his eyes and took a deep, calming breath. "A guy like Sutton's got something wrong inside. He's never gonna go straight. He can't behave himself in the real world. The moment he got out, he was one bad decision from going right back in."

"What did he do?" Travis pressed.

Jake leaned forward on his knuckles, his face looming into his little brother's. "This doesn't leave this room. We think he shot a liquor store owner the same night he beat up his girlfriend."

Travis's jaw dropped. "That son of a bitch."

"Detectives are nailing the case down," Jake said. "We wanted Sutton to think that he was only in for felonious assault."

"Only ... " Travis shook his head.

"Now, thanks to my little brother who can't shut the fuck up, Sutton knows we got more." Jake eased into a seat. "So does Blevins."

"Sorry," Travis muttered again.

Jake sighed and leaned back, closing his eyes in exasperation. He put his booted feet up on the conference table, just like his father, and rubbed the bridge of his nose just like his mother.

"We're going for a capital conviction, right?" Travis said. "Jake, please tell me we're gonna fry this bastard."

Jake set his feet. Adjusted his grip. Pulled back slow and measured, just like he'd been taught, then let his swing go, strong and true.

His club connected with the tiny white ball, sending it off the tee and sailing out over the rippled green landscape. The shot was high and long, if a little curved, and Jake lost sight of it against the trees. Two-hundred-fifty yards if it was an inch. Not bad.

That one was Carlisle.

Jake rolled another golf ball onto the battered green Astroturf pad. This one was going to be Velasquez. He smiled as he gripped his club.

"You're gonna hook it."

Jake's smile dropped in an instant. He refused to look up and pretended he hadn't heard a thing. Beside him the other golfers continued their practice, littering the driving range grounds with white balls that looked like nothing so much as huge hailstones. Jake prepared to execute his backswing.

"Your shoulders aren't square."

He threw the club to the ground. She'd completely blown his concentration, forcing him to acknowledge her.

"You're not getting your credentials back," Jake snapped.

Christine Morton smiled and brushed her hair from her neck. "I hadn't noticed you pulled them."

There it was: the smug grin that made Jake's blood boil. He grabbed his club from the ground and turned his back to her. "We're done talking, Morton."

"Do you know you only call me 'Morton' when you want to get official?" she said. "We go back a long way, Jake. You can call me Christine all the time."

Jake rolled a ball into place. He tried to settle in but it just wasn't happening. He took aim anyway. This time the little white sphere wasn't Velasquez: This time it had dyed blonde hair and a condescending smirk. He drew back and let go, whacking the ball savagely.

"Told you," Morton said as the ball sailed from right to left, cutting a wide arc in the sky. "Mean hook. I know a guy who can help you fix that."

"I'd ask how you found me at a municipal golf course," Jake said, still refusing to look at her, "but I don't care."

"Usually you go to the country club," Morton answered anyway, "and when I heard you were here I wondered why. But then it hit me. Here, no one knows who you are."

"I don't care who knows me," Jake growled. He lined up another ball. This one also had blonde hair.

"Plus, if you go to the club, there's every chance you're going to run into Dave Carlisle." Morton's words dripped with self-satisfaction.

Jake pushed the ball back and forth, pretending to find a smoother spot on the worn mat. The one thing he absolutely hated about Morton—over everything else there was to loathe—was her talent for pinpointing exactly what was on his mind. It was uncanny, like she knew what he was thinking. His face grew warm, and he continued to line up his shot.

Morton shook her head. "The Jake Lynch I know never ran from a fight in his life."

"I'm not running," Jake snapped. Heads turned his way, and Jake took a deep, calming breath. He glared at Morton, wishing her dead on the spot. "I'm just working out a little tension."

"Of course." Morton held his gaze steadily, like a cobra sizing up a mongoose.

Jake broke first, turning toward the driving range. "You really suck, Christine, you know that? 'Rich Kid Murders'? How do you come up with that crap?"

"Your words, not mine," Morton reminded him. "From your press conference."

Jake whacked another ball, this one falling far short of the hundred-yard marker. His father had mentioned the same thing, even though Jake didn't remember saying that…

"I heard the cops picked up two suspects," she continued. At least she was keeping her voice down. "But no official word from your office yet."

"No comment," he barked as he whacked another ball.

"Jake, are you gonna make me burn a favor in the police department?" Morton chided.

"I can't *make* you do anything," Jake muttered.

Just as he lined up another shot, Morton grabbed his shoulders and turned him. "Seriously, you're stressing me out with this terrible form. Square up."

He raised an eyebrow.

"Golf team in college," Morton explained. "Why don't you know that?"

"All right, fine," Jake surrendered. "Off the record."

"Jake …"

He turned back to the range.

"You owe me, Jake," Morton said. Her voice had changed. No longer filled with a knowing superiority, now it held a subtle threat.

"I thought you owed me," Jake said as he rifled off another shot, this one driving like a laser straight downrange and dinging off the three-hundred-thirty yard sign.

Morton sighed. "Off the record."

Jake leaned on his club. "Because of your media circus the other day, I have to tread very lightly with this case. You know if this was just another drug deal gone bad, your anchorman would mention it once and never again."

"Drug deal?" Morton's eyes lit up. "Were the rich kids buying or selling?"

"Off the record," Jake reminded her. "It's pretty muddy. Lots of stories, and none of them line up. I don't need any speculation or 'details' getting out in the media before we've had a chance to run everything down."

Morton shrugged. "The beast is unleashed. I can't push it one direction or the other."

"Bullshit you can't," Jake countered. "You do it all the time."

"All right, say I pull a few strings, keep things quiet for you," Morton offered. "I get an interview with the suspects."

Jake shook his head. "That's against policy and you know it. But, if my office gets to examine the leads before they're presented in the media, I can see to it that you get the press releases fifteen minutes before anyone else."

"An hour," Morton countered.

"Half an hour," Jake replied.

"Half an hour and I get my credentials back."

Jake mulled the proposition over, hoping he was making Morton sweat. "No leaks. First time I hear something on the news I don't already know—your station or not—the deal's off."

Her brow furrowed, and Morton crossed her arms over her chest. Finally she nodded.

"Why do I always feel like I'm making a deal with the devil?" she asked.

"I was going to say the same thing," Jake replied.

He rolled another ball into place and tried to calm the fury that talking with Morton always seemed to stoke. As he lined up his shot, he could still feel Morton's eyes on him.

"What do you want now?"

"Do you remember the first time we had this conversation?" Morton asked.

"No," Jake lied. He settled in and addressed the ball.

"I do," Morton replied, "and it's been on my mind lately. What with Sutton's execution the other day. I saw Travis there."

Jake's jaw tightened. "It's been ten years. It's done. Let it go."

Morton's eyebrows raised. "He was your first one, wasn't he? The first man you got a capital conviction for, and the first one executed. There's blood on your hands now, Jake. Did it affect you in any way, or were you the tough-guy DA to the very end?"

Stone-faced, Jake stared her down. Morton returned the stare, but with an investigative reporter's gleam in her eye.

"Your grip's off," Morton said as she walked away. "You're gonna slice it hard."

Jake wound up his swing and let loose with a monster hit. The ball sailed high and cut left-to-right as if a gust of wind had caught it. A dramatic slice, the worst one he'd ever seen.

He looked up, expecting at least a knowing smirk from Morton. But she was gone.

"Are you being proud, Trav," Claire asked, "or just stupid?"

Straining under the weight of the window-unit air conditioner, Travis didn't have the breath for a reply. His older sister stood under the shade of his front porch—decked out in her very ladylike yet all-business suit—heckling him instead of offering to help.

Travis heaved and strained, hoisting the "new" air conditioner onto the struts that had supported the old one. His arms quivering, he stepped back and bent over, gasping like a fish out of water.

"My client … couldn't … no money …" he panted, gesturing at the air conditioner. "And the old one finally …"

"That's not what I'm talking about and you know it," Claire said, tossing her auburn hair back. "If I wasn't your sister, you'd probably say yes."

Claire was the middle of the Lynch children, coming between Jake and Travis—the only girl. She was the one who took the family legacy seriously, working in the law firm their ancestors had built up when neither Jake nor Travis would. She was an excellent attorney, with a wiser legal head than either of her brothers, but she was an even better businesswoman. She'd taken the Lynch law offices from a boutique, almost nostalgic practice to a thriving modern legal firm, increasing the staff half over. She was also easy on the eyes, as Travis understood it, but to him she just looked like his sister.

"No, I'd say what I've been saying for ten years." Travis fit the bolts to the bottom of the air conditioner, a convenient excuse not to make eye contact with his sister. "I didn't come to work for Dad, and I'm not changing my mind for you."

"Lynch and Brockhurst is as much your legacy as it is mine," Claire insisted. "You wouldn't be working for anybody but yourself."

"I'm doing that right now," Travis muttered.

"Really? What part of your law degree involved studying how to install old air conditioners?" Claire stood with her hands on her hips, a taller mirror image of their mother, right down to the piqued twist of her lips.

"Things are just fine," Travis said, hoping Shirley couldn't hear him.

"You're bartering like a starving college student," Claire replied. "Doesn't look 'just fine' to me."

Travis turned the last bolt, securing the air conditioner to the struts. Now all he had to do was plug it in, cross his fingers, and pray it worked. Or at least worked better than the old one. He leaned against the shady side of the house, facing his sister.

"Can we talk about something besides my practice?"

Claire sighed and took a seat on the patio chair Travis had received as payment from another client. Her cheeks were turning a little red—a blush less than Jake or their mother would have shown—

but she kept her composure. She folded her hands demurely in her lap, like she was at a cotillion waiting to be asked to dance.

"Did I tell you about the new landscaper the Prochazkas hired?" she offered.

"You were telling Shirley," Travis replied. "He was tall and dark and gorgeous, and that's not a conversation I want to have with my sister."

"Come on, Trav," Claire said. "Doesn't my little brother care about my love life?"

"When have I ever?" Travis answered. "Last I heard, it was some guy named Thom."

"That was six months ago," Claire scoffed. "He was at Mother's Christmas party the last time I saw him. If you'd just come to a family function once in a while you could keep up."

Travis shook his head. It had been ten years since he attended any of his mother's gatherings. Ten years since he decided to follow his conscience and strike out on his own. Ten years since he'd cut himself off from the Lynch family fortune. Ten years since he'd exchanged a single word with his big brother.

"How about this?" Claire said, dabbing daintily at a drop of perspiration behind her ear. "I'll give you a call when I know Jake isn't going to be there."

"Jake's always there," Travis replied. His brother didn't miss a chance to press the flesh with the kind of old-money politicians and cronies their father and mother counted as friends; it was how he kept getting re-elected.

"I can fix it so that he's not," Claire said, and Travis had no doubt she could. "You can help Daddy prune the roses, build a model, something."

"What something?" Shirley asked as she emerged from the house.

"Nothing," Travis replied.

"Come by the house," Claire urged Shirley. "Sunday brunch. Mama always does brunch up big."

Travis saw the initial sparkle in his wife's eyes dim almost immediately, and the eager smile on her lips turned into a sad curve as she shook her head. It was a ritual she had become all too familiar with, politely declining invitations to brunches, dinners, fundraisers, open houses, social gatherings of every kind. She had married into the Lynch family, but she wasn't getting any of the benefits.

"I don't think so, Claire," Shirley couldn't keep the note of resigned disappointment from her voice. "Travis doesn't really … well, you know. Just not in the cards."

"Come on," Claire replied, trying to strong-arm him like she had when they were kids, "what's the big freakin' deal? Even if Jake is there, so what? He can sit at his end of the table, you sit at yours, and nobody touches anybody else. Like you're eight years old again in the back seat of the wagon."

"I don't think so," Travis said. When his sister pushed him like this, the last thing he was going to do was agree. "You know how he is."

"I know how *you* are," Claire said, and Shirley laughed out loud. "Stubborn little cuss, that's what Grandpa used to call you. But damn, he didn't know the half of it."

"Maybe we should try just once," Shirley said, grabbing Travis's hand, double-teaming him. "You never know, you and Jake might get along."

"Oh, that won't happen," Claire said, agreeing with Travis's silent sentiment. "You put them in the same room, it's like a match and gasoline. Have you actually seen it, Shirley? Trav thinks Jake starts it, Jake thinks it's Trav, when it's really both of them poking at each other's sore spots. Always has been."

"It's him," Travis said defensively.

Claire opened her mouth to try her closing arguments on him, but her cell phone began to vibrate.

"Sorry, I have to get this," she apologized. She brushed her short hair back and raised the phone to her ear, suddenly becoming all about the business. It was amazing: She was the bubbly, laughing big sister one minute, then a stern, tough woman-in-charge the next minute. Claire talked fast, listening closely and firing off instructions like she was a sergeant on the battlefield. In less than thirty seconds she was finished, closing her phone as she stood.

"I have a little emergency," she said, smoothing the fabric on a suit that cost more than Travis made in a month. "You remember Frank Morales? Dad's friend? He wants to go with another firm. We can't lose him—he's been a client for too long."

"Oh!" Shirley said, hurrying to Claire's side. "Do you have those recipes?"

Claire pulled a small accordion file from her bag and handed it to his wife. An odd moment passed between his wife and his sister, just an instant, but Travis caught it as Shirley quickly took the folder and held it close to her pregnant belly. Was that a guilty look on her face?

"I thought we might try something new," Shirley said quickly. "Claire used to date …"

"The chef guy," Travis interrupted. "I know. The one with the biceps and abs. You told me."

"Take care," Claire said, grabbing Travis by the chin and squeezing as she headed for her car. "And I need to see you at Mama's house one of these days."

In seconds she was behind the wheel of her showroom-gleaming German auto, backing out of the driveway and tossing a wave over her shoulder as she drove off.

"Maybe we should think about what she said," Shirley replied, perhaps a little wistfully. "Maybe it wouldn't be so bad, working for the family business."

Travis watched the sunlight glint off Claire's car as it disappeared from sight. Everything about her, from her styled hair to her manicured nails to her perfume to her ridiculously expensive shoes reminded him of the privilege he'd given up. And of the reason he'd given it up.

"It's Claire's place," Travis said.

"And she wants you there," Shirley responded. "Let her run the business, you go be the best attorney you can be."

She looked at him so earnestly, so eager to share his burden, that a crack almost formed in Travis's armor. He almost broke. Almost admitted that he wanted everything Claire had and more besides. But the moment passed and the urge left him.

"Let's see if this air conditioner works," he said. "Then I need to get some paperwork done."

9

C**LEAR AS MUD."**
In his memory, Jake heard the words his old boss used to describe the worst cases, the ones with no independent witnesses, with lies piled on lies, with hostility and criminality on both sides—legal and political minefields. Daring to argue one side or the other in court could only end badly for everyone involved. This case—Morton's "Rich Kid Murders"—was clear as mud.

His briefcase lay open on his dining room table, with papers spilled from its insides like the silty Mississippi draining into the Gulf. Every page his office put in front of him in the past week was either incomplete, flawed, or possibly a falsehood. He wanted to see the case as a complete picture, but half the painting was smeared and the other half was missing.

"Here you are," a soft voice called from the kitchen. Bundled in her nightgown, Rita leaned against the doorway, shaking her head slowly. "Do you know what time it is?"

"I'm avoiding clocks lately," Jake replied. Outside it was dark and didn't seem to be getting any less so, that was all he knew.

Rita yawned and stretched, running a hand through her blonde hair. "What is all this?"

"Work," Jake muttered.

"At home?" Rita asked. "You never bring work home."

"I'm doing it now, all right?" Jake snapped.

In a moment Rita was behind Jake, her hands kneading his shoulders, her soft skin pressed against his stubbled face. "Fourteen years, and you've never once brought work home. You spend the night at the office a few times a month. You stay late, you go in early. But you've never taken over the dining room table at five in the morning."

Jake's head drooped as his wife worked her magic on his aching, tense muscles. Suddenly bone-tired, he relaxed and his eyelids drooped. If he hadn't shaken himself out of it, he would have fallen asleep right there.

"We don't talk like we used to," his wife whispered, her warm breath caressing his cheek. "Tell me what's going on."

A huge sigh escaped his lips and Jake deflated, loosening even more under his wife's gentle hands. "It's this … this thing with Peter Carlisle. With *Dave* Carlisle."

Rita's hands stopped. "It sounds horrible. That doesn't happen here. The Carlisles live three houses away. I'm afraid for Eric."

"Eric's only ten," Jake said softly. Of their two children, Eric was definitely the more level-headed. "And he's a good kid."

"Peter was a good kid, too," Rita replied, her voice trembling like her hands. "He used to come trick-or-treating, remember? He cut our grass when he needed money. I don't understand how he could have … how someone could have …"

Jake pulled his wife onto his lap and gathered her into his arms. She felt warm and soft and tender. She leaned into him, clinging tight.

"There's more to this than you might think," he said.

"Our kids are going to go to the same high school Peter Carlisle did," Rita said. "I never thought it was a place where they might get killed."

"They weren't at school," Jake said, trying to be comforting. "There are a lot of questions I need answered before I can say for sure what happened."

Rita pushed back, her blue eyes searching. "What do you think happened?"

"I can't tell you, it's an ongoing case."

"Honey, you always tell me about your cases," Rita replied.

"This is different," Jake replied stiffly. "These are people we know."

Rita snuggled in close, laying her head on Jake's shoulder. It was good, like the days when they were first married, before the kids, before his election, before everything their lives had become. He felt her heart beating against his and Jake melted. Rita reached up and stroked his chin softly, slowly, like she hadn't in a very long time. Jake tangled his fingers in her hair, inhaling her perfume with every breath.

"You would not believe the rumors flying around here," she said softly, her breath caressing his skin. "There's been nothing but bad blood in the entire neighborhood."

"I've seen that too many times," Jake replied. "Crime tears communities apart, especially something like this. I just thought that we were … that maybe the people around here would leave the Carlisles alone."

Rita stroked his chest. "The Carlisles are fine. We're the ones they need to leave alone."

Jake's hand dropped from his wife's hair. "What?"

"That's why I need to know what happened. So I can set the record straight, get them back to hating the Carlisles."

Jake took her by the shoulders and turned her to look into her eyes, so he could see if she was joking. She wasn't.

"You want to know the details of a murder investigation," he said slowly, "so you can get one over on the neighbors?"

"Don't you dare," Rita said, her eyes flashing angrily. "Don't you belittle me. Do you know what the neighbors are saying? Why isn't Jake Lynch going after the men who killed poor Peter Carlisle?"

"'Poor Peter Carlisle' got shot at three a.m. in an abandoned construction area," Jake said. "You tell me he was there to build houses for the homeless and I'll call you a liar."

"What do *you* think he was doing?" Rita pressed.

Jake stood, pushing his wife from his lap as gently but firmly as he could. "I need sleep. We're not having this conversation."

He collected the documents scattered across the dining room table, pointedly ignoring the poisonous glare his wife shot his way.

"Your career isn't just yours," Rita said sharply. "You have standing in the community. *We* have standing. And we're taking a beating because that stupid kid got himself murdered."

"Stupid?" Jake couldn't help himself. "Just a minute ago you were almost crying."

"I need ammunition," Rita said. "I need to get out in front of this, so I need to know what happened."

"This is none of your concern," Jake spat.

Rita tried to read the pages over his shoulder as he gathered them up. "You're lots of things, Jake, but you're not naive. All the politicking you do with people like David Carlisle, all the meetings, all the talking, all the cameras. Who takes care of things behind the scenes? Who takes care of everything else so you can ride your white horse to work every day?"

A flash shot through Jake, and tinges of red crept in at the edges of his vision. She knew all the buttons to push to get him to lose control. But he wouldn't let her get to him, not this time.

"You do," he said slowly, carefully. "And I love you for it. But this isn't a property line dispute, Rita. It's not like the time Paul Barnhart cut down the Jewett's magnolia. It's all a fog, all shades of gray. Two kids are dead, a third is probably never going to walk again, and, God help me, it looks like they were just as much the criminals as whoever shot them."

Her face paled but Rita stood strong. "What are you talking about? Drugs? Was Peter Carlisle dealing drugs?"

"The evidence isn't clear on anything yet," Jake replied.

"In *our* neighborhood? Three houses away?"

Jake said nothing.

"All right, I can work with this," Rita muttered.

"There's nothing to work with," Jake protested. "You have no details."

"This isn't a court room. I can connect the dots," Rita said, dismissing the notion with a wave of her hand. "I know what Janet Carlisle said, and I know what she didn't. Looks like her little golden child had feet of clay."

"Rita ..."

She kissed him on the cheek and ran her hand across the top of his head where his hair used to be. "David Carlisle's coming after you."

"That's an empty threat," Jake said. "He's a grieving parent."

"He's a vindictive son of a bitch," Rita said. "I've heard things at the club, in the grocery store, pieces of conversation before people realize I'm in the room. He wants to get rid of you. But don't worry, we're gonna fight this. You and me. Like always."

With a swirl of her nightgown and a parting whiff of her perfume, Rita left Jake alone in the dining room. And he was glad, not for the first time, that his wife was on his side.

The front door closed behind Travis's previous client; before the man could descend the front steps and cross the yard, Shirley was shoving another file folder in Travis's hands, murmuring the details of his next client's troubles as far as she could ascertain. The woman—a brand new client, just like the last two—waited patiently on the front porch. The porch had become a de facto waiting room, with yet another prospective client waiting his turn behind her.

With four new clients on the schedule this morning, Travis barely had time to catch his breath. His day had started three hours ago, with a phone call waking him up at seven o'clock, and had continued at constant clip since then. It seemed that as soon as he got off the phone with one potential client, another would call. He liked being busy— better to have too much work than too little—but Travis hadn't eaten breakfast and his stomach was letting him know about it.

"What is going on?" he asked his wife as he scanned the file.

She cast him a sidelong glance as she prepared yet another new client folder. "What do you mean?"

"This." He gestured at the stack of work in front of him, at the people waiting on his porch. "It's like somebody turned on a faucet. Where are these people coming from?"

Shirley shrugged. "Word gets around, I suppose."

"It's been a week, and they just keep calling," Travis mumbled. "Business always comes in chunks, but this is insane. Do you know each of them is willing and able to pay? Nobody's blinked twice at the fee schedule."

"That's not a bad thing, is it?" Shirley said, still not looking at him. "What can I get you to eat? I can hear your stomach growl from here."

Travis shook his head. "Let me get through these last two. Who knows? Before long, I may need to schedule an actual lunch hour."

Shirley shrugged. "You've paid your dues doing what you love. Maybe it's time for you to start making some money, too."

"Hell, if this keeps up, we might be able to start using the company credit card again."

Travis waited for his wife's reply, but she had already retreated to the kitchen. Almost like she was avoiding him.

He shook his head. No, couldn't be. Her moods had been up and down since she'd been pregnant, this was probably just more of the same.

And yet....

He didn't want to seem ungrateful, but his practice had never seen the kind of traffic it had in the past week. Word of mouth did carry a lot of weight, especially for an attorney, but Travis's reputation had always circulated in the less-than-financially-blessed circles. These new people were from miles away—Round Rock, Georgetown, Buda—nowhere near his office, nowhere near the people who usually needed his services. They weren't drop-ins, either: These people had made appointments, sought him out specifically, almost like they'd been steered his way.

Shadows danced in the kitchen, where Shirley was busy making him the meal he didn't ask for. He didn't like using his trial attorney skills on her, but she certainly was acting like a guilty party. It couldn't hurt to ask.

He'd taken one step toward the kitchen when the phone rang.

"I'll get it!" Shirley called from the kitchen. Did she sound a little panicked? Or was he imagining things?

Before she could make it out of the kitchen, Travis picked up the phone.

"Law office of Trav … Oh, Claire. Listen, this isn't really the best time, I've got a porch full of … Is Jake going to be there?"

Shirley reached for the phone but Travis shook his head. "Then no. Sorry, we can't make it. Yeah, maybe some other time."

"Sunday brunch. Again," Travis explained as he hung up the phone. "Did you have something else you needed to talk to her about?"

"Of course not," Shirley said, looking away. Was she angry? Embarrassed? "You ready for Mrs. Rouhier?"

"Shirley, if you know something I don't about these new clients—"

Heavy footsteps on the front porch interrupted him. A knock sounded and the door opened onto two familiar faces.

Min and Bae Park. Both with red eyes and haunted expressions, they had clearly been weeping but pulled themselves together for this visit.

"Shirley, were you expecting the Parks?" he called over his shoulder. But his wife didn't answer. Instead, she stood in the doorway to the kitchen with her arms folded over her growing belly, her jaw set and one eyebrow raised. No, she hadn't been expecting them at all, and she was clearly not happy to see the Parks on her doorstep again.

Carefully, slowly, and waving apologetically at his other clients, Travis ushered the Parks in. He could feel them holding their composure like a cracked shield, ready to splinter at the slightest touch.

"Come in, sit down," Travis said gently.

"Thank you," Bae said, brushing his graying black hair out of his face and saying something to his wife in Korean. He held a newspaper in one hand, the sheets folded into a tight square.

"We don't know where else to go," Min said, haltingly, her lower lip quivering.

"Soon is arrested," Bae said, angry and helpless at the same time. His face was pale, and it seemed he had aged ten years in the few days since Travis had seen him last.

Travis took Min's arm, leading her to a chair. "Give me the details."

"The man the state sends … " Min said, obviously searching for the proper words.

"Sam has a court-appointed attorney?" Travis said.

"A man named Mitchell," Bae replied, spitting the name as it left his mouth.

"He is a bad lawyer," Min said. "Not like you. You are a good lawyer. You know what you are doing."

"And this guy doesn't?" Travis asked.

"He was late to the first meeting," Bae said, his anger and frustration coloring his voice. "He does not look me in the eye."

Min took a ragged, gasping breath as sobs wracked her body. "I don't want my son to die."

"Excuse me?" Travis gasped. Had he heard her correctly?

In reply, Bae handed over the newspaper. Travis unfolded it quickly, to reveal the headline: "DA May Seek Death in Rich Kid Murders."

"Oh my God," Travis gasped. He recognized the story, it had been all over the news for days, but he'd had no time to pay attention to the details. He only knew that Peter Carlisle was one of the two dead. "*This* is what Sam was arrested for?"

Min and Bae nodded, tears streaming down their proud faces. Travis's heart broke. All they knew was that their son had been arrested for murder; they didn't know who Dave Carlisle was, what strings he could pull, or the considerable influence he could levy. As bad as the Parks believed this situation was, with Dave Carlisle in the equation, it was ten times worse.

"Soon did a bad thing," Min said between sobs.

"If he did it," Bae replied.

"He must go to prison," Min said. "But not die. Not die."

Bae wrapped his arms around his wife as she buried her face in his chest. Travis couldn't imagine the agony they were experiencing. They'd already had one son swallowed up by the system, and now they saw their remaining child poised on the precipice.

"Travis," his wife's voice carried a warning. Still in the doorway to the kitchen, she shook her head slowly. "We're just starting to dig ourselves out."

The Parks stood together in their grief as Travis went to Shirley, searching her face for the slightest hint of compassion and finding none.

"They don't know," Travis whispered, gesturing with the newspaper. "They have no idea what they're in for if Jake makes it a capital case."

"This is not our problem," Shirley said, resolute as a statue.

"This is exactly why I started my own practice," Travis replied. "To keep poor kids like this from being railroaded by the system."

"I thought you started your own practice to provide for your family."

Her words hit like a slap, but Travis shook it off. "I've been through a capital case before, they're not like anything else."

"They take more time," Shirley interrupted, "and more resources, and more energy. We can't do it for free."

Her eyes locked onto the Parks.

"Shirley …"

"No more pro bono," his wife interrupted again, her green eyes flashing. "Definitely not a murder case, and *especially* not a death penalty case."

Travis turned to the Parks, who clung to one another. Bae glared at Travis while Min pleaded with him silently, her eyes so full of hurt and anguish that Travis had to glance away. His gaze fell on the newspaper in his hands, and words leapt at him. Sam Park. Capital murder. Death.

"This is my son," Min said, her voice small. "Please."

"If he's anything like his brother," Shirley said, "he was into some pretty bad stuff. I'm sorry, we just can't … "

"I'll do it. Mr. and Mrs. Park, I'll take Sam's case."

Travis's words hung in the air. The Parks eyes widened as if they didn't quite believe what they'd heard. Travis turned to his wife and saw that his defiance had prompted the exact same stunned silence from her.

"Thank you," Min gasped.

"We do not have much," Bae said, a tiny flash of hope in his eyes, "but we can pay."

"You can make arrangements later," Travis said as he hurried the Parks to the door before Shirley could recover her composure. "I'll let you know as things develop."

Min broke from her husband and clutched Travis tight. "Thank you. You are a good man."

"Let's see what I can do for Sam first," Travis replied.

In a moment, the Parks were out the door and on their way, walking as if ten tons had been lifted from their shoulders. Still stationed in the doorway to the kitchen, Shirley glared at him, her anger smoldering just beneath a carefully-neutral facade.

"If Sam were our son," he explained, "you'd want the best attorney possible. And that's me."

"That's not what this is about, and you know it." Shirley turned back to the counter, her back stiff and her mood black as midnight. "I hope this ten-year-old grudge against your brother doesn't bankrupt us."

10

TRAVIS SHIFTED UNCOMFORTABLY. HE DIDN'T *want to be here, he didn't see what he could add, and he didn't know why Jake insisted he come along. They sat inside one of the smaller, older houses Austin had to offer, sweltering without air conditioning. Travis glanced again at the worn carpet and the wallpapered-over paneling, noted the paintings bought from the starving artists' show and the mismatched, hand-me-down furniture, and grimaced at the collection of plates hanging along the wall. He could think of nothing besides his mother's cousin's place in Denton. Mama called it "Wal-Mart chic" when she was trying to be kind.*

Amanda Grojean sat on her couch, her left arm in a cast, running her free hand nervously through her home-dyed red hair. Deep purple bruises ringed both her eyes, the color darkest near the bridge of her nose, working through blue, green, and then yellow toward the edges of her eye sockets. A set of stitches started just past her hairline and ran back across her scalp, and her lower lip sprouted its own crisscross set. She kept one leg propped on the couch, her ankle wrapped tightly with tape and gauze. Reilly Sutton had beaten her savagely, and she was just beginning to recover from his attack.

"Do you remember what time he got home?" Jake asked. He looked at Travis, pointing to the notepad. He expected Travis to take notes even though they were recording the conversation.

"About five thirty," Amanda said. Travis noticed she was missing one of her lower teeth. "Regular time, right after work. Except he wasn't working, he was looking for work. I guess, that's what he told me."

"Was he drunk?"

Amanda shook her head. "Not yet. Least not that I could see. Reilly can hold his liquor, though. I saw him drink almost a case of beer one Fourth of July. Schaefer Light. He called it cow piss."

"You told the police that he was upset about dinner?" Jake asked carefully. When he was like this, Travis almost didn't know his brother. Usually brusque, sometimes vulgar, when Jake interviewed delicate witnesses he transformed into a sensitive, gentle man. To Travis, it was like watching a charging bull transform into a lop-eared rabbit before his eyes.

"We was gonna have steaks," Amanda said. "That's what I told him in the morning. When I went to work. But it was so expensive, I just bought cube steak instead."

"He didn't care for that?"

Amanda shook her head again and she put a hand to her lip, feeling the stitches gingerly. "I tried to apologize, I did, but he got that look in his eye. I went for the door because I knew what was coming next. But he got me."

The tears welled up in Amanda's eyes and she shrunk into herself, lost and alone. Travis wanted to reach out to her, comfort her, but Jake had given him explicit instructions against touching. According to police records, she was just three years older than him, not even thirty, but she seemed over forty, lines of care and worry already etched deep into her face. Jake had a tissue ready, and Amanda dabbed carefully at her wounded eyes.

"He hit me in the mouth first," Amanda said, her voice now calm, detached. "Then he grabbed me by my hair and ran my head into the cabinet over there," she pointed into the kitchen. "I don't remember much after that." She sobbed once, a great heaving exhalation that made her gasp and grab her side. "I don't remember him breaking my arm or my ribs. The doctors say he probably kicked me after I passed out."

"Take your time," Jake said softly. "I'm going to ask you more questions, and if you don't remember, don't make anything up. Just tell me what you know."

Nodding, Amanda raised a shaking hand to her neck, trying to soothe herself as best she could. It wasn't right, Travis thought, she was just trying *to get by, trying to make a living, and she happened to hook up with someone like Sutton. She hadn't done anything wrong, not one thing, and that monster beat her within an inch of her life. No one deserved this. No one.*

"We're going to get him, Ms. Grojean," Travis said, his voice husky with rage. "Don't you worry, he's not going to do this to anyone else ever again."

Jake couldn't keep a small, satisfied smile off his face as he read the pages laid across his desk.

"DA May Seek Death in Rich Kid Murders"

"Lynch's Next Move Uncertain"

"District Attorney Tight-Lipped about Direction"

It looked like Morton had been keeping up her end of the bargain. There had been no leaks in the past week, and judging by the website banners, newspaper headlines and nightly news lead-ins, none of Austin's political reporters had anything solid to go on. Even rumors had evaporated like morning fog.

Just like it should be.

He swept up the newspapers and the print-outs and tossed them all in the recycling bin. Then he turned to the pink message slips that Susan had been dutifully adding to the pile day after day. As he flipped through them, Jake knew what he'd see: Dave Carlisle demanding to know what the District Attorney's office was doing with his son's murder case.

Jake threw all those into the recycling bin as well. Carlisle wasn't leading this investigation, no matter what he might have thought. And no one but Jake was going to set the DA's office agenda. Not media bottom-feeders, not grieving parents, not men with more political weight than common sense. It was time Austin remembered who was holding this horse's reins.

"Susan," Jake called through his open door, "phone Mr. Carlisle back, ask him to come in for a lunch meeting."

"He's already suggested that," Susan replied, poking her head in. "He wanted today or tomorrow."

"I'm busy then," Jake said, glancing at the bin and the messages he hadn't really read. "Tell you what, let's change it to breakfast. The earlier the better."

"I'm pretty sure Mr. Carlisle golfs in the morning," Susan said. "He mentioned it when I suggested times from your calendar."

"Seven-thirty a.m. it is, then," Jake said, leaning back in his chair and folding his hands behind his head. "Half an hour. My schedule is just too packed for any other time."

Susan rolled her eyes, but nodded and retreated to her desk to make the call. No doubt Carlisle would be furious, but it was time he learned that the DA's office was not going to give in to manipulation.

"Is he in?" Before Susan could intercept him, Velasquez invited himself into Jake's office, practically standing at attention in the center of the room. As always, his suit was pressed, his collar and cuffs blinding white to match his teeth, and his salt-and-pepper hair set just-so. To Jake, he looked like an op-ed caricature of an attorney, but Velasquez obviously took his appearance very seriously.

Jake waited patiently as Velasquez smoothed his lapels.

"Hey, boss, you going for lunch today?"

"I might," Jake replied. "What do you need?"

"Why do I need something?" Velasquez tugged nervously at his collar, trying to smile, which only made him seem more suspicious.

Absently rubbing his chin, Jake felt stubble; he'd rushed through his morning routine and missed several spots. "Do you mind if I shave first?"

Velasquez bristled but quickly hid it. Jake could sympathize, he'd always hated it when his old boss made him wait. But Velasquez needed to learn his place too.

"I need to talk with you about the Rich Kid ... about the Carlisle case," Velasquez mumbled.

"What about it?" Jake said, running water in his sink. One of the perks for the DA was a private bathroom in his office. It was tiny, hidden behind a door that could have been a wall panel, but no one else had one.

"We're going to have to make some decisions, sooner rather than later," Velasquez explained carefully. Jake hated when people tried to soft-pedal their intentions; Velasquez was so concerned with the way people saw him that it could take him ten minutes of fumbling to express a thirty-second question.

"You saw the newspaper," Jake prompted. "You want to know if this is really a capital case."

"Well, yes, but that's not … " Velasquez trailed off. He caught Jake's eye in the mirror then looked away quickly. "The families of the murdered boys have been very patient."

There it was. Velasquez was running interference for Dave Carlisle, as if four calls a day wasn't enough.

"They'll have to be patient a while longer," Jake said. He lathered the shaving cream onto his face. "Capital cases take time."

"I need to tell them—"

"Just because Carlisle wants the death penalty," Jake interrupted, "doesn't mean he's going to get it."

Velasquez's eyes flew wide; he clearly thought he'd been keeping his motives secret. "That's not it at all."

"I'll ask you the same thing I asked in that press conference," Jake said as he scraped the whiskers from his cheeks. "There were two men murdered the week before these kids. Why aren't you all over me about the status of that case?"

Velasquez's perplexed expression eased. "So we're not going for death?"

Jake sighed. Velasquez just couldn't take a hint. Or maybe he was under so much pressure that he wouldn't take "maybe" for an answer.

"I've been involved in a lot of cases in my time. A lot of gray areas, a lot of murky interpretations," Jake said. "The facts of a capital trial are usually very cut-and-dried. But the politics behind them aren't. And the public confuses the politics with the facts."

"I don't follow." Judging by his expression, Velasquez wasn't lying.

"Do we have all the facts in the Carlisle case?"

"Well, not exactly."

"Not exactly?" Jake sputtered, nearly cutting himself. "Right now, we know next to nothing about the circumstances surrounding the shooting." He paused to scrape the bit under his bottom lip. "But we know the politics of the case. Rich kids, poor kids, obviously illegal business in the middle of the night on the wrong side of town. When we uncover them, the facts are going to be ugly. I guarantee you, when Carlisle finds out what his boy was up to, he'll want this dealt with quietly. Very, very quietly. You ever see a quiet capital case, Bobby?"

Jake finished shaving, wiping his now-smooth chin with a clean towel. He turned, finding Velasquez staring at the floor, hands clenched together as if he were praying.

"Does that answer your question?" Jake said.

"I suppose so," Velasquez muttered, sounding extremely disappointed.

"Let's go get some lunch, then," Jake said, ushering Velasquez out of his office. "Burgers okay with you?"

Susan appeared in his doorway, clutching a pink message slip. "Jake, you're going to want to see this."

"After lunch," Jake replied. He advanced on Susan but she didn't give ground; she was practically blocking the doorway.

"It's about opposing counsel in the Carlisle case."

"Mitchell?" Jake scoffed. "Complete hack. We'll steamroller him."

"Sam Park has a new attorney," Susan replied. She glanced down at the message slip as if the words might have changed.

"Anybody we know?" Jake asked. He tried to move past his assistant but she blocked him again, and stared him in the eye.

"Travis Lynch."

Jake's world went silent, like the moment before impact in an auto wreck. He hurtled toward destruction, waiting for the squeal of tires and crunch of metal.

"I see." Jake walked stiffly back to his desk, lunch with Velasquez forgotten. "I guess that means I have some work to do."

"Do you understand what I'm saying to you?"

Travis sat at a battered metal table across from the angriest young man he'd met in a very long time. Sam Park radiated vicious fury, like his body had no way to contain his rage; he practically vibrated with the effort of keeping it in. His jaw was set like stone, his cuffed hands clenched so tight his arms trembled. His dark eyes stared straight ahead.

They'd faced off like this for half an hour, Travis trying to explain himself, his client steadfastly refusing to answer, even to nod his head. It was a grade-school version of a grown-up drama, Travis playing the bleeding-heart attorney and Sam playing the tough-guy defendant. The act had been tedious after the first five minutes; now it was becoming absurd. Travis's patience was nearly shot.

"Come on, Sam," Travis tried again, "I just need the answers to a few questions."

"Fuck you, man."

The first words his client spoke echoed off the cinderblock walls, surprising Travis. It wasn't much, but it was a start. Sam glanced at Travis, just a brief flick of his eyes, the barest moment of recognition.

Travis leaned back in his chair and waited. After a few seconds, Sam resumed his lock-jawed pose, but the crack was there. Travis had his opening.

"This is serious," Travis said. "More than I think you realize. And every minute you keep up this front is one minute less I have to work on your defense."

"You know where you can stick your questions." Sam barely moved his head, but he shifted in his chair, tugged at the orange county jail jumpsuit. Looked like he was getting tired of the charade, too.

"Who brought the gun?" Travis asked again.

Sam's mouth worked, the huge bruise on his lower lip rolling like a buoy on the tide. He'd been in several jail yard fights since the cops brought him in two days ago, but there had been no official report; evidently Sam refused to rat on any of his fellow inmates.

"How many of you were there?" Travis pressed. "Just you and Roger, or was there someone else?"

Sam turned his mouth down in a grimace and he closed his eyes, but he shook his head—a slight side-to-side—and said nothing.

"Maybe you could start by telling me what happened," Travis continued. "I need to see things from your perspective."

Sam's chin lifted and his eyes widened. He turned to Travis, his eyes glinting with a sinister light. "I remember where I know you from."

"I told you, I represented your brother," Travis replied. "You would have seen me arguing his case."

Sam shook his head. "My parents never let me close to the courthouse while that was going on. You were on TV. I remember, years ago. I was in, like, elementary school."

It was Travis's turn to stare straight ahead. "You probably have me confused with—"

"No, it was you," Sam interrupted. "That was seriously fucked-up, man. Even I could tell that, and I was ten."

Travis sighed. "If you remember anything about that case, then you know I'm one of the few people who can help you with yours."

For the first time, Sam relaxed, just the tiniest bit, and he cocked his head to the side. "What the fuck are you talking about?"

Travis took a newspaper from his briefcase and slid it across the table so Sam could see the headline: "DA May Seek Death in Rich Kid Murders."

At first Sam refused to look at the paper. But the longer Travis sat there, saying nothing, the wider the crack in Sam's defiance became. Finally, he glanced down and his facade broke. His face went pale, his mouth hung open, and he grabbed the paper with his shackled hands. He shook his head slowly. "Would they do that?"

"If you let me represent you," Travis said, "I'll do everything I can to keep that from happening."

Sam's face fell, but he recovered quickly, shoving the paper back across the table, pressing his chin upward. "Like you did for Charlie? I don't need that kind of help, man. I want to stay out of jail."

"Charlie was guilty," Travis said, staring Sam down. "What about you?"

"Does it make any difference?"

"It does," Travis said without thinking, still holding Sam's gaze. He hadn't intended to admit it, he had a series of prepared answers to that question, provided by rote to his clients. But something about Sam's demeanor made him want to wield the truth like a cudgel.

"Why?"

Travis looked away. It shouldn't make a bit of difference if his client were guilty or not. But it did. "Did you do it?"

His answer was nothing but silence. Travis waited, still turned away, a tactic that sometimes worked. When Sam still didn't answer, Travis turned to his client, who sat with his head in his hands, breathing deeply.

"Can they hear me?" Sam asked, his voice hoarse and gravelly. His eyes flicked toward the ceiling, toward the closed door.

"This is a confidential conversation," Travis said. "No one's listening to anything. And if someone were, they couldn't use what you said."

Sam's shoulders relaxed, and he slumped onto the table. "There was a gun," he said, "and it … went off … I guess."

"Who was holding the gun?"

Sam shook his head. "Charlie told me what they do to snitches in prison."

"Did you know Death Row is solitary confinement?" Travis tapped the newspaper. "Those guys are in their cells twenty-three hours a day. For years. Decades."

Nodding, Sam bit his lower lip. "How'd they find me?"

"Kenny Galipo," Travis replied. "Evidently he woke up and your name was the first thing on his lips."

"That's the one with the blonde hair?" Sam said, his voice catching.

Travis nodded. "How many of you were there? Just the two of you, or more?"

Sam shook his head, refusing to answer. Travis became suddenly weary of the whole dance, the back and forth. He gathered the newspaper and his own pages and prepared to leave. There were paying clients he could be seeing.

Sam mumbled something under his breath.

"I'm sorry," Travis said, "I didn't catch that."

Sam paused, staring Travis down, once again the thug he had been when he walked in. "Just two."

11

TRAVIS HAD NEVER INTERVIEWED A *policeman before, never been alone with one. His eyes kept flicking to the pistol at the man's side, at the gleaming badge, at the bulletproof vest bulging under his uniform. Sitting ramrod straight, the officer stared at Travis coldly, as if he were moments away from slapping on the cuffs. Travis fumbled with his pen as he tried to disguise his trembling hands.*

"We arrived at twenty-two hundred hours," Officer Porter said. Travis noticed a bit of a globe-and-anchor tattoo barely visible under the rolled sleeve of the officer's upper arm. Marine. That explained the high and tight haircut. "There was no one visible. My partner cleared the aisles while I took the counter. I found the owner lying face down near the cash register. There was a lot of blood. A lot. I checked for a pulse and found none. I radioed for an ambulance."

He fell silent, and it took Travis a moment to realize the officer wasn't going to elaborate, he was going to answer the question and no more. It began to dawn on Travis that the officer thought of this as an interrogation, maybe as some desk-jockey lawyer second-guessing necessary actions in the field. Maybe, just maybe, this officer was as intimidated as Travis was.

Remembering his preparation, Travis flipped through some papers. "I saw in your report that you had been to this liquor store previously."

"*The week before,*" *Officer Porter replied. "Not a robbery, shoplifting. Two kids, came in for beef jerky and sandwiches, ended up running out with a couple of forties of malt liquor.*"

"*Did you catch them on the recording?*"

"*What recording?*" *the officer said.*

Travis held up a crime scene photo taken after the murder. He pointed to the camera set high on the wall. "The one that connects to this."

Officer Porter shook his head sadly. "It's a fake camera. The guy didn't have the money to get a real one, so his cousin or something sets him up with this fake. There's one outside the back door that's a fake too. Not connected to anything."

"*Damn,*" *Travis replied, shaking his head ruefully, pretending experience he didn't have. "It's never easy.*"

"*Tell me about it,*" *Officer Porter said. He shifted in his seat, slowly relaxing. "Those kids were in and out so fast the owner could barely describe them. But I knew who it was, local punks, always in trouble. I knew it, but I couldn't prove they did anything.*"

"*Did you talk to them?*"

"*Went right to their parents' house,*" *Officer Porter said. "Confronted them and their folks. Little bastards said they hadn't been anywhere near the liquor store. I could smell the beer on their breath.*"

"*Did you take them in? I mean, at least for underage drinking?*"

Officer Porter shook his head. "What would be the point?"

"*Well, it's the law, for one,*" *Travis said. "And then there's justice for the victim.*"

"*You're new, I can tell,*" *the officer said with a stiff smile.*

Jake hated the smell of a hospital.

The antiseptic sting hit him first, making his eyes water and filling his nostrils with astringent vapors. Underneath that harsh major note lingered a hint of bleach, beside the flat olfactory slap of sterile bandages and tape. It was a fraud, though, the presentation of hygiene—Jake still smelled everything they couldn't scrub completely clean. Stale sweat and dirty laundry. Vomit and urine. Blood.

"My sister's a doctor," Velasquez said at Jake's side, his voice far too cheery. Too loud. "Spends eighteen hours a day in a hospital. I couldn't do it."

"I can take it or leave it," Jake professed as every cell in his body screamed at him to turn back, to get out.

"My grandpa said people go to the hospital to die," Velasquez continued, blissfully ignorant. "Can't say I disagree with him."

As they passed the nurse's station Jake caught sight of his reflection in the glass, noting the queasy bend at the edge of his eyes. He looked like he might retch at any moment. But so did many of the doctors and nurses they passed.

They rounded the corner, headed for the room at the dead-end of the hallway. Beside the door stood a uniformed officer, his hand resting casually on his sidearm, staring them down as they approached.

"Is this really necessary?" Velasquez whispered. "We got the shooter."

"We got two guys in custody," Jake replied. "No idea for sure who they are yet."

He reached into his jacket and produced his identification, even though he'd known Officer Roth for over ten years. It took Velasquez a moment of fumbling before he found his ID and the officer stood aside to allow them in.

The room smelled like ointment and gauze and desperate sickness. Velasquez coughed, catching a whiff the same time Jake did. Someone stirred, and the curtain around the bed parted as the nurse emerged. Her smooth mahogany skin contrasted remarkably with the green scrubs she wore, and the severe way she eyed Jake spoke to how seriously she took her job.

"You're the DA, right?" the nurse practically demanded. She didn't wear a name tag; she didn't work for the hospital. A private nursing staff cared for Kenny Galipo twenty-four seven, paid for in full by Dave Carlisle. "Officer Roth said you were coming."

"How is he?" Velasquez asked, pointing vaguely toward the curtain.

"He got shot three times and he's had four surgeries," the nurse snapped. "How do you think he's doing?"

"I'm sorry," Jake said, "I don't know your name."

"Karen," the nurse said. "And, no, you don't have to get a court order. His parents say it's okay. You can talk to him, but don't get him excited. He's already pulled some stitches in his sleep. The kid's strong."

"Thank you, Karen," Velasquez said, too politely. Karen rolled her eyes and pulled the curtain aside.

Kenny Galipo lay in his bed, his arms on the covers, bandages bulging on his stomach and right shoulder. His skin was pale, and the shadowy wisp of a boy's mustache crept along his upper lip. White ear buds sprouted from either side of his head, which bobbed in time to the music he listened to.

"Hello, son. I'm the District Attorney." Jake didn't extend his hand.

"You play golf with Peter's dad," Kenny said, his voice surprisingly clear and strong for someone who looked like he did. He took the pods out of his ears and nodded at Velasquez. "I've seen this guy over at their house too."

Velasquez coughed nervously, but Jake pretended he hadn't heard that part; he didn't know Bobby and Carlisle had any sort of relationship outside of work. Though the news caught him off guard, it didn't really surprise him. Velasquez was a version of Jake himself, ten years ago.

"I'm going to ask you a few questions," Jake said, "and it's important that you tell me the truth. No matter how uncomfortable that truth is."

"Is that why my mom's not here?" Kenny's sunken eyes searched Jake's face.

"It's usually easier this way," Jake said. "You're seventeen, you're almost officially a man. But it's not easy when your parents are listening. There are some things I still can't tell my father, and I'm way older than you."

Karen pushed past the curtain with her hands full, barely glancing at Jake. "Don't mind me."

Jake's objection died on his lips when he saw what she held. Bile rose at the back of his throat as a syringe glinted in the light. Karen raised it to her eye and then punctured a small vial of medicine, drawing the clear liquid into the plastic cylinder.

"Can you not do that right now?" Jake asked, his voice small. Sweat coated his upper lip.

"It's an antibiotic," Karen said absently, still holding the syringe high. "It won't make him sleepy or anything."

Jake grimaced as his stomach protested. "Please, we're trying to conduct an interview."

Karen glanced out of the corner of her eye. "Needles bother you?"

Jake shook his head, forcing himself to keep eye contact. It wouldn't do to show weakness. "Couldn't care less. But we're talking to Mr. Galipo right now."

"No more than ten minutes," Velasquez offered. "Right, boss?"

The best Jake could manage was a short nod.

Karen put the syringe down as she brushed past. "If you're gonna lose your lunch, aim for the trash can."

Jake turned so he could see Kenny Galipo but couldn't see the syringe on the stand beside him.

"So what were you doing at a construction site at three in the morning?" Velasquez prompted. He held a pencil to a small note pad, ready to write.

"I don't wanna …" Kenny stammered. He licked his lips nervously. "This is, like, on the record, right? This is official for court and stuff?"

"I am the DA," Jake said. "Doesn't get more official than me."

"It's just, I don't want people to think …" Kenny closed his eyes, pursing his lips.

"Whatever it is," Karen's voice carried across the curtain, "it's going to hurt less when it's out of you than when it's in you."

Kenny glanced toward his nurse's voice, then back at his interrogators. Jake could see the thoughts work through the boy's head, options considered, discarded, then considered again. It was a war between Kenny's conscience and his cowardice.

The boy glanced at his bandages and laid his hands on legs that would never again carry his weight. He sighed sadly and shook his head.

"It was Peter's idea," Kenny said. "He said it was why he was going to get the biggest cut. By the time I got involved, they had most of it figured out."

"Peter and Shane?"

"Yeah," Kenny said, "though I think Shane was the one who knew people. Or he knew that one guy Sam, anyway. I never heard any other names. I didn't ask too many questions."

"So it may not have been Peter," Velasquez offered. "He may not have put things together. It may have been the other kid, Shane."

"Just let him talk, Bobby," Jake growled, "don't put words in his mouth." *Was Velasquez coaching the kid?*

Velasquez puffed up. "All I was saying …"

"Let's continue," Jake interrupted. "What was it you guys were planning?"

Kenny winced as he shifted nervously. His body only moved from the waist up. "It's stupid. Really, really stupid. I mean, like I don't know that now, right?"

"Shane's idea?" Velasquez prompted.

Jake turned, fire in his eyes. "Bobby, that's enough."

"Shane was after some cash," Kenny replied, "but it seemed like Peter was looking for some kicks. You know? He was doing it for the rush, like a skydiver or something."

"We'll get to that later," Jake said before Velasquez could chime in. "Just tell me what you were planning."

Kenny hesitated, glancing toward the curtain and Karen just beyond it.

"We were going to buy meth," Kenny said, the words coming quickly, as if he had to get them out before he changed his mind. "A lot of it. Five thousand dollars. We were going to supply Westlake."

Velasquez wrote furiously, far more than Kenny's words.

Jake paused for a moment to let it sink in. He'd imagined it would be bad, but not this bad. Rita had read the situation dead-on perfect. His neighbor's son wanted to bring meth into the neighborhood. Across the street from his house. Across from Eric and Heather.

"I see," Jake replied carefully, only his nausea keeping his temper in check. "Why did you think you needed to do that?"

A few mumbled, unintelligible words dribbled from Kenny's mouth. He stared at the foot of the bed.

"If Shane needed money, do you think he came up with the plan?" Velasquez said.

With a hollow thud, Jake's hand landed on Velasquez's chest. "You don't want to prejudice our findings, do you, Bobby?"

Velasquez glared at Jake. His fingers reached for Jake's hand but never actually touched. "I didn't …"

"You're done here," Jake snarled. "Wait for me in the hall."

Velasquez turned stiffly, his legs shaking as he exited the room. Through the curtain, Jake saw Karen watching him closely, her eyebrows raised. No doubt word of this would get to Dave Carlisle sooner rather than later.

"We all needed money." Kenny seemed paler, weaker than he had been when Jake walked in. "Maybe we just wanted it. Shane got cut off when he trashed the house at his Vegas party. He didn't even have the cash for a candy bar. Peter's dad wouldn't give him money for a new computer. My mom wouldn't let me use the car until I paid for my own insurance. Like I said, stupid."

For a brief moment Jake felt a tickle of compassion, a tiny spark of sympathy he seldom allowed himself. He imagined his little boy Eric laying in a hospital bed, wounded and bandaged like Kenny, his future shattered, his life forever changed by one bad choice. But his son would never do something so irresponsible. So thoughtless. So *selfish*.

"Stupid's an understatement," Jake snapped.

Kenny's composure started to crumble and his lip trembled, tears welling in his eyes but not falling. He looked away as his hand rubbed absently on legs that couldn't feel the touch.

"One more thing, then I'll leave you alone." Jake crossed his arms over his chest, presenting as stern a father figure as he could. "If Peter had the idea, and Shane knew someone to supply the meth, what was your role?"

Kenny's eyes filled with tears again, and his lips trembled. "I was the muscle. I was there to take care of things if they got out of hand. I guess I didn't do a very good job."

"There is a lot of case law on that," the librarian had sighed. "Unfortunately."

Travis sat in the university law library, head down, methodically reviewing every death penalty case on the books. One case at a time. With the heavy stack of volumes towering over him, he remembered doing the same thing his first year of law school, trying to pay attention to every detail because he didn't know which tiny point might come up in class. But now, today, there was more at stake than a simple grade; he had more at risk than mere embarrassment if he weren't prepared. Sam Park's fate could hinge on this preparatory work.

Travis groaned—quietly—and leaned so far back in his chair he almost fell over. His eyes ached; it hurt to open them, it hurt to close them, it hurt to rub them, it hurt to leave them alone. His desert-dry mouth and the throbbing pulse in his temple exactly matched the symptoms of drinking far too much, except he hadn't gotten to enjoy the warm belly and pleasant flush of a good scotch. Between this research and all the new, paying work that had come his way, he'd managed to scrape together only about five hours of sleep a night for the past week. His body felt like it'd been run over by a dump truck and his brain felt like a fuzzy lump in his skull. He needed to take a break but there just wasn't space in his schedule.

He closed his eyes, a painful exertion, and took several deep, cleansing breaths. It would be so easy to let go of consciousness, to let his mind drift and shut down. Surely no one would begrudge him a few stolen moments of slumber.

"You attorneys bill for sleeping on the job? How cush a gig is that?"

Of course she'd tracked him down here.

"I don't want to talk to you, Christine," Travis muttered, not bothering to open his eyes.

"That's where you're wrong." Travis heard a chair being pulled out, and the crinkle of fabric as Morton sat. A whiff of her perfume tickled his nose. "In a minute I'm going to be your favorite person."

"Unless you have some information pertinent to Sam Park's defense," Travis replied, still not opening his eyes, "I don't have time for you. Go away."

He waited. He didn't hear her moving, though he could hear her breathing. And the perfume still lingered.

Slowly, his muscles protesting every movement, Travis sat straight. His eyelids fluttered up like broken window shades to reveal Christine Morton sitting beside him, amused as she took in his discomfort.

"Burning the candle at both ends, are you?" Morton said, her tone cloyingly friendly. "I hear your one-man operation is starting to take off. About time, right?"

Travis gestured at the peaks and valleys of law books littering the table. "I really don't have time for small talk."

"Your wife must be happy," Morton continued, undeterred. "She's very patient, you know. With you."

"What do you mean?" Travis asked, immediately regretting engaging her.

"This whole genteel poverty thing," Morton said, brushing her blonde hair from her eyes. "It's very Austin, don't get me wrong. Very granola and dolphin-safe. But Christ, doesn't it get old? Don't you want a new car? A house that isn't falling apart?"

"It's not about the money." Travis turned to his notes, knowing she wouldn't take the hint.

Morton snorted, a coarse laugh that belied her expensive makeup and just-so hairstyle. "It's always about the money. Especially when you're a Lynch. You're about to have a child: Don't you want it to have all the advantages you had?"

"They didn't do me much good," Travis muttered.

"What are you talking about?" Morton replied. "You had opportunities other kids would kill for. And you took advantage of all them. Until you decided you had a conscience, for some reason."

Travis slammed the law book shut, the loud snap echoing from the walls and shelves, turning heads. "I'm done being polite. You need to go. Now."

Morton didn't budge. That infuriating, superior smirk still showed on her lips.

"I heard about your case," Morton said. "Sam Park."

"Who hasn't?" Travis snapped.

"I mean, I heard about it on the street," Morton said, her smirk widening. "Details. Stuff you may not know. Interested?"

"What do you want?" Travis asked, settling back into his chair.

"You lawyers are so suspicious," Morton said. "Can't I just be a good citizen?"

Travis could feel the jaws of an invisible trap closing on him. Morton didn't give anything away, all her exchanges were strictly *quid pro quo*. But in the days since he interviewed Sam, Travis had generated absolutely nothing on his own. No tips, no leads, no breaks. A wall of silence had gone up, both on the DA's side and on the street. Even Sam had stopped talking.

"So be a good citizen," Travis replied.

Morton took her notepad from her purse, flipping back several pages. "I talked to a few people who saw Sam around, at a noodle house, a dive of a coffee shop, that kind of thing."

"Who are these people?" Travis asked.

Shrugging, Morton didn't look up from her note pad. "My people. Sources are confidential, Travis, you know that. Mind if I use this?"

Morton grabbed Travis's pen and started writing on his notes. Before he could object she had given him three business names, places he'd never heard of.

"You'll work out a timeline when you start asking around here," Morton said, tapping the names. "Put A before B, that kind of thing."

There was that smirk again, that infuriating twist to her mouth that said she knew far, far more than she would tell him.

"This is the kind of investigation the DA's office does," Travis said. "I can get that from them during discovery. Or Sam could tell me."

"But he's not being the most cooperative client, is he?" Morton replied. "And before you ask, no, I'm not going to tell you how I know that."

"Thanks for the information," Travis said, stuffing his temper deep in his gut, "but it's nothing remarkable. Don't think I'm going to owe you anything for it."

He snatched his pen from Morton's hand and buried his nose in the thick law reference in front of him. Even though she'd been dismissed, he could feel Morton's eyes on him, and she didn't budge.

"Mark Kidd." Morton's voice was barely a whisper.

Travis raised an eyebrow. The name sounded familiar for some reason.

"I'm not going to say it again," Morton said softly, "and if you say you heard it from me, I'll deny it, but he's the missing piece. He's the third man on your boy's team. You get three sides to the same story, and you're getting real close to the truth. Know what I'm saying?"

Already the wheels spun in Travis's head. Sam insisted it had been just him and Roger, and both of them denied firing the gun that killed Peter Carlisle. Stalemate. Neither mentioned anyone else. But if there had been a third man....

Morton's grin seemed to take up her entire face. "*Now* you owe me."

12

WHAT KIND OF COP DID *you say you are?"*

The large black man leaned over the pool table and lined up his shot. A cigarette dangled from his lips, adding to the smog hovering four feet off the floor. According to the investigators, this was Carl Nelson, unmarried, age thirty-two. Occupation: welder. Just the kind of guy who would feel at home shooting pool in Smitty's.

"I'm not a cop," Jake said, slapping a business card on the rail. "I'm with the DA's office."

"What's the difference?" Carl smacked the cue ball, which careened wildly across the table. Jake raised an eyebrow; either Carl was sandbagging or he was a truly miserable pool player.

"Pay attention," Jake said. He leaned over the table and lined up the cue. "This is about a murder."

"What's that got to do with me?" Carl said. "I didn't murder anybody."

Jake took a neat, quick shot that sank two balls. "You know Reilly Sutton?"

Carl tensed, then shook his head. "Not really. I mean, he comes in here from time to time when I'm here. So, sure, I've seen him around. But do I know him? No way."

"You see him here last Friday night?" Jake sank another ball.

"Payday, yeah," Carl replied. He fidgeted, glanced at the door.

"We have him in custody," Jake said. "He's not getting out any time soon."

Carl's entire body relaxed and he leaned against the table. "Thank God. That guy is nothing but trouble."

Jake took a sip of his beer. "Was there trouble that night?"

"Damn straight," Carl said. "You should probably talk to Smitty about that."

"I'm talking to you."

Carl glanced at the door again. "Sutton was out of cash. If he even had any when he walked in."

Jake nodded knowingly. Smitty's had been his hangout from his undergrad years into law school. "Yeah, Smitty's not fond of deadbeats."

"Sutton tossed a few things around, tried to get loud, tried to puff up like he was back on the prison yard." Carl pointed at the room with his cue stick. "Do these people look like they give a rat's ass about how tough you were in prison? Half of them are packing heat right now."

"So he couldn't pay," Jake prompted, "and Smitty threw him out."

"Sutton starts yelling how he's gonna get Smitty, make him sorry, all that crap." Carl shook his head. "I need to hang out in better places, man."

"Did you see if Sutton was driving a car?"

"Some old beater, white or beige or silver, hard to tell at night," Carl said. "Looked like something he hot-wired, you know? I mean, if you're gonna steal a car at least steal a nice one."

"One last question," Jake said. "What time did this happen?"

"About ten-thirty," Carl replied. "I know because I had two beers left in the bucket."

Jake sank the last ball, leaving the white cue ball alone on the green felt. "Thank you, Mr. Nelson, you've been very helpful."

"You're keeping that crazy bastard locked up, right?" Carl looked worried.

Jake nodded as he put on his suit coat.

Carl smiled. "Damn straight."

This was the stupidest thing he'd ever done.

Before Travis could turn around to get back on the elevator, the doors closed, leaving him stranded. On this floor. The same floor as Jake's office. The same floor as the whole stupid DA's office.

He jabbed the 'down' button, then jabbed it again and again and again. What had he been thinking? How was this anywhere close to a good idea?

Two pressed-suit attorneys marched into the silent lobby, the woman pulling a rolling satchel, the man lugging an oversized accordion briefcase. No chitchat, no hesitation, both of them focused. They stood next Travis without a glance, like they hadn't even seen him.

This place had Jake written all over it.

Travis pressed the elevator button again, as if the more he insisted the faster the car would come. This visit was unavoidable. Inevitable. They were on opposites sides of the same case now; after ten years of staying away from one another, they were going to have to meet. They were going to have to negotiate. Discuss terms. Talk.

Just not now. Not today.

The elevator chimed and Travis teetered on his toes, ready to sprint inside the moment the doors opened. Sam's case was going to take a long time; he could afford to give this place a pass for a little while longer.

The door opened to reveal a wiry, white-haired, and sun-darkened man who glanced into the lobby as if he were about to walk onto the moon. He took a halting step out, uncertain whether he was in the right place.

The two attorneys waited, though not particularly politely. The woman put her hand on the door to keep it from closing and did nothing to hide her impatient scowl.

"Reception's that way," the male attorney said brusquely, pointing over his shoulder.

The wiry man nodded and sidled out of the elevator as the attorneys pushed in. Travis paused, looking first at the attorneys on the elevator, then at the confused old man beside him. He let the door close.

"Follow me," he said to the man. "I'm going there myself."

"Oh, thank you, son," the man replied. "This whole building is a maze. I swear I've been wandering around for an hour."

Travis went slowly; the man seemed to be in no hurry to get anywhere. "It's not all that bad once you know your way around."

"You're dressed pretty casually for someone who works here," the old man said, with a glance at Travis's jeans and T-shirt.

"It's been a while since I worked here," Travis replied. "But things haven't changed much."

The man regarded Travis with a quizzical eye. "Have we met before?"

"No, sir," Travis said as he pulled open the door to the District Attorney's office, "I'm pretty certain we haven't."

The old man did not seem convinced, but he reached the front desk before he had a chance to exercise his memory of events ten years past. The receptionist smiled pleasantly but noncommittally at the old man, then her gaze fell on Travis. Her eyes widened in shock before she recovered her composure. She frantically dialed a number with one hand as the other covered her headset mouthpiece.

"Her name is Emily," Travis told the old man. "She'll answer any questions you have."

Emily kept her whisper very quiet, but Travis could still hear "brother" and "what should I do?" Travis waved at her and shrugged.

In less than thirty seconds, the door to the rest of the office opened and Susan Cullen bustled out with a flash of her multi-colored scarf, accompanied by a waft of floral perfume. Once she had been Matthew Caroll's assistant, now she was Jake's: one constant in an ever-changing political environment, the pivot around which the entire office rotated. With more gray in her hair than Travis remembered and perhaps a few more pounds around the hips, her demeanor hadn't changed one bit. She lifted her glasses to her face and regarded Travis with cool detachment.

"Well, Mr. Lynch, it's been quite a while since you've graced us with your presence."

The wiry old man glanced up from the reception desk, and Travis heard him mutter "I knew it."

"I wouldn't be here now unless it was extremely important," Travis said, meeting her gaze steadily if reluctantly. His stomach churned; this was even tougher than he expected it would be. He took a deep breath. "I need to talk to Jake."

Susan folded her arms over her chest and regarded him like a protective mother hen. "He's not in the office right now. If you don't believe me, I can escort you back and you can see for yourself."

Travis almost laughed out loud; it was too good to be true. All this torment, all the knots he'd tied himself into, and it didn't matter in the least. Jake wasn't even in the building.

"I trust you," Travis stammered. "I could just wait."

"I don't think that's such a great idea." She stared daggers at him, practically daring him to take a seat. Waiting was not an option.

"I need to talk to him about the Park case," Travis pressed.

"You mean the Carlisle case?"

A tall man emerged from the office behind Susan, his slicked-back hair and ready, phony smile screaming *weasel* at top volume. He tugged at the sleeves of a far-too-expensive suit and inspected Travis like a turkey vulture peering at a carcass.

"I'm Roberto Velasquez," the man said proudly, with an emphasis that said Travis should clearly have heard of him already. "Maybe I can help?"

Travis glanced at Susan, whose expression had soured considerably.

"I'm the DA's second in command," Velasquez said. He extended a hand, on which shone two gold rings. "You must be Travis."

"Mr. Lynch hasn't assigned a second," Susan replied dryly.

"Well, when he does, I'll be the one he chooses," Velasquez replied, hand still extended.

Reluctantly, Travis shook the man's hand. He and his brother may not have spoken in a decade, but he did know Jake like only a brother could. And there was absolutely no way this smooth counterfeit of a man would ever become Jake's right hand.

"Will Jake be back tomorrow?" Travis asked Susan, pointedly ignoring Velasquez.

"Mr. Lynch's calendar has been … erratic lately," Susan replied. "He should be in tomorrow, but he was scheduled to be in this afternoon, too. He's not out of town, though, so I assume he'll be back home tonight, you could catch him there."

"Jake's house? That's not gonna happen," Travis blurted before he could think better of it. "I mean, this is business. I need to keep it professional."

"I'll be happy to discuss the case with you," Velasquez said, "and fill Jake in on the details later."

Travis wondered if the man realized how completely insincere he sounded.

"I need to talk to Jake about this," Travis addressed Susan again, still ignoring Velasquez, "not anyone else."

Velasquez's back stiffened, but he wiped away the momentary frown and flashed his gleaming white teeth. "I'd think you'd want to take advantage of every possible chance to keep your client away from the needle."

Susan frowned as Travis turned to Velasquez. "So you *are* going for the death penalty for Sam Park?"

Velasquez paled slightly. "I wouldn't say that."

"You just did," Travis replied. "Thank you, Mr. Velasquez, you've been a big help."

"Now, hold on a minute," Velasquez gasped as Travis turned away. "We need to talk, don't we? Work something out?"

Travis shook his head. He'd come here to tell his brother about Mark Kidd, about the third person in Sam Park's crew. He'd come to ask for Jake's help finding Mark and searching for the gun. He'd come to give his brother every opportunity to do the right thing as far as Sam Park was concerned. He had not come here to give this ladder-climber a boost.

A strong hand took Travis's arm and spun him around. For the briefest instant, Travis felt an uncharacteristic spark of rage flare within him—rage more suited to his brother—as he looked down at Velasquez. His hands balled into fists.

"I'm not going to have you running to your brother, telling him how I blabbed about a capital case," Velasquez hissed.

"What I say to my brother is none of your Goddamned business," Travis replied coldly. "But I will tell you this: You might want to consider other career options. As long as Jake is the DA, you're not going very far."

With wide, shocked eyes Velasquez let his hand fall from Travis's arm.

Travis tried to ignore his shaking legs as he hurried back to the elevator.

Ten minutes later, he raced—futilely—to the corner of 10th and Guadalupe, trying to catch the driver's attention as a city bus pulled away. It was no use: The bus made the light and sped down Guadalupe, its tail lights fading into the distance. Defeated, Travis crossed the street to the park, clutching his side and trying to catch his breath. He thought he was in better shape; a dash down half a city block shouldn't have winded him like this.

Nodding to the rumpled man already on the bench—either homeless or a university professor—Travis settled in. There wouldn't be another bus for half an hour, enough time to eat the sandwich Shirley packed him and down the bottle of water she insisted he take. Travis was glad her mothering instincts were kicking in, otherwise he'd have been wheezing *and* famished.

Looking around, his heart sank. He saw Christine Morton's TV-ready face behind the wheel of a sedan parked at the curb; she touched up her makeup in the rear-view mirror and pointedly ignored him, not even glancing his way.

Travis seethed. How did she do it? How did she track him here, to downtown Austin? Was she following him? Had she hacked his cell phone GPS?

"This has to stop," Travis muttered under his breath. He shoved his sandwich and water bottle into his backpack. It was time Morton learned she couldn't just tail him through the city.

Before he could stand, a tall man wearing an expensive suit approached Morton's car. Gold rings flashed in the sunlight as Roberto Velasquez dashed across 10th Street and leapt into the passenger seat.

Travis ducked his head and turned away, glancing out of the corner of his eye as Morton drove off quickly. Neither she nor Velasquez gave him a second look; he might as well have been another vagrant whiling away the afternoon on a park bench.

Velasquez and Morton. Travis wondered for a moment if Jake knew, then realized if his brother had known, Velasquez would no longer be employed at the DA's office, and probably wouldn't have a career as an attorney in the city. Jake hated Christine Morton almost as much as Travis did.

Travis wanted as little as possible to do with the DA's office. With Jake. With Morton. With Velasquez. But this was big. *Family obligation* big. Something he just couldn't ignore. No gray areas, no room for interpretation. This was something he needed to tell Jake.

But as he thought it over, Travis really had no idea if he would.

"It's good to see you, Jake. Why don't we sit outside?"

Dave Carlisle stepped onto his front porch, graciously offering Jake a seat on the patio furniture.

Jake accepted warily. "If this is a bad time …"

Carlisle shrugged helplessly as he settled into a chair opposite Jake. "There's never really a good time these days, honestly. What can I do for you?"

Gray. That was the only word Jake had for it. Dave Carlisle had become a gray man, someone you'd never look at twice if you passed him in the grocery store. He'd once stood tall and spoken with conviction, now he'd deflated, caved in on himself. Diminished.

"I wanted to keep you apprised of developments in your son's case," Jake said, as delicately yet directly as he could. "We have more details."

Carlisle perked up a tiny bit. "Do you know which of those bastards pulled the trigger?"

Jake shook his head. "That's still under investigation. We do know there were three assailants, for lack of a better term."

A bit of color came into Carlisle's face. "Bastards. What other term would you use for the man who killed my son?"

Jake opened his mouth to reply, but Janet Carlisle bustled onto the front porch carrying a tray with glasses of iced tea. Carlisle's gaze darkened as his wife set out the glasses, oblivious to the building tension.

"It's good you've come by, Jake," she said, running a hand across her dark ponytail. "Gives me a chance to do something for someone else. Don't get me wrong, I'm grateful for all the help we've had, all the food and all the calls and whatnot. But after a while it just starts to remind …"

She broke off with a sob, putting her hand to her mouth. She wasn't wearing any jewelry, and she'd bitten her fingernails down. She wasn't wearing makeup, either, none at all. Her skin seemed stretched across her cheeks, with paper-thin wrinkles at the corners of her eyes.

"I'm sorry," she mumbled. "Can I get you something to eat? A cookie, maybe? Or a brownie? For some reason, people keep bringing us brownies."

"Jake was just going to update us on Peter's case," Carlisle said. He leaned forward on his elbows, fingers together in front of his chin; that was the old Dave Carlisle, the hardass Jake knew.

Without another word, Janet Carlisle sat. She tried to still her shaking fingers and finally clasped her hands in her lap.

Jake would rather have been in front of a hundred TV cameras. He licked his lips and took a sip of iced tea to soothe his suddenly-dry mouth.

"I was telling your husband," Jake said, "that we know there were three men. Three other men, that is, besides the three in your car. We don't have many details on the third one, but we're going back to interview the two we do have …"

"Hang 'em all," Carlisle barked. "Every last one."

"Now, David," Janet Carlisle said, rubbing her husband's arm. "Don't work yourself up."

Carlisle grumbled, but he let his wife assuage his temper. He still stared daggers at Jake.

"There is a bit of a problem, though," Jake continued. "We know what Peter was doing at the construction site. What he intended to do."

Janet Carlisle shook her head. "I told him he needed to give that up."

Her words hung in the air. Dave Carlisle averted his gaze, staring down into his iced tea.

"I'm sorry," Jake said, softly and evenly, "told him to give up what?"

"The pot," Janet said, smiling wanly at him. "It was just a phase. All kids go through it."

"Not all of them," Jake replied. He could feel the heat rising from deep in his belly. "But you knew about him smoking pot?"

"I don't think he ever smoked it, did he, David?" Janet said. "He just helped friends who wanted to buy it."

Carlisle refused to raise his head, refused to meet Jake's gaze.

"So he was *dealing* pot," the words almost refused to leave Jake's mouth. "And you knew?"

Wide-eyed and oblivious, Janet Carlisle nodded.

"How long?" Jake demanded. The heat in his belly had grown into a fire of righteous indignation.

"It's over, Jake, he's gone," Carlisle interjected, still not looking up. "Let it go."

"My kids play on these sidewalks," Jake growled. He jabbed his finger at his house, across the street and down three. "Peter brought that garbage to my neighborhood, and you *knew*?"

"It's no big deal," Janet insisted. "I don't know what you're getting so worked up for. It was a little pot."

"'A little pot,'" Jake spat. "Do you know what Peter was doing that got him killed? He was trying to buy methamphetamines. That's why he was in that construction area at three in the morning. To make a drug deal."

Janet Carlisle blinked, frozen where she was. A tiny tear sparkled at the corner of her eye. "That can't be true."

"We'll find the truth in court, when we have Kenny Galipo's testimony alongside the others'." Jake's lips curled back and his hands curled into fists. He hadn't been this enraged in years. Not since Travis found a conscience.

"I said, let it go," Carlisle muttered. "You can take care of this, can't you, Jake? You can charge these kids, get a plea, lock them up, all without a trial. You can make that happen, right?"

Carlisle's hand fell on his wife's, holding her trembling fingers tight.

"You've gotta be fuckin' kidding me." Jake's temper rose even higher.

"Remember who holds the reins around here," Carlisle warned. His voice was flat, without affect, and he stared sorrowfully at his wife. "You need to recognize when it's time to go along to get along."

Jake stood slowly, his heart pounding in his chest, his pulse throbbing in his skull.

His eyes like black pits, Carlisle raised his head. "One hand washes the other—you know that. You didn't get to be DA all by yourself. Now it's time to return the favor. Make this go away."

"No."

Janet Carlisle started weeping; soft, almost-silent sobs wracked her slender frame. Carlisle pulled his wife close.

"Now's not the time to take a moral stand, Jake."

Jake almost vibrated with rage. "Your son was dealing drugs. And you *knew*. You're complicit in everything that has happened, and everything that will happen. The community deserves to know the truth. All of it."

Before his hands could betray him, before he could wring Dave Carlisle's neck, Jake turned and marched stiffly down the sidewalk. He was going to need to set up the heavy punching bag in the garage to work off this fury.

Behind him, Janet Carlisle sobbed loudly. Pitifully.

"All right, Jake," Dave Carlisle called after him, "have it your way."

13

I'M STILL NOT CERTAIN WHY *you came in."*

Jake leaned back in the conference room chair, putting his hands behind his head. It was a very uncharacteristic move. Travis had never seen his brother do that before.

"I ... um ... I need to let someone know about what happened to me." The blonde woman, slight and pretty, barely more than a girl, stared up at Jake with big eyes.

"The police downstairs would have taken your statement," Jake replied. "You should talk to a desk sergeant."

The woman shook her head and passed her hand over a line of new, pink skin on her cheek, a scar from a recent injury. "They're not really interested in anything I have to say."

"I was intimidated by police too," Travis offered, "until I talked ... "

He trailed off as both his brother and the woman shot him withering glances.

"I recognize you, Ms. Gibson," Jake said, his hands still clasped behind his head.

A flash of panic shot across her face but she covered it almost immediately. "Have we met?"

"Not the way you think," Jake said. "You obviously don't remember, but I was low man on the totem pole at your arraignment two years ago."

She shrank, her hair falling across her face. "No, I don't remember you."

Jake grinned at Travis's confusion. "Karla's a hooker. On the street, she goes by Michelle."

She looked at Travis, her earnest blue eyes pleading. "I'm here to tell you about Reilly Sutton. About what he did. To me."

"Let me guess," Jake said, "he robbed you. Gave you a little something to remember him by on your face."

Her hand went to her cheek again, to the scar. "That's the start of it. I didn't know who he was until I saw his picture on the news this morning."

Jake shot a concerned glance at his brother. "The news?"

Karla turned to Travis again. "Look, I know the police and DA don't care if we get beat up, or robbed, or even killed. We're prostitutes, so we're less than human."

Jake sat up, his face coloring. "It's not that we don't care, it's that juries don't. Putting a prostitute on the stand is an extremely hard sell."

"We can still take her statement, can't we Jake?" Travis urged. "More evidence is better, and this speaks to his character."

Jake threw his hands up. "Be my guest. Just don't expect to see it at trial."

Karla grabbed Travis's hands and squeezed. "Thank you. I want him put away where he can't hurt anyone else."

"Put away?" Travis scoffed. "We're probably going for capital punishment."

"Dammit, Trav," Jake sighed.

Karla pulled her hands back. "Oh, no. No. You can't do that."

Travis glanced at his brother, whose face was now bright crimson. "It might be a little premature for an announcement, so please don't say anything."

"It doesn't bother you?" Karla asked, searching Travis's face. "The idea of executing someone?"

Travis shrugged. "It's the law."

"It's irrevocable," Karla replied. "If you get new evidence, you can always let someone out of prison. You can't un-kill them."

For a long time, Travis couldn't reply.

"Karla's also an undergrad at the university," Jake grunted as he got to his feet. "Get her statement on my desk by four o'clock."

"Don't get too comfortable. We have more clients this afternoon."

Shirley poked her head into the living room-office-disaster area and raised an eyebrow. "Did you hear me?"

Travis barely glanced up from the pile of documents on the coffee table in front of him. "Right. More clients."

"Trav, I'm serious," his wife continued. "You don't even have an hour. Enough time for lunch and to read through their files."

He shook his head, her words barely registering. He flipped through a second set of creased, stapled papers, growing more and more frustrated. The pages told him exactly what he did not want to hear.

Mark Kidd was nowhere to be found.

Two weeks shot to hell. Fourteen days of a private investigator's time that Shirley didn't know about and a bill that would make her mad enough to spit nails, all for nothing. All because he couldn't get up the courage to talk to his own brother.

The DA's office could find this guy, the third man. Finding people was what they did, they were good at it. But they needed somewhere to start, they needed a name, and Travis hadn't come through with this one. Now Jake and his pinstripe-suited minions were two weeks further along in the death penalty case against Sam Park, because Travis was behaving like a frightened little boy.

"You didn't have much of a breakfast, you need to eat." Shirley put a plate in front of him, a salad, of all things. She turned her attention to the wreck of papers and files that Travis generated while he worked, attempting to inject some kind of order into the chaos that was her husband's work space.

"You ever have to do something you really, really didn't want to do?" Travis mumbled. "Only you knew you had to do it for someone else's benefit?"

Her arms full of case files, Shirley paused, giving him an odd, almost guilty look. "What do you mean?"

"The Park case," Travis sighed. "I have a name, and I need to give it to Jake."

"So call and leave a message," Shirley snapped.

Travis shook his head. "After ten years, I'm going to leave a message with his assistant? For this kind of case? This needs to be in person. I need to look him in the eye."

Angrily gathering folders, Shirley muttered under her breath as she turned her back.

"You know I hate it when you do that."

"I said what you need to do is take care of these paying cases," Shirley barked, turning around with fire in her eyes. "We're in the black, Trav. For the first time in forever, we're actually ahead on our bills. If this keeps up, I'm even going to pay off a few completely. The last thing we need is you spending your time and your energy on a pro bono death penalty case."

She was an unstoppable force, taking every opportunity to urge him to give up on Sam Park. He was the immovable object, committed to seeing the case through to the bitter end, regardless of the consequences. Regardless of the strain it put on his relationship with the mother of his unborn daughter.

Travis blinked and looked away, breaking the tension.

"You just don't understand."

"You've said that before," Shirley replied, her voice surprisingly soft. "But if you explained it, maybe I would."

Unbidden, Reilly Wayne Sutton's face loomed large in Travis's memory. Not the man he was at his execution, but the man he had been ten years ago. Strong, arrogant, dangerous, reckless. But also beaten and trodden down, abandoned and neglected.

And angry. So angry. Just like Sam Park now.

He thought back ten years to that woman, the prostitute, also beaten and abandoned and neglected. As much a lost soul as Sutton, but instead of directing her hurt outward, instead of sharing her pain and spreading it around, she'd been the voice of reason. The person who'd changed Travis's mind, and his life, forever.

"You hear people say the death penalty is a deterrent," Travis said, talking to himself as much as his wife. "But that's not true. Murder is a crime of passion: No one stops to think of consequences in the heat of the moment. So they'll say it's punishment. But it's also retribution. And vengeance. They'll say it's a way to remove those people who have proven that they can't function within the bounds of society. Which is true, I suppose. But all those reasons sound to me like justification after the fact."

Shirley put down the files and knelt in front of Travis.

"But the arguments against capital punishment are usually calls for compassion and rehabilitation," Travis continued. "Which are really just appeals for clemency, and don't address the nature of capital punishment itself."

His wife grabbed his hands and squeezed, bringing him back from his memories. He looked her in the eye and smiled sadly.

"I've only ever heard one cogent argument for or against the death penalty that makes any sense. Ten years ago, I realized that when you allow capital punishment, you're granting the state the power over an individual's life and death. And I just can't abide that."

He could feel Shirley's heart beating through her fingers, a steady, warm pulse that rooted him to the here and now. Her eyes glistened with tears that wouldn't fall as she leaned forward and kissed him softly on the cheek.

"Okay."

With one word, she released him. Even as she let go of his hands and disappeared upstairs, Travis felt light. *Free.* He stood up, feeling as if he were breaking loose from cement. For the first time in ten years, he'd come very close to really opening up, and it felt good.

Travis grabbed the stack of files Shirley had left, and then a few more besides. She was right, their office was busy enough that he couldn't keep to his old sloppy habits. Things needed to be filed promptly and properly. And it would be a nice gesture to help Shirley, a way of saying thank you for her permission to continue with Sam Park.

Her footsteps sounded from upstairs, tiny, delicate echoes that matched her petite frame. Travis smiled. He was lucky to have someone like her, someone who would put up with him and all his tilting at windmills.

He scanned the temporary pressed-cardboard file cabinets—all they could really afford right now—looking for the proper drawer for the first folder. Shirley was very organized; each client's name was typed neatly, last name first, and arranged just-so on a tab. Travis flipped through the files quickly, glad that someone in the office took the time to create a system.

Files flipped by and Travis scanned the names, looking for the proper spot for the one in his hand. He was pleasantly surprised by just how many clients they had now, more than he had realized. He almost flipped past an odd file—the name wasn't typed neatly, it was written in pen.

Travis looked at the folder in his hand. "Malone, Sean" was typed and neatly centered on the tab. Yet there in the file cabinet he saw "Malone, Sean" written in a feminine hand.

It wasn't Shirley's handwriting. Whose was it?

"What are you doing?" Shirley's voice startled him so much he nearly dropped the files. "Give me those, you need to eat. I don't want you messing up my system."

Shirley grabbed the stack and closed the drawer. She stood in front of the file cabinet protectively, waiting for him to leave her to her task.

"I was just trying to help," Travis replied weakly.

His wife looked down and away from him. "I appreciate it. But stick to the lawyering, I'll take care of running the business."

Travis dutifully sat on the couch and began devouring his lunch as Shirley continued to straighten up. But even as he scanned the folder for his next client appointment, his mind never wandered far from the file cabinet.

Why would a strange woman's handwriting be on one of his client folders?

Jake grumbled as he paced back and forth in his office. He'd put pins into a large map of Austin hanging on one wall, and he discovered he needed to squint to see them when he stood a few feet away. Either he was so tired he couldn't see straight, or he finally needed glasses. Probably a little bit of both.

He did not need something else to worry about.

Ever since he was a little kid, when Jake needed to think, he needed to move. In a never-ending battle with his parents, teachers, and even bosses who told him to quit fidgeting, Jake knew the only way to get his thoughts out was to jostle them loose. When he had been in college he walked the university campus, from 26th Street to 19th Street and back again, over and over and over. As a junior DA he'd made a circuit of downtown Austin, from the Capitol down to the river. But as the boss, he couldn't just disappear when he needed to digest information, so he'd taken to pacing in his office. The scenery never changed, but if he kept his door closed no one bothered him. It was a fair trade.

He went to the map, standing less than a foot away. Each pin was a drug arrest, in his neighborhood and for a two-mile radius around. It was just a preliminary analysis—no record of any convictions or their severity—but it was a veritable forest of pins. Far too many, and too many of those clustered around Peter Carlisle's high school, the same high school Jake's own kids would attend one day. It seemed that Peter Carlisle and his foolish friends hadn't been innovators at all, they'd just been following a trend. All the cool kids were doing it.

Jake turned his back as his temperature rose. There were going to be even more pins, because the DA's office was actively working to uncover every single illegal activity at that school. The investigators were the best Jake had, and they'd started with an advantage. Kenny Galipo. Once he'd resigned himself to being a snitch, it was proving almost impossible for the kid to stop talking. He was quiet, but he had big ears and he named names.

There were other pins scattered across Austin, and they clustered, too. University neighborhoods, of course, and some of the lower-income areas, even a few surprising parts of the suburbs. But none of them bothered Jake as much as all the pins within walking distance of his house.

When Travis got ahold of this information ...

Jake tried to calm his nerves by taking a huge gulp of cold coffee that had been in the mug since before breakfast. He could almost make Travis's argument for him: Sam Park had been enticed into an illicit transaction by privileged rich kids who had been getting away with all sorts of illegal activity at their high school for years. The point was not germane to the fact of the murders, but all Travis had to do was plant that seed of doubt in jurors' minds. His little brother would consider any tactic a fair one if it turned the jury's opinion away from a capital murder charge for the two suspects.

Three. Jake needed to remember there were three assailants. Kenny Galipo had been very clear on that, even if he couldn't provide the third name. Three. Sam Park, Roger Laubach, and Mr. Nameless.

The primary investigators on the Carlisle case had canvassed every place Sam and Roger had been in the past two years and come up completely empty-handed. No one who knew anything was talking, and if they were talking, they didn't know a thing. That whole part of town circled the wagons when anyone with a badge came around.

Infuriating.

All Sam Park had to do was wait out the process, let the justice system run its course. Sure, the DA's office would file charges, and the case would come to trial, but with no eyewitnesses and neither of the two suspects breaking rank and turning on each other, there was almost no way to get any conviction, let alone a capital conviction.

Jake was about to begin another round of pacing between the map and his desk when voices outside his door caught his attention. Were those children? In the DA's office?

"I'm sure it's all right, Susan, we'll only be a minute." The door opened and Rita ushered herself in, followed by two little blonde whirlwinds, Eric and Heather, who raced to hug their father in a competition to see who could cling the tightest.

Susan caught Jake's eye and shrugged. He'd never given her instructions on what to do if Rita were to come in with the kids because it never seemed like something he'd have to plan for.

"We just had checkups at the dentist," Rita explained, "so I thought I'd bring the kids by. To remind you what they look like."

Jake carefully held his temper as he tried to pry his son and daughter loose from his legs. "Now? Why not any other dentist visit?"

"Yeah, Mommy," Eric said, his forehead creasing just like Jake's did when he got to thinking hard, "why haven't we ever been to Daddy's office before?"

Rita smiled a plastic beauty-queen smile. "Well, your Daddy hasn't been quite so busy before, has he? He's missed dinner three nights in a row this week."

"We had lasagna last night," Heather said, lisping past her missing front teeth. "That's your favorite."

"Daddy had lasagna too," Rita explained, "he just had it after you went to bed. Long after."

"This isn't fair, Rita," Jake hissed. "You know how important this case is. And with Travis on the other side …"

"That's why I'm bringing the family to you," Rita said breezily. She took in his office, a pig sty compared to the way she kept house, raising an eyebrow. When she caught sight of the map she approached it curiously. "Pins, Jake? You can't use a computer?"

"Sometimes I need something to touch."

Rita leaned closer, passing her fingers over the pins clustered around Peter Carlisle's high school. She looked up with panic in her eyes. "Is this…?"

He shook his head and glanced pointedly at their children.

"Eric, Heather, did you see the candy dish in the lobby?" Rita suggested.

"But we just went to the dentist," Heather said suspiciously.

"Think of it as a reward," Rita said. "And a chance to try out your new toothbrushes later."

The kids scampered off toward the lobby, earning a scowl from Susan that Rita completely ignored. As soon as they were alone, she drew near her husband.

"Is that what I think it is?" she hissed, pointing at the map.

"Arrests, only arrests," Jake explained half-heartedly. "The number of convictions is going to be much lower."

"Oh my God, Jake," Rita sighed. "So many."

"It's not as bad as it looks." He could feel his face getting hotter.

"But it's worse than it should be."

"Don't you think I know that?"

The sharp snap of his words drew Rita's undivided attention. Outside his door, Susan raised her chin and glanced his way.

"Honey, I didn't mean—" Rita began.

"I don't know what's worse," Jake interrupted, "that there are so many arrests, or that I had no idea what was going on in my own back yard."

Rita's expression melted and she reached for Jake's chin. He turned away, angry and embarrassed.

"Goddammit, Rita, I'm the DA." He kept his back to his wife, ashamed to let her see his face.

Rita's hands landed softly on his shoulders, kneading gently.

"How can I be doing any good for anyone if I can't even keep my kids safe in our neighborhood?"

"Don't second-guess yourself," Rita whispered.

"How can I not?" Jake muttered. "My job is to *stop* this kind of thing."

Rita's fingers kneaded harder. "Don't."

"Years," Jake mumbled, "it's been building for years. Probably as long as I've been in office."

"I said don't." Rita pushed on his shoulders, turning Jake around. "You always think everything is your responsibility, and when things go bad it's your fault. This isn't anything you could have controlled."

"You don't know that," Jake objected.

"What would you have done differently?" Rita challenged.

Jake hesitated.

"See?" his wife said softly. "All you can do is deal with the problem you have. You can't go back and fix it before it happened."

Eric and Heather raced back into the office, lips and fingers smeared with chocolate. Rita gave Jake a quick peck on the lips.

"Are we going to see you for dinner?"

Jake nodded as he leaned down to kiss his children on their sticky faces. He'd try.

Rita grabbed his chin as she ushered their children out of his office. "You be the best DA you can be."

He waited until his wife was out of earshot before he replied.

"I don't know how good that is any more."

14

THIS WAS IT. DEFINITELY. THE address on the house and the license plates on the car matched the private detective's report. Even the detective's descriptive asides were spot-on: 'Shabby' and 'run-down' did indeed describe the property. The entire neighborhood was nothing but tilted fences, bad-tempered outdoor dogs, and weeds growing through sidewalks.

All Travis had to do was get out of his car, walk across the street, and knock on the door. The private detective hadn't done that. Travis only paid her for information on Mark Kidd, not to confront him or anyone else. Yep, all he had to do was open the driver's door, unfold himself from the broken front seat, and march on over. Simple. Nothing to it.

A bead of perspiration trickled down his face; it wasn't even ten a.m., and already the temperature soared. He couldn't sit here another day, in a car without air conditioning in the middle of a Texas summer, sweating out of every pore in his body. He was wasting time, the one thing he absolutely could not spare. He had to pull the door handle and get the job done.

He couldn't.

Mark Kidd's last known address was yards away. Across a narrow residential street and a brown, weed-choked lawn. Mark wasn't there— he wasn't anywhere as far as Travis or the private detective could discern—but maybe there was someone in there who knew where he was. Travis needed to knock on that door.

He sighed and stayed put. It looked like this was going to be another wasted morning, more hours he could have been spending with paying clients.

He shook his head, trying to dislodge the notion. If he didn't represent Sam, someone like Mitchell would, a hack who hadn't cracked a law book since he'd barely passed the bar. No, this was important, even more important than paying the bills, as much as Shirley didn't want him working this case.

"Hey!"

The sharp exclamation accompanied a heavy rap on the roof of Travis's car.

"Who the fuck are you?" The words had a North Texas twang and a drunk's slur.

A thick, heavy man leaned on Travis's car, his face thrust through the window, his gin-blossom nose looming large in Travis's vision. The man's breath was more liquor than air, cheap, sour tequila that made Travis gag.

"I seen you sittin' here for three days now," the man said, his eyes struggling to focus on Travis, "and I had enough of it. Whatever bill you're collectin' for, I'm not payin'. Got it? So get on out of here before I go get my shotgun and encourage you."

"I'm not a bill collector," Travis replied. "I'm just looking for someone. He lives in that house over there."

The man half-turned the direction Travis pointed. "That's my place."

Travis's eyes flicked toward the private detective's report on the passenger seat. She'd mentioned someone else in the house, the father presumably. No other names listed on any bills or credit reports. No mother.

"Are you Mr. Kidd?"

Nodding, the man moved back a few steps as Travis opened the car door. He eyed Travis suspiciously, as if a gunfight might break out in the middle of the street at any moment. His eyes went wide when he saw how tall Travis actually was.

Travis stuck his hand out, putting a friendly smile on his face and in his voice. "I'm an attorney, but don't worry, I'm not here to sue anybody."

It took the man a few moments to make the decision, but he finally shook Travis's hand. His grip was strong, his palms wide and rough. When he worked—which might not be very often—Mr. Kidd used his hands.

"My name's Travis."

The man's eyebrows came together. "Kevin. Do I know you?"

"We've never met," Travis replied. "Let me get right to it. I'm looking for Mark Kidd. I assume he's your son?"

For a moment the man's face fell, his mask dropped and a look of supreme anguish washed over him. He covered it quickly, clearing his throat and raising his chin. "Well, I'm his father, you just gotta stand us next to each other to see it. Mark's never been much of a son."

"Sorry to hear that," Travis continued. "Would you know where I might find him?"

Kevin took a deep breath, one that shuddered his chest, then he closed his eyes sadly as he shook his head. "Haven't seen the boy in weeks. And, tell you the truth, I'm getting worried. You got any kids?"

Travis shook his head.

"Do yourself a favor: Don't bother. Not worth the trouble."

"Could I ask you a few questions?" Travis said. "I promise it won't take long."

Mark's father considered the request, peering at Travis out of the corner of his eye, sizing him up. Finally, after what seemed like minutes, he nodded.

"We gotta talk out here," he said, leaning against the fender of Travis's car. "I don't let strangers into my house without a warrant."

Several neighbors watched Travis and Mr. Kidd intently, not even bothering to pretend they weren't eavesdropping. No doubt some of them recognized Travis from ten years ago, even if Mr. Kidd hadn't made the connection yet. Travis resigned himself to a public interview, with a drunk man, in middle of a neighborhood where he was the rich intruder. He reminded himself it was for the cause, for Sam's defense.

"Do you know Mark's friends?" Travis asked. Mr. Kidd shrugged, tossing a vague sort of nod. "How about a guy named Roger Laubach?"

Mr. Kidd scratched his chin. "I dunno. Fat kid? Dark hair? Kind of stupid looking?"

"That's him," Travis replied. "Did Mark spend a lot of time with him?"

"This Laubach kid get into some trouble?"

Travis's eyebrows raised, but he kept his cool. Obviously Mr. Kidd wasn't in the habit of reading newspapers. Or of watching local news, assuming there was a working television in the house.

"He's in jail," Travis replied.

"Then Mark probably hung out with him," Mr. Kidd sighed. "I don't know what's up with that boy. He's smart. Scary smart. Always was. I thought that would get him out, you know? He graduated high school, so he beat me there. Barely. He's in community college, but I don't know how that's going, he doesn't talk to me much. I just want him to skip the mistakes I made and get the fuck out. Get away from here. Away from me."

"Maybe that's what he did?" Travis offered.

Mr. Kidd shook his head. "He'd want to rub my nose in it. Show me how he made it and I didn't. And I'd let him. I'd probably hug the little bastard too. Not showing up for weeks … it's not like him at all."

"What about guns?" Travis asked. "Did Mark own any?"

A huge guffaw erupted from Mr. Kidd's lips, and he bent nearly double. He laughed until he coughed, and coughed until he choked. He turned red and then blue, and Travis was worried he might be having a heart attack. Neighbors even craned their necks, trying to see what the commotion was about.

Finally Mr. Kidd composed himself enough that he could stand straight again. "Sorry, but if you knew my boy that would be Goddamned funny to you, too. No, I can tell you for sure that Mark does not own a gun. I own eight or ten. Ten. I think. Anyway, whenever I tried to teach that punk to shoot, he'd tell me he wasn't interested. Like he was too good to hold a pistol. Wouldn't touch a BB gun. Wouldn't pick up a bullet."

Travis frowned. This was not the answer he was expecting. Or the one he'd been hoping for.

"So, he's never actually fired—"

"Wouldn't even touch a holster," Mr. Kidd interrupted. "I guess he wanted to make himself as different from his old man as possible. Good for him."

"One more question, if I may?" Travis asked.

Mr. Kidd patted his pockets absently. "You know, I could use a smoke. But I think I'm out. Don't think there's a pack in the house either, if you catch me."

Travis handed over a twenty-dollar bill, which Mr. Kidd promptly stuffed in his pocket. "Fire away, stretch."

"Did you ever meet one of Mark's friends by the name of Sam Park?"

In an instant Mr. Kidd's placid, if flushed, expression hardened into a mask of pure hatred. His jaw tightened and worked as if he were trying to chew his own teeth while his eyebrows collided in the center of his forehead.

The veins on Mr. Kidd's nose threatened to burst and he breathed so hard he was almost hyperventilating. "If you know him, you remind him the last place he wants to come around is here."

"He's in jail too," Travis said hastily, glad he hadn't introduced himself as Sam's attorney. "Can I ask what he—"

"Stealing," Mr. Kidd interrupted again. He gestured across the street. "Look at my fucking house. Does it look like I got anything worth taking? But that little bastard, he'd swipe anything that wasn't nailed down. I caught him. Twice. Trying to take one of my pistols. Warned him the first time, punched him the second. Told him there wasn't gonna be a third."

Travis's smile tightened. "Just wondering, sorry to upset you. If I do ever see him, I'll be sure to tell him what you've shared with me."

Mr. Kidd's thick, workman's finger landed in the center of Travis's sternum. "No, you tell Sam Park if I ever see him again, I'm gonna put a shotgun in his mouth and make a doughnut out of his skull."

Built by a cattle baron and former Confederate colonel Jesse Driskill, the Driskill Hotel had overseen Austin's business at 6th and Brazos since 1886. A large Victorian structure, the establishment had gone from diamond in the rough to neglected icon back to lavish showplace in its century-plus of existence. Many Texas politicians had adopted the Driskill as their own special haven, from Governors Hobby, Moody, Connally, and Richardson to President Johnson, who had his first date with his future wife in the hotel's restaurant.

The lobby set visitors' expectations, with two-story columns advancing across marble floors, huge leather-covered furniture, and a large portrait of Colonel Driskill watching over it all. People who frequented the hotel felt a sense of privilege and entitlement when they came back, not only like they belonged, but that they deserved such opulence.

The lobby staff greeted Jake cordially as he entered, briefcase in one hand and his suit coat draped over the other arm. This wasn't Jake's first time in the Driskill: The Lynch family had been regulars here since the hotel opened. Distracted, Jake acknowledged the staff with a nod and a wave and mounted the grand stairs to the upper lobby. His father had insisted on meeting Jake today, and "no" was just not an answer Jake was allowed to give. Of course Val Lynch wouldn't say what the meeting was about; when he got secretive like this the topic could be literally anything. Six months ago it had been a living will Val didn't want Mae to know about, but the time before that it had been a puppy for Claire. Anything.

Jake waved off the waiter approaching him discreetly in the upper lobby and scanned the low, heavy leather furniture for his father—who was, of course, nowhere in sight. Since he'd given up day-to-day operations of Lynch & Brockhurst, Val had become almost Bohemian in his attention to time. He'd get here when he got here and not a moment before.

The overstuffed chairs beckoned Jake, enticing him to sit, just for a moment, put his feet up and relax. Instead, Jake put his briefcase on a table and stood while he scanned the latest report from the team working the Carlisle case.

As he read, Jake's blood pressure rose. Nothing new. Since the last report, his staff had produced exactly zero insights and provided him precisely zero analyses that he hadn't already seen. Even after multiple rounds of interrogation, Sam Park and Roger Laubach steadfastly maintained they had been the only two in that construction area. Yet Jake heard with his own ears Kenny Galipo saying there had been three assailants, but the only name the boy knew was Sam's.

Deadlock. Stalemate. Without either Park or Laubach naming the third man, they could each maintain they hadn't pulled the trigger. All they had to do was keep their mouths shut until the trial and Jake had nothing but circumstantial evidence. Not even enough to bag a murder conviction, let alone capital murder.

Who was Sam Park protecting? That kid definitely was not the giving sort: he was loyal only so far as there was something in it for him, and he clearly wasn't afraid of anyone or anything. So why wouldn't he give up the third guy? What game was he running?

"Oh, *there* he is."

Jake watched his father coming up the stairs with a big smile on his angled face. Beside him walked another man, shorter, heavier, with sweeping waves of snow white hair on his head and a huge white mustache dominating his face. A dapper man whose eyes danced with mischief, he wore a suit three or four times more expensive than Jake's, and Jake never went for the cheap stuff. Light glinted from the extremely costly, understated watch on the man's wrist and on the eyeglasses framing his rugged face. When he shook Jake's hand, it was a firm rancher's grip, not a limp city person's.

"Sorry we're a little late," Val Lynch said, though he didn't sound sorry in the least, "but Mel was showing me his heirloom tomatoes. Son, you remember Mel, don't you?"

"Of course," Jake said, masking his confusion with a smile. His father never said anything about a guest. "Mr. Davis and I worked together during the last election."

You couldn't be a power player in Austin and not know Mel Davis. If functionaries pulled the strings of the political machine, Davis pulled the functionaries' strings. He was *the* mover-and-shaker, the one who got things done, the one who made or broke careers. You couldn't survive Austin politics if Mr. Davis decided he didn't like you.

"Oh, right. After a while, all that stuff kind of blends together," Val said. Still with that big, suspicious smile on his face, he clapped Jake on the back. "Good to see you."

"How about we sit?" Davis said, beckoning a waiter. "I don't know about you boys, but I'm parched."

A suggestion from Mel Davis really was not a suggestion at all, so Jake sat. Beside him, his father sank casually into one of the big comfortable seats. Jake envied his father's ease, the same kind of manner Travis had. They could talk to almost anyone and make a friend. Jake was too focused on results to allow himself the niceties that would have made people like him. He sat last, after Davis leaned back into an overstuffed chair.

"Good to see you in office for another term," Davis said, his gaze locked on Jake.

"It was tougher this time," Jake said, recalling the hard-fought battle to keep his job. "We squeaked it through, thanks to you."

Davis brushed the notion aside with a wave. "People give me too much credit. The people didn't elect me, they elected you."

A waiter approached, quiet, deferential, ready to take Jake's drink order.

"Mineral water, please," Jake said to the waiter as he nodded politely to Davis.

"Hell, give him a beer," Val called out. "He's old enough."

Jake's father and Davis laughed, but Jake shook his head. "I'm still technically on the job. Back to the office after this, another few hours of work. Really busy, if you know what I mean."

He looked pointedly from his father to Davis and back again. If there were a polite way to demand that these two stop wasting his time, Jake hoped he'd just found it.

"Keep your boots on," Davis drawled. "We're waiting for one more person."

Jake raised an eyebrow at his father, who refused to return the look and instead studied his fingernails.

"What's going on Dad?" Jake asked, keeping his voice low. "You're not running for governor again, are you?"

Davis and his father exchanged a brief, guilty glance.

"Hell, no," Val said with a laugh. "Once was too much. How Mel convinced me to have a second go is a mystery."

Davis patted Val on the arm, a familiar gesture that was also the tiniest bit condescending. "Just wasn't your time."

"Sorry I'm late."

The deep voice caught Jake by surprise, and Dave Carlisle leaned across the table to shake hands. Jake kept the pleasantly neutral smile on his face, even as inside he railed against the subterfuge. There was absolutely no way Jake would have agreed to meet Carlisle here in a public place.

"What are you fellas having?" Carlisle asked as the waiter appeared at his elbow. "It's five o'clock somewhere, right?"

Jake glared at his father, furious at the violation of trust.

"Don't worry," Carlisle turned to Jake as the waiter hurried off, "I'm not here about the case. Peter's case. I know it's one day at a time for you and me both, and we'll just have to see how it all plays out."

"I appreciate that," Jake said. He didn't believe a word of it.

"We were just talking about Val's runs for Governor," Davis said, his eyes twinkling.

Carlisle nodded sagely; he'd been involved in those campaigns. "I remember them well. Too bad it didn't work out."

"I'm not the political one in the family anyway," Val said. Even though his own ambitions had been thwarted, Val made no secret of his pride in his son.

Jake shifted uncomfortably, as three sets of eyes focused on him. His father looked as if he were about to burst at the seams, Davis wore an enigmatic smirk, and Carlisle's hostile smile never quite reached his eyes.

Davis leaned forward, clasping his hands and focusing on Jake. "Even if your father isn't going to run, there's no reason another Lynch shouldn't."

"No reason at all," Carlisle echoed.

His pulse rising, Jake glanced around the table. "I don't think you're going to get Mama to run."

"We're not talking about your mother," Val said.

All three men stared at Jake expectantly.

The waiter delivered the drinks, and Jake downed half his glass of water in one gulp. "I'm going to guess you're not talking about Claire or Travis either."

Davis swirled his bourbon and leaned back, surveying the table like the power broker he absolutely was. "How does Governor Jacob Neill Lynch sound to you?"

For the first time in a very long time, Jake had no clue what to do or what to say. He'd been so focused on being the District Attorney, the only job he really wanted, that he hadn't considered for a moment doing anything else. Higher office was the next logical step, if he were determined to stay in public life. But governor? Now?

His father beamed with pride, Davis stayed infuriatingly unreadable, and Carlisle's insincere grin made him look like a pageant queen forced to endure another public event. Clearly there was far more behind this offer than Jake knew.

He gestured to the waiter. "I think I will take that beer after all."

15

THE CRACK OF A BALL connecting with pins echoed across the nearly-empty bowling alley. The lunch league players were long gone and the evening league players had yet to arrive, leaving the place a ghost town.

Karla Gibson shivered as she wiped her bar clean; her fingers were freezing and the tip of her nose tingled. Outside the temperature rose steadily, it was probably in the mid-nineties, but inside, the manager Ravi kept the cavernous space almost thirty degrees cooler. With her slender build, it was like tending bar in the walk-in freezer.

She flipped a page in the textbook propped against the beer tap and squinted as she read. Tending bar in a bowling alley wasn't a career she'd settle for, not anymore at least, but for right now, it kept her in an apartment and paid her tuition. While Ravi wasn't completely on board with her using company time to study, he didn't hassle her too much when she did. Especially not when it was during the dead part of a weekday.

Karla rubbed her hands together, trying to get some feeling back into them before she had to reach into ice-cold water again to clean the bar glasses. Maybe Ravi would let her sneak outside for a few minutes, to bask in the warm sun like a rattlesnake.

The automatic doors clicked and clattered as someone came in, sending a welcome draft of hot air through the space. And, thank the

Lord, whoever it was stood in the doorway, letting more air in. As Karla enjoyed the brief heat, she noticed the counter was vacant. Cesar was probably out back sneaking a smoke, and Mike was probably sneaking a beer. Ravi pretended not to notice anyone had come in; he was in the middle of his game and kept his back turned. Karla sighed; she hated doing someone else's job in addition to her own. She fumbled with her apron and tried to see who the customer was; she hoped it wasn't the homeless guy who stuck his hands down his pants.

"Hello?" The woman at the door sounded confused. She probably wanted to know where everybody was, too.

There was a crash from the lane, and Ravi raised his hands with a triumphant shout, another strike. Karla came around the bar, heading for the door. She stopped dead in her tracks as she recognized the woman.

"Oh. It's you."

"I get that a lot," Christine Morton said with a snide smile. "Do you have a few minutes?"

It had been years since Karla had seen her in person. Though Karla guessed Morton was a few years older than herself, she looked younger. She still stood tall, her hair carefully set and now very blonde, her clothes tasteful and understated and probably worth more money than Karla made in a month.

"Actually, I'm busy." Karla headed back to her bar.

The crash of pins echoed in the empty hall as Ravi rolled another strike.

"Are you sure?" Morton's voice carried the same condescending note it had ten years ago, like fingernails on a chalkboard.

Karla went to work, her back still to Morton. "What the hell do you want?"

"Just to talk," Morton said, following. "No camera, no tape recorder. I don't even have my pad and pen."

Grabbing a bar towel to stop her hands from shaking, Karla avoided eye contact as she wiped the expanse of bar she'd already cleaned. "Why now? It's done, over with, you know? Weeks ago."

"I was there when they executed him." Morton eased onto a stool.

Karla's hand went to her cheek, to the side of her head, and her eyes closed. She didn't remember what she had for lunch yesterday, but she remembered that night like she'd just woken up from it. She could still feel the blows, still feel each knuckle of his fist on her face, still taste the blood.

"Then there's nothing more to say."

"I was going over my old notes, looking at everything in a new light," Morton said. "I found two loose ends. I hate loose ends."

"Not really my problem, is it?"

Morton's smug grin was exactly the same as ten years ago. "We'll see. You remember the trial. The Lynch boys. You know, that cute younger brother, the tall one with the dark hair?"

It had been in the interview room, the one that smelled like cigars, when she'd first met him. Karla had felt herself caught in his blue eyes, at first so fierce and then so compassionate. And so distant. He moved in different circles, his family had friends and connections that put him in a league far above Karla's own. But that didn't mean she hadn't hoped, with a tiny part of her soul, that he might look past who she was, past what circumstances had forced her to become.

Karla plunged her hands into the freezing rinse water in her sink, shaking her had to get the memory out. To erase the look in his eyes when they'd last spoken. Ten years ago. "Like I said, it's been done for a long time. Nothing more to it."

"Jake and Travis," Morton muttered, picking at a bowl of peanuts. "Fire and water. I've seen family drama before, but that situation was a trash fire."

Shaking her head, Karla refused to engage. She polished glasses that were already spotless, trying to ignore the reporter.

"I studied my notes," Morton might as well have been talking to herself, "and I was never able to wrap that up. Not then, not now."

With a sigh, Karla looked Morton in the eye. "If you're not going to buy a drink or roll a game or two, you should probably go."

"What changed Travis's mind?" Morton pressed. "Do you have any idea? Did he mention anything to you?"

"Do you want to know what I remember?" Karla snapped, as warm anger bubbled up inside her. "Cameras. *Your* cameras. Always there. And you in front of them, destroying my life to make your career."

A stiff smile showed on Morton's face. "That's hardly fair. I was just doing my job. Like I'm doing right now."

"You're a vulture," Karla countered.

Morton's lips pursed, and she glanced away. "I don't think you understand the role of the fourth estate."

"I understand this: You *liked* ruining me. Ruining Travis Lynch. Tearing us down a little bit every day. You didn't need to do that to make a name for yourself, but you did it anyway. Because cruelty makes you feel powerful."

The reporter's face changed from impassive to thoughtful. She nodded slightly.

Karla busied herself with cleaning another glass. "I'm done talking to you."

Morton's finger traced the book propped against the beer tap. "This looks like it's for a class. I thought you were a couple of semesters away from graduating ten years ago. Then on to a master's, maybe a PhD. Isn't that what you told me then?"

"Get out." Karla shoved her finger in Morton's face. "Right now, or I'm calling the cops."

"I get that a lot too," Morton replied as she strolled for the door.

"Don't come back," Karla called after her.

Morton stopped and turned around.

"Michelle."

Karla suddenly went as cold as the water in her sink. "What did you say?"

"That was my second loose end. When you were, you know, a prostitute. Why did you pick the name Michelle?"

"No … no reason," Karla replied. Despite her best efforts to keep them down, images of that room leapt to her mind's eye. *Her* room, the place where she worked, with its flaking white paint, its yellowed wall fixtures, the horrible rattan hanging lamp suspended over a cheap motel table. The chair where the men would usually hang their coats. Their pants.

"It's ultimately not important," Morton said. "I mean, not germane to Sutton's trial. But I always wondered."

Karla's hands shook. That part of her life had been over for eight years, but Morton took her right back there, as if she'd never left.

"I did a little digging last week." Morton locked eyes with her. "At first I thought it might be totally random. Maybe you chose Michelle because you didn't know anyone with that name, or it was a movie star. Like that. But then I looked over your high school yearbooks."

"You need to go." Karla's panic and trauma rapidly turned to rage.

"You were bookish, kind of a nerd, a few close friends," Morton continued, almost disinterested. "Just one more random kid biding her time until high school ended. But then I found Michelle Dowe."

Karla seethed, and her fingers curled around a thick, heavy bottle of amaretto. She could do serious damage with something that heavy. It would be everything Morton deserved.

"Kind of your opposite: cheerleader, artist, student council, very popular. I'm guessing you and she didn't get along. But where did the bad blood start? With you? With her? I'll bet it was middle school. Middle school is the worst. But was it terrible enough to make a girl take her enemy's name when she becomes a prostitute?"

"GET OUT!" Karla yelled. The outburst was enough to make Ravi glance over from his game, even take a few steps in Karla's direction.

"I'll take that as a yes," Morton said calmly. She hadn't flinched, hadn't even moved when Karla screamed. "You'd think I'd get tired of being right all the time, but it never gets old. Maybe we'll talk again."

The door opened and closed, sending another blast of air through the bar, but this time it didn't warm Karla.

"That'll be a cold day in hell."

16

TRAVIS HAD BEEN DISTRACTED ALL *week as the prostitute's words played over and over in his mind, so he only half-heard what the widow in the liquor store said.*

"I'm sorry, there's a lot to think about with this case."

"I said I have to be out by Friday," the woman replied as she bustled from shelf to shelf, "so you talk while I work."

The place smelled strongly of disinfectant and bleach, and Travis noticed the woman, Marina, avoided the counter area, the place where her husband had been stabbed. They were Persian, had immigrated fifteen years earlier, and she spoke with a charming, subtle accent, though her words were tinged with the kind of grief Travis hoped he would never understand.

"My brother wants me to interview you again," Travis apologized, "but I don't know what I can ask that you haven't already told the police."

Marina boxed a few more bottles of gin, then paused. "Sayeed was a gentle man. He never woke me when he left early or when he came home late. He made tea just the way I like it, and never too hot." She bit her lower lip and swallowed, trying to hold back the tears. "They didn't ask about that."

"I'm sorry," Travis said, his heart going out to her. "Can I help you carry something?"

Marina shook her head. "I have to do it by myself. Inventory was my job with the store, and it's the last thing I can do for Sayeed."

"When we prosecute this guy, what would ... " Travis stammered, finally trailing off awkwardly.

"What would I do with the man who killed my husband?" A sad smile played on her face then faded. "If you asked me that last week my answer would have been different from today. And if you ask me a year from now it will be different again. This is, I think, why justice needs to be impartial. This is not a matter of personal honor, it is a matter of law."

Chagrined, Travis could only blush and look away.

"Oh, since you are with the police, I have something for you."

"I'm not with the—" Travis started to say, but in an instant she disappeared into the back room.

In another moment she returned and firmly pressed a flash drive into Travis's palm. "This is from the camera."

She pointed to the security camera mounted high on the wall behind the counter.

"I thought that was fake." Travis's heart fell into his stomach. He'd never bothered to verify what Officer Porter told him.

"It used to be, but Sayeed put in a real camera just a few days before ... " Marina stopped, choking back a sob. She mumbled a few words in a language Travis didn't understand before she composed herself. "It is the file from that night. I can't watch it."

The flash drive suddenly felt heavy in his hand. Chances were very good the camera caught the last moments of Sayeed Homayanpour's life. The perpetrator was probably plainly visible.

"The police ... " Travis stammered. "This should ... I can't ... "

"You are a good man," Marina said. "You will know what to do with it, where I do not. Please, watch it, use it as you can."

"What is up with you?"

Susan looked over her glasses at Jake, who stood at her desk without the slightest idea what he'd come to ask her about. It was the second time today his mind had gone blank, which was two times more than usual.

"Got a lot to think about lately, I suppose," Jake replied. The words sounded weak to him, like something Velasquez would say.

Susan waited patiently as he tried to make up a reason for his intrusion in her work day, but his mind just wouldn't cooperate. Finally, he just shrugged and strolled back into his office. He closed the door and stood there for a few seconds before he realized there was work waiting for him at his desk. His mind was still back in the Driskill three days ago.

Governor Jacob Neill Lynch.

Those words had lodged in Jake's head from the moment Mel Davis had let them slip past his white mustache. Governor. It just didn't sound right.

District Attorney Lynch: *That* sounded right. That sounded like someone with purpose, someone who accomplished things. Someone who kept the wheels of justice turning. District Attorney was an office he'd prepared for, an office he'd sought out, a job he was good at, that he knew forwards and backwards.

Governor? Jake wasn't anywhere near prepared to hold that office, not even in Texas, with its extremely weak executive. The governor's mansion was somewhere he visited, not a place he ever thought he might live.

And why now?

Jake grabbed the new bottle of bourbon from his bottom desk drawer, cracked it open and poured himself two fingers in a glass he was pretty sure hadn't been cleaned since the night Sutton was executed. Jake knocked back the bourbon in one gulp, wondering about the motive behind this seeming gift of the governorship.

He could still see Carlisle's smile, that Cheshire cat grin, as if things were falling into place in a scheme Jake wasn't privy to. If Carlisle was involved, it had to be related to the "Rich Kid Murders." But Jake couldn't see the connection. Carlisle would rather cut his own arm off than shake hands with Jake, but he sat in the Driskill's upper lobby and offered Jake the kind of job that capped a career.

It made no sense. Jake hated things that made no sense.

Still, it wasn't a problem he was going to solve this afternoon. He'd play Carlisle's game and hope he figured things out before it was too late to change the rules. He dropped the bourbon and glass back into his desk drawer and sat heavily, resigned to the work he had been avoiding all day.

The case file for the Rich Kid Murders sat on his desk, a thin, sorry excuse of a thing: Jake had seen misdemeanor case files five times that size. By this point, weeks after the murders, the DA's office should have been awash in paperwork. There should have been clerks regretting their choice of careers because of all the transcription and busy work associated with the reams of evidence and depositions they were obligated to work through. But there had been no progress in over a week, and Jake's clerks were woefully underworked. The case had hit a brick wall.

Jake had never seen anything like it. Each case had its own rhythm, but he had never had one shrivel up and die like this. They had the two men—kids, really—in custody, but that was as far as things had gotten. The Galipo kid hadn't seen who held the gun when Peter Carlisle took a slug to the skull, and the two in custody each insisted it hadn't been either of them, steadfastly denying the existence of a third person Kenny clearly recalled. What Jake had at first thought was a by-the-numbers murder investigation had turned into some sort of chess game.

Then there was Travis.

Jake almost reached for the bottle of bourbon again. Why did it have to be Travis? The Parks could have chosen anyone else; by hiring his brother, they had gotten under Jake's skin. Eventually he and Travis were going to have to sit across from one another in open court, and it would be even money on which of them threw the first punch.

A knock sounded at his door, and Velasquez peered in timidly, clearly expecting to encounter Ogre Jake in his lair. "Got a second, boss?"

Jake nodded and waved his subordinate in. Dealing with Velasquez was just one more stone on the pile that was already crushing him.

"I think we may have an opening in the Carlisle case," Velasquez said. He placed a stapled document in front of Jake. "Forensics found both Sam Park's fingerprints and Roger Laubach's fingerprints on the inside of the BMW."

A raised eyebrow was all the reaction Jake gave. He waited for Velasquez to continue, but that was the extent of his revelation.

"So we have fingerprints inside a vehicle," Jake sighed, "that the two of them admit to entering? What kind of opening is that?"

"But their fingerprints place them—"

Jake flipped open the case file. "It's right here, Bobby. Both of them, independently, admit to entering the car and taking money from the bodies. Of course their fingerprints are going to be all over it."

"Yeah, okay, that makes sense," Velasquez mumbled.

"Dammit, Bobby, we have to be better than this!"

"Of course, Jake, I don't know what—"

"Sit down."

Velasquez took one look at Jake's commanding stare and hastily took a seat. Jake stood and handed over the case file.

"Susan told me my brother was here last week," Jake said quietly. "And that you spoke with him."

Velasquez went white as a sheet and could only nod.

"What did you think of him?"

For several seconds, Velasquez considered his answer carefully. Jake could see him discard words before they crossed his lips; it seemed Velasquez couldn't avoid politics.

"He seemed a little … casual," Velasquez said finally, with a tremendous gulp.

"Wrong answer," Jake growled. "He may look like an average Austin slacker, but Travis is the second-best attorney I know. Don't let his wardrobe fool you into complacency."

"Absolutely not, I would never …"

"Look in the file," Jake interrupted. "Three-quarters of what we have comes from the law office of Travis Lynch. Filings, notices, briefs, look at them, what do you see?"

Velasquez shrugged as he scanned a few pages. "All very thorough, completely professional."

"Wrong again," Jake spat. "They're not just 'professional.' They're *perfect*. All the i's dotted, all the t's crossed, even the *line spacing* is dead-on. There is nothing in there we can challenge on any kind of technicality. Now take a look at the garbage we put together."

His brow furrowed as Velasquez read.

"Kind of embarrassing, isn't it?" Jake snapped. "My little brother, in his one-man living room law firm, is outclassing the District Attorney's office like we're a bunch of snot-nosed clerks!"

Jake paced in front of his desk, his powerful stride taking him across the room and back in a few steps. Velasquez quailed, cringing as if he were afraid he might get hit.

"Travis doesn't make mistakes," Jake declared. "Which means we can't either. Nothing riles him, nothing makes him lose his cool—he sets his sights on the horizon and marches on until he reaches his goal. We have to match him strength for strength. That's the only way we're going to beat him."

"Um … Jake? Can I speak plainly?"

Jake stopped pacing and turned his furious glare on the assistant DA. Since when did someone like Roberto Velasquez speak plainly? Jake crossed his arms over his chest and perched on the edge of his desk, practically daring Velasquez to speak.

"I think your brother's gotten into your head."

His mouth opened, but Jake never uttered the denial. It was true. The war had started, and Jake had been caught unprepared, his own personal Pearl Harbor.

Travis had already won the first battle.

"Well, how about that," Jake muttered. "You're right, Bobby. One-hundred percent."

A flicker of a smile worked across Velasquez's face. "Maybe we should have someone else review all the documents from our side. You've got an entire office to run, plus with your brother being opposing counsel … "

"Are you suggesting I put you on this case?" Jake snarled.

Velasquez looked away, a beaten dog preparing himself for another kick. "I don't want to step on any—"

"I think it's a good idea," Jake replied. He gestured at the manila folder Velasquez still clutched. "You're in charge of the investigation."

An eager smile flashed on Velasquez's face before he stifled it. He tried to maintain decorum as he stood and headed for the door, but Jake could see him twitch, as if he were forcing himself not to jump for joy.

"You won't regret this, Jake, I promise," Velasquez gushed as he held the case folder tight.

Jake nodded, turning his back. "I'm sure I won't."

"Thank you for coming by, Mrs. Rohde, we'll get that filed as soon as possible."

Shirley escorted the last client of the day out the door, but Travis barely noticed. To his right on the coffee table sat a large stack of files, all the work he'd been doing this past month or so, the paying jobs. To his left sat the Park file, all by itself. He should have been focused on the larger stack, the one that had his practice booming like never before, but the Park file still drew all his attention. The gears of justice turned, slowly but inexorably, and Sam Park was well on his way to being ground up in the machine. Sam had become his own worst enemy, forcing Travis to fight on two fronts.

The prosecution was proving as formidable as Travis knew they would be. Jake was confident, maybe even arrogant, filing a capital case with nothing but circumstantial evidence linking Sam to the two dead boys. The newspapers were full of speculation as to Jake's real motives—given his connection to Dave Carlisle—but the consensus seemed to be that the DA's office had a very winnable case. Travis couldn't disagree.

"And now I have another hour and a half of billing," Shirley said, grabbing the larger stack of files. "It's good to be busy, don't you think?"

Travis nodded, still staring at the Park file. That defense wasn't going to mount itself, but he'd done all he could. Mostly. He had never quite gotten around to sharing Mark Kidd's name with Jake's office.

How hard was it? He could have done like Shirley suggested and just left a message. He could even have made it anonymous, there was no reason anyone needed to know he was involved. But he just couldn't do it. The name ate at him, kept him up at night, made him short-tempered. Mark Kidd. The third man on Sam's crew. The guy who could clear all this up, the man whose testimony would answer the question as to who had pulled the trigger, who had killed Shane Ablin and Peter Carlisle. So why couldn't Travis hand over the name?

He frowned as the answer bubbled up in his conscience. He needed Sam to be innocent. Right now, as far as he was concerned, Sam *was* innocent. But if Mark Kidd were in police custody, if he were interviewed by the DA's office, then the uncomfortable truth would almost certainly come out.

Travis suspected the truth would not be kind to Sam Park.

With a flash of polished chrome and the purr of a well-tuned engine, a car pulled up in the driveway.

"Oh, by the way, Claire's coming over," Shirley said as she arranged her work at her computer. "When I have the baby, I won't be able to do all this billing and scheduling and filing. Your sister has some names of people who might be interested. We're going to have an office staff, isn't that great?"

"Fantastic," Travis mumbled. He didn't know where he'd fit another person in his tiny living room.

He stood up as his big sister breezed through the front door accompanied by the jangle of bracelets and the scent of expensive perfume on the hot afternoon air. Claire and his wife exchanged hugs and pecks on the cheek as Travis watched, barraged by their rapid-fire chattering. Shirley brushed Claire's lapels, she mentioned the bracelets, gushed about the perfume, her eyes sparkling the entire time. It was as if she were window-shopping and Claire was the display mannequin.

"Travis and I are going out to eat Friday," Shirley said proudly. "Date night."

Claire nodded appreciatively. "About time. You deserve it."

"Things are definitely looking up," Shirley agreed, waving a hand at their cluttered living room. "I might need to hire a maid soon."

Travis shook his head. "Let's not get crazy. We've had one good month. We don't know how long this is going to last."

Shirley frowned, but she still nodded agreement. Claire reached out to stroke her shoulder sympathetically, raising a judgmental eyebrow at her brother. Like it was his fault Shirley was already planning ways to get them deeper in debt.

"Since you're in a celebrating mood, is there any way I can convince you to come to brunch Sunday?" Claire asked.

Travis's temper had been turning sour since his sister arrived, and now immediately darkened. Why did she insist on torturing his wife this way? He shook his head.

"Maybe some other time," Shirley offered, unable to keep the disappointment from her voice.

"You always say that and it never happens," Claire replied. She was talking to Shirley but she was looking at her brother.

"Every time you ask, the answer's always the same," Travis said. "You'd think a smart businesswoman could take a hint."

Claire rolled her eyes then turned back to Shirley, reaching out to touch her sister-in-law's slowly-growing belly. This time it was Claire's turn to window shop, and their conversation quickly turned to maternity and female body issues that Travis would rather not hear.

"If you don't need it, I'm going to take the car," Travis called out as he scooped up the Park file and the car keys. "Gotta get to the law library."

"Well, don't leave on my account," Claire remarked.

"Don't flatter yourself," Travis replied. "I just need to do some more research for Sam Park's defense."

"Oh, that's part of the reason I came over," Claire said. She intercepted Travis before he could escape out the front door. "I had a couple of our junior staff put in a few hours on this, I told them to look off the beaten path, come at it sideways. Maybe it's something you haven't seen before."

She handed Travis a manila folder with "For Trav" scrawled across it, and "Park" written very carefully on the tab. Travis was about to give his sister a grudging thanks when he paused. He'd seen that handwriting before.

In a flash it came to him, and he yanked open the top drawer of his file cabinet.

"Travis, don't mess up my system," Shirley called.

Travis barely heard her as he flipped through the files, searching for the one with a hand-written label instead of a typed one.

There.

He grabbed the file from the back of the cabinet, holding it side-by-side with the one Claire had given him. The same handwriting graced the tabs of both files.

Claire's handwriting. Travis's hands trembled as his heart dropped into his stomach. He turned to his sister, brandishing the file.

"*You've* been giving me these cases."

Claire froze, a deer in headlights. Travis glanced at his wife, who looked like she'd been caught with her hand in the cookie jar.

"You're in on it, too."

"Trav, don't jump to—" Claire began.

"What the hell, Claire?" Travis interrupted. "Since when do I need your charity?"

"It's not like that," his sister replied carefully. "These are referrals."

"Bullshit they are!" Travis yelled, his voice shaking the rafters. "When you refer someone, you call them and let them know! How many? How many cases from the last month came from you?"

"Trav, it's not wrong for family to help each other out," Claire said, keeping her voice neutral, even as her red face betrayed her rising temper.

"It's not enough that you pity me, you don't think I can make it on my own?"

"We weren't," Shirley said softly.

Travis stopped cold. His wife stood at Claire's side, watching Travis with compassion and hope and sadness and disappointment all at once.

"We weren't making it," his wife continued. "I told you over and over, we can't pay bills with IOUs and good wishes. We needed paying clients. People with cash. I talked to Claire, Trav, I asked her to help us out."

Travis felt a cold knot tighten around his heart. Finally, after all these years, he understood. This was what betrayal felt like. "Did you have to lie about it?"

"Would you have taken the cases if you knew where they came from?" Claire replied.

Silence hung in the room. The answer was as plain as the anguish on his face.

"Who else knows?"

"Trav, that's not important," Claire replied. "What is important is that family helps each other out. Always."

"Who. Else."

Claire refused to meet his gaze. "Dad. Maybe Mama, if he told her."

"He tells her everything," Travis said. "She knows. Which means Rita knows. Which means *Jake* knows. Jesus, Claire, why didn't you just write it on a billboard?"

Her face shining crimson to match her auburn hair, Claire walked stiffly to the front door. "I'm not going to apologize for helping you. If your pride got wounded, get over it. You have a family to support now. That comes first."

"Call you later?" Shirley said as Claire pulled the door open. "We need to talk about office staff."

Claire nodded. "I have some more cases for you in the car. No sense pretending they're recipes now."

"Hold on." Travis glanced from his sister to his wife. "I changed my mind. I think I will go to brunch on Sunday."

Claire's eyes went wide. "Do you really think that's best?"

Travis glared at his sister. "A minute ago you were practically begging me. Let Mama know so she can make enough food, Shirley and I are going to be there."

"Travis … " Claire was giving him the big sister's warning, the admonition to be on his best behavior even though she knew he wouldn't be.

"Come on," Travis said with a humorless smile. "It'll be fun."

17

TRAVIS EASED TO A BRAKE-SQUEAKING stop in front of his parents' rambling ranch-style homestead, his knuckles white on the steering wheel. Beside him, Shirley smoothed her hair and checked her makeup in the visor's tiny mirror. She seemed a little pale, which Travis chose to attribute to the increasing heat of the morning and not her nerves. He grabbed her hand and squeezed, trying his best to be reassuring when his own stomach was doing backflips.

"Claire is here," Shirley said, pointing at his sister's shiny German prize, glinting in the dappled sun.

"I'm guessing that one's Jake's," Travis replied, pointing at a not-so-new but still ridiculously fancy American car beside it. "I thought Claire said they had a mini-van. Huh."

They both fell silent, warily watching the front door as if it might explode outward. Towering old trees shaded them and the droning of cicadas swelled like an ocean tide, rising and falling in sonorous waves. Travis held his wife's hand, neither of them moving.

"Ready?" Shirley finally asked. Her slight, sad smile showed that she was prepared to drive away, another sacrifice for her husband.

"Not at all," Travis sighed.

He reached for the door but Shirley wouldn't let go of his hand. She pulled his chin toward her, and looked him in the eye.

"Behave yourself, understand?"

Travis shrugged. "It's him you need to worry about, not me."

Shirley held tight as he tried to turn away. When did she get so strong? "Promise."

"Okay, best behavior. I promise."

His wife reluctantly let him go. As he came around the car to help her out, Travis reminded himself that this was maybe the fifth or sixth time Shirley had been to the Lynch home in all the years they'd been married. She'd enjoyed a few meals with his parents, even been shopping with his mother several times, but most of the functions held at this house—where Travis had grown up—included Jake. And where Jake was, Travis wasn't. Until now.

"I forgot how big the yard is," Shirley said as Travis escorted her to the front door. "Like three of ours."

"Imagine having to mow it all by yourself," Travis said. "With a little push mower. That's how my father would punish us. 'Get out there and mow the lawn, boy.' I think Jake secretly liked doing it."

They stepped up to the front door and Shirley squeezed his hand reassuringly. "You're sure about this?"

"I told Claire and Claire passed the word," Travis said. "Mama's expecting us. And trust me, you don't want to disappoint Mama. Not at Sunday brunch."

He reached for the doorbell but stopped before his finger could land. Shirley stretched up to kiss him on the cheek and hug him tight. It helped, a little, but Travis's insides were still collapsing into a black hole in his stomach. He passed a shaking hand across his clammy forehead, ashamed that his body refused to obey him and just press the damned button.

Ten years.

He hadn't seen his brother in person for a decade. Almost a third of his life. Sure, he'd watched the returns on TV the first time Jake got elected. He'd occasionally watched a press conference, and the re-election commercials were unavoidable. He knew how far Jake's hairline had receded and how growly his voice had grown. He could guess how pompous and authoritarian his brother had become, that was no challenge at all. But it had been so long since they shared breath in the same place.

"The last time we were together," Travis sighed, "it ended badly."

"I remember," Shirley said. "I had to come get you. Find you."

Travis kissed his wife's hand. Of course she'd been there to pick up the pieces. She always did. His heart broke as he looked down into her lovely green eyes. He'd stolen so much from her.

The doorbell echoed through the house and past the front door. Travis looked down at his hand as if someone else had moved it, as if some force had put his finger on the button. Footsteps approached the door and Shirley's hand tightened on his.

"Hitting the mimosas a little hard, aren't you, boy?"

Jake looked up as his father walked through the living room, casting a stern eye on his way to the kitchen. Jake felt a touch of chagrin; brunch wasn't even close to being ready and he was already two glasses in.

His father snatched the glass from Jake's hand. "I'll get you some water. Probably do you good to stay sharp today."

Val Lynch disappeared into the kitchen carrying Jake's half-drunk mimosa and leaving that odd remark echoing from the walls. Jake reached for the TV remote and settled into the cushions of his parents' overstuffed couch. Things had been off between him and his father for days now, ever since that meeting in the Driskill. Val said he didn't mind his oldest child running for the same office he'd failed to secure—twice –but his actions didn't match. If Jake didn't know any better, he would have sworn his father was jealous.

It was far from a done deal, though. Jake had not accepted the offer and had come no closer to a decision. Most people would have leapt at the opportunity, but Jake kept it at arms' length. The deal didn't pass the smell test. He was used to fighting for every professional accomplishment, scratching and clawing his way toward a goal. But he had no opposition with the offer of the governorship, nothing standing between him and the nomination. There was something wrong with this—the way such a prime opportunity came out of nowhere, handed to him like a medal he hadn't earned.

"Oh, there you are," Rita said, poking her head in from the den. "Everything okay?"

Jake raised an eyebrow. "Any reason it shouldn't be?"

"Just checking," his wife replied. She plucked at her hair absently. Maybe a little nervously? "I'm helping Mae set up, anything you want?"

"A beer," Jake replied.

Rita frowned; she'd been after him about his drinking lately. "I think we're going to stick with iced tea today."

"Fine," Jake grumbled. "Everybody's a Goddamned babysitter."

He clicked through a few channels, the images on the TV screen nothing but color and motion. His mind was still back in the dark-paneled hotel lobby.

Mae Kerr Lynch, mother to Jake, Claire, and Travis, bustled in, stacking, adjusting, gathering, and straightening, a blur of house-cleaning motion. She was short but solid, a physical and metaphorical contrast to her lanky husband. She and Jake shared their stature, their temperament and their florid complexion, though where his hair was gradually disappearing, hers had become a grand halo of white and silver.

"Feet off the coffee table," she commanded as she worked around her son.

"What's gotten into you?" Jake sighed. "You're just moving stuff around. The place looks fine."

"I thought I'd straighten up before—" his mother began.

"Mae." Val's admonition interrupted his wife and startled Jake. He hadn't heard his father come back.

Jake looked from his father to his mother as he slowly got to his feet. Both of them refused to meet his gaze, like kindergarteners caught in a lie. "Before what?"

The doorbell rang, and for a brief instant his parents froze, statues captured at the moment of their greatest surprise. His mother broke first, dashing for the door as if she were on fire and the extinguisher was in the driveway.

Rita appeared at Jake's side, grabbing his arm protectively. "You need to be nice, do you understand?"

"What the hell is going on?" Jake demanded.

Rita's nails dug into his arm savagely, painfully. "Be. Nice."

Jake's mother took a deep breath, exhaled dramatically, and pulled the door wide.

His heart pounded in his chest as the big oak door creaked open, and for an instant Travis felt the overwhelming urge to turn and run. But then his mother's beaming face appeared, blinking back tears. She grabbed him and squeezed him so tightly he couldn't catch his breath. His father's hand landed on his shoulder, and for a moment Travis was smothered in parental love.

"Good to have you back, boy," his father said.

"Isn't this perfect?" Mae said, clasping Shirley close and laying a protective hand on her belly. "The whole family together. It's about time."

Val ushered Shirley inside, leaving Travis by himself in the doorway. Across the living room, Jake radiated fury like a beacon. Rita whispered something to her husband, which he brushed aside with a brusque nod. His eyes shot icy daggers at Travis, and he folded his arms tightly across his chest.

Shirley cast one last look over her shoulder as Val and Mae ushered her into the kitchen, and Rita followed, so nervous and flustered she was visibly perspiring. In a moment, the brothers were alone together, for the first time in ten years.

"Okay, now it makes sense," Jake muttered. "Seems I'm the last one to know."

"If Mama told you we were coming over, would you be here?" Travis asked.

Jake shrugged. "Probably not. Rita and I are going to have a few things to discuss later."

Though his face had flushed crimson, Jake held his temper admirably. He turned away from the door and perched on the edge of the couch, peering intently at the television. Travis closed the door and tentatively approached his brother.

"It's been too long—"Travis began.

"Why are you here?"Jake interrupted, without glancing at Travis.

Travis's own temper instantly sparked into a roaring blaze, but he took a moment, took a breath, and forced himself to remain calm. Jake certainly wasn't going to be the voice of reason, so it was up to Travis to be the adult.

"Claire invited me,"Travis replied. "I thought that Mama should see Shirley."

"That's a lie," Jake grumbled. He glanced at Travis, then resumed glaring at the television. "See what you're doing with your fingers? You do that when you're lying."

Travis jammed his hands into his pockets. "There are some things you and I need to discuss."

Jake still refused to do anything more than glance at his brother. "Yeah, I heard you came by the office. Not interested."

His brother's offhand rejection was like salt in an open wound. So much had happened in ten years, so many things had changed in their lives, but they were both stuck where they'd left off, angry and betrayed and hurt. Like Travis had rejected Jake hours ago instead of ten years ago.

"Hear me out,"Travis said, unable to keep the exasperation from his voice. "Before you do … what you always do, just listen."

"No!"Jake said, rising sharply, his face red. His index finger jabbed into Travis's face. "You can't just come in here like nothing's happened."

Travis wanted to bat the finger away, but he held back. He didn't give any ground either, squaring off against his brother as if he were going up against the middle school bully.

"Oh, for God's sake, already?"

With a heavy sigh, Claire pushed between her two brothers. Travis hadn't heard her come into the room.

"That's enough out of both of you," she declared. "You're grown men. Stop it."

Travis took a step back, and then, grudgingly, Jake did too. But Travis still stared his brother down, and Jake's flushed, red face hadn't returned to a normal color. If looks could kill, they'd both be dead on the spot.

"Seriously? You're going to make me do this?" Claire shook her head. "All right. Jake, go help Mama on the patio. Travis, into the kitchen. Now."

Jake felt his ire ease—slightly—as he stalked off, putting Travis out of sight but definitely not out of mind. His brother had been away for ten years, but he'd been back ten minutes and he was already usurping Jake's position. Jake had been put outside like the family dog. Incredible, just incredible. If Jake hadn't been on the receiving end, it might have been something he admired.

He wasn't going to let Travis do this. He wasn't going to let his little brother take over and make everything all about him. Not this time. Jake counted to five, put his hand on the back door, and turned the handle.

Mockingbirds chirped in the huge ash tree in the back yard, and a cool breeze flowed across the terra-cotta tiled porch. A trellis supported an ancient wisteria bush that had grown to monstrous proportions, providing shade from the already-relentless sun. A wrought-iron table with a thick glass top would hold the family's brunch, though now it only held stacks of plates and silverware.

Mae brushed past her son, carrying two vases overflowing with flowers she'd no doubt just picked from the garden. She hummed softly while she snipped and arranged, as happy as Jake had seen her in a very long time.

Jake felt his temper rise again. This was what Travis had taken from them, from his family. For ten years, his mother had waited for her youngest child to come back to the fold, and for ten years Travis had denied her. For what? Some bankrupt principle he didn't even really believe in anymore?

"Time to lean means time to clean," Mae said, tossing Jake a dish rag. "Make yourself useful."

Jake knew better than to disobey his mother. He got busy wiping down the glass tabletop. But after a few half-hearted, swipes his temper got the better of him. "What's he thinking, coming back like this? Why now?"

"Just be glad your brother is here," his mother said, without looking his way. A warning crept into her voice. "Leave well enough alone."

"But don't you think—"

"Jacob Neill Lynch!" his mother snapped. "I am not going to tell you twice."

It had been a very long time since his mother had scolded him. Jake took the reprimand with outward calm, though inside he seethed.

"Claire did a good job keeping this from me," he mumbled.

"It was actually my idea," Mae said.

Jake froze. His mother didn't seem like she was joking.

"You lied to me?"

"It wasn't a lie, honey," his mother said soothingly. "We just never told you Travis and Shirley were coming over. I guess it was a secret. Give your sister some credit—*she* wanted to tell you."

"But you said no."

Mae moved stems from one vase to the next, eyeing the arrangement with a critical gaze. "Don't get pouty. Sometimes it's better for everyone if you don't know certain things."

She carried on as if she'd said nothing out of the ordinary. She brought the vases to the table and placed them as carefully as she'd placed the flowers inside.

"What do you mean?" Jake could barely choke back his anger.

His mother patted his hand gently. "Sweetie, don't get your back up. You know the way you react to things. It can't be a surprise that you don't get the full story all the time."

"You're serious."

"Oh, now you're hurt," Mae said.

"How could I not be?"

His mother waved away his concern. "It's not like we do it all the time, just every so often."

She said it so matter-of-factly that he knew it had to be true. "We? It's not just you? So this is, like, a family thing?"

Mae shrugged. "You're a lot of work, Jake, and people need a break from time to time."

Her vases set just-so, Mae hurried off to attend to the next detail. Jake stood at the table, words failing him, his stomach tied up like he'd just taken a punch.

If Travis hadn't come back, Jake would still have been blissfully unaware.

A gentle breeze rustled the wisteria branches, washing dappled sunlight across the table. Jake felt resentment boiling over in his heart, but he pushed it down until it burned in his belly, alongside all the other emotions he kept caged there.

He picked up the dish rag and finished wiping the table.

Travis's parents had remodeled the kitchen.

He stood in the doorway, familiar with the layout but not the details. The appliances all matched now, sleek stainless steel, and the floor was wood instead of linoleum squares. The cabinets were all brand-new, some of them not even in the same places. Travis missed the crazy-quilt feel of the kitchen he grew up in, the one where the stove was a different color than the refrigerator which was a different color than the oven, and nothing matched the color of the walls.

He felt just the tiniest bit lost. They'd erased part of his childhood. Where was the loose tile by the sink? Where was the stain on the back wall? Where was the dent in the refrigerator? It was like looking at a family portrait where all the faces had been swapped out with strangers'.

Claire, Shirley, and Rita had descended on the breakfast table, where they chattered about pregnancy, babies, and children. Rita, mother of two, held court like the wise old matron, even though she was just six years older than Travis, two years older than Claire. Already they were making plans for showers and parties, and a phone tree for when the blessed event arrived and Shirley delivered Travis's first child. Travis turned away; it was getting too real far too fast.

"First, let me say it's great to have you back," Val said, clapping his son on the shoulder. "But you're going to have to give your brother time to get used to having you around."

Screw him, Travis thought, *he can get used to it on his own time.* But he just nodded thoughtfully and behaved himself like Shirley made him promise. It seemed like everyone—his wife, his father, his sister—imagined this was Jake's territory, sacred ground where Travis was an intruder.

"You want a beer?" Val asked, reaching into the refrigerator.

"Before we eat?" Travis asked. "You sure about that?"

A bottle clutched in his hand, Val stopped and squinted out the kitchen window, searching for Mae. He could change the kitchen, but Val still had the same mannerisms, the same gentle, easy nature. And he was still afraid of his wife. Val considered the bottle thoughtfully.

"Probably not worth the trouble," he said, returning the beer to the fridge. "Besides, I think your mother's made sangria. Normally she doesn't, but since you're here, she's getting fancy."

"I didn't mean to shake things up," Travis said.

Val's eyebrows arched, and he leaned against the counter, giving Travis one of his knowing-father stares. "Uh-huh. So why are you here?"

"I can't just decide to come see my family again?" To Travis's ears, his words came out petulant, whining, as if he were back in high school.

"Nope," Val replied. He continued to stare at Travis, a patient parent waiting for his child to confess.

"Well, I mean," Travis mumbled, "I just … it's about time, don't you think?"

"It was about time a week after you stopped coming," Val replied. He cocked his head to the side, looking his son up and down, taking Travis's measure. "Did you know your mother used to cry when you weren't here?"

"She did not," Travis scoffed. His father fixed him with a gaze that could stop a cobra in its tracks. "Mama? Since when does she cry about anything?"

"I'm telling you, boy," Val said softly but oh-so-seriously, "if you're here for any reason other than to make my wife happy, it would probably be better for you if you turned around and left right now."

Travis couldn't help feeling like a little kid again, caught lighting firecrackers or jumping off the roof. His father always could see right through him.

"All right," Travis bowed his head as he confessed. "I need to talk to Jake. Where other people can hear."

"You were hoping your mother and I would take sides?"

Once again, Travis was a little boy called on the carpet. "I was, yes sir."

Val reached out and clapped his son on the shoulder. "I don't take sides with my kids, you know that."

I don't take sides. The words were a bellows stoking the fire in Travis's chest. He caught Shirley's eye across the room, and she shook her head slightly. Behave himself. He'd promised.

But this was too much. "That's bullshit and you know it."

"Excuse me, boy?"

"How many times have I been in your house in the past ten years?" Travis accused. "We don't talk, you don't tell me anything. I didn't even know you'd completely redone the kitchen. But I'll bet you and Jake discussed it. I'll bet he helped Mama pick out the colors."

"You're the one who walked away, Travis," his father replied.

"I didn't move to Europe," Travis countered. "For God's sake, I live five miles away. How many times have you been to my house? Could you even find it on a map?"

His father hesitated, one of the few times Travis had ever seen him anywhere close to being flustered. "Just because I might not ..."

Shirley was at Travis's side, tugging him toward the door, away from his father. Travis allowed her lead him off, but he turned back after a few steps.

"You picked sides ten years ago." He let the words fall. "And you picked Jake."

Jake sat where his mother told him to, at one end of the long table. It wasn't where he usually sat, in the middle, at the center of things, but since Travis had disrupted everything else there was no reason that should stop with the seating arrangements. Jake sipped at his iced tea—tea!—and tried to maintain what little decorum was left in him.

Shirley led Travis from the house; she looked pale and frightened, while he looked sullen. Jake stared his little brother down as Shirley steered him toward the open seat at Mae's right hand, diagonally across from Jake, as far apart as his mother could possibly get her sons and still have them at the same table.

Rita and Claire followed, both uncharacteristically silent. Jake's father came last, his long features seeming even longer and sadder. Jake shook his head: It seemed Travis's influence was already well on its way to ruining a perfect day.

They held hands and said grace, but as Jake reached for the French toast, Mae cleared her throat, demanding everyone's attention.

"It's nice to have everyone together," Mae said. "Most everyone, anyway. Rita, where did Eric and Heather go again?"

"Church camp," Rita replied. "But I know they would have loved to see their Uncle Travis and Aunt Shirley."

"Next time," Shirley offered. Jake groaned; he hoped there wouldn't be a next time.

"Oh, I've got a third grandchild right here!" Mae said, smiling as she patted Shirley's belly. "Why isn't anyone eating? Help yourself."

For a while, less than a minute, the air filled with the clink and scrape of people grabbing food. Then: nothing. No questions, no comments, no conversation. It was as if they were each stuck in solitary confinement, not allowed to communicate with anyone else. The only sound was the scrape of forks on plates and the clink of ice in glasses.

"With more adults at the table, you'd think there'd be more talking," Rita finally said.

The uncomfortable silence continued for a few more moments. Jake caught his little brother's eye, finding the same glint of animosity that gleamed in his own.

"All right, here's something," Jake said. "Travis, what changed your mind? Why are you gracing us with your presence today?"

Everyone stopped. Jake settled back into his chair, eager to hear what his little brother had to say.

"I think we just wanted to see the family again," Shirley said with a nervous laugh. She patted her husband's hand. "Isn't that right?"

With a stiff smile and a stiffer nod Travis agreed. "It's been too long."

"I don't know about anyone else," Jake said, "but I could have used more time."

"Be nice!" Rita admonished him, with a not-so-gentle slap to the arm.

"It's okay," Travis said. "To tell you the truth, I do have an ulterior motive."

"Need more clients from Lynch & Brockhurst's slush pile?" Jake could barely keep the sadistic glee from his voice. It would kill his little brother to know where all his new business was coming from, and Jake was only too happy to break the news.

Maddeningly, though, *infuriatingly*, Travis merely kissed his wife's hand. "No. Shirley's handling that with Claire. I'm talking about the Park case."

Travis was glad to see the disappointed scowl on Jake's face, happy to be the fly in Jake's ointment.

"I know you haven't been here in a while, Trav," Jake said, color slowly creeping into his face, "but we don't really talk shop during brunch."

"Since when?" Travis countered. "When we were kids, Dad would have clients over, when we were in law school he'd grill us on what we were learning in class. All we *do* is talk shop over brunch."

"You do kind of go on about it, Jake, honey," Mae said.

Rita nodded, as did Claire and Val. Outnumbered, Jake surrendered. He put his fork down and folded his hands across his chest. "Okay. Fine. Say what you have to say."

Travis took a deep breath, glad to have Shirley's warm hand on his. "You need to re-think the death penalty for Sam Park."

Jake was shaking his head before Travis finished the sentence. "I got three words for you on that, Trav. No. Fucking. Way."

"You pompous, self-righteous … " Travis began, but he caught himself when Shirley squeezed his hand hard. "I really think you should consider other options for charges."

Jake's face was growing redder by the second, and his voice grew strained. "Sam Park and his friends pumped eight slugs into that car. Two of the three kids are dead, one is paralyzed for life."

"We don't know that Sam was the one who killed those two boys," Travis insisted. "We don't know who pulled the trigger."

"He admitted he was there when it happened," Jake replied. He slapped the table with authoritative finality. "As far as the law's concerned, that's enough."

Travis's breath came faster. "But it's not *right*."

"You're his attorney," Jake said, leaning forward, his face now crimson. "You've seen his rap sheet. Your kid is a career criminal, starting when he was ten. Petty vandalism, burglary, assault. He's been working his way up to multiple homicide for years now."

"That's my point," Travis insisted. "The system failed him, just like it failed his brother Charlie."

"No!" Jake's voice rang loudly across the patio. "There are hundreds of kids just like him who aren't murderers. The system didn't fail him, Sam Park failed himself."

"And now you think the only solution is to execute him?"

Jake sighed, a long, infuriatingly expansive sigh, like he was trying to keep his patience with a child. "There's no more frontier, Travis. No place to put criminals like this, no wilderness to make them walk into. People like Sam Park have proved they can't operate by the rules of modern society, and they're never going to adapt. They're predators. They're cancer. So we have to cut them out."

"Where does it stop?" Travis almost vibrated with fury. "Do we start cutting the hands off of thieves so they don't steal? Do we brand adulterers? Vengeance isn't justice. It's just more killing."

He was so sure, so smug. Jake's little brother sat there, presuming to lecture the District Attorney on justice. Jake's pulse throbbed, and his face radiated heat. But he stayed in control.

"We're not stringing him up like it's the Wild West," Jake growled. "There's nothing my office takes more seriously than a capital case. You should know that better than anyone else."

Travis clenched his fists, the same way he had since he was little boy. "If this case goes to trial …"

"*If?*" Jake interrupted. "You think I'm going to let that bastard plead?"

Travis slammed his hands on the glass table and stood so sharply he knocked his chair over. "Dammit, Jake!"

"Here we go," Claire said. She gathered up the glass items, as Rita grabbed the two larger platters.

"What? What's happening?" Shirley demanded as the rest of the family cleared away anything breakable.

"Just keep your distance," Claire said. "Don't get between them."

Jake stood quickly, backing toward the yard as Travis stalked around the table, even though every instinct told him to move forward. "We're not kids any more, Trav. If you want to do this, it's gonna hurt."

His little brother stopped a few feet away, glaring, furious. "Why don't you ever listen? Why can't you admit that other people can be right?"

"If the time comes you're right about something, I'll let you know."

For a moment, it looked like Travis might actually step up. He locked eyes with Jake, waves of pure malice vibrating between them. But Travis shook his head and turned away.

"You don't have to try this as capital murder," Travis muttered.

Jake closed the distance as he spoke. "I have multiple homicide, drug trafficking, and felony robbery. I'm not gonna let this one get away."

"There are a hundred other ways to get what you need without going for a death sentence," Travis said.

"Sam Park deserves this," Jake replied.

"Like Reilly Sutton did?"

Jake's eyes went wide and he stepped forward, fists up around his chin. Travis turned, his own hands raised, and let a punch fly, his fist landing square on Jake's jaw, snapping his brother's head back.

It took Travis a moment to register that, yes, he had indeed thrown the first punch. And it seemed to take his brother just as long to realize that he'd *taken* that punch. That his little brother had hit him first. Travis looked down at his fist, which had betrayed him again, just like it had at the front door.

A guttural growl vibrated the air, and Travis caught a glimpse of Jake's flushed, furious face just before his brother launched himself forward, ham fists aimed straight for Travis's chin.

Travis backpedaled onto the lawn, blocking his brother's blows as best he could while Jake threw punch after punch, each potentially devastating blow narrowly avoided. Travis evaded, constantly circling, constantly weaving and retreating, hoping to be the matador that tired out the bull with trickery and strategy.

Jake wasn't stopping.

He'd slowed down after the first flurry of punches, but now Jake was picking and choosing his attacks, jabbing and feinting.

Travis used his height to his advantage, staying just out of Jake's reach. He batted his brother's hands away as he danced backwards, trying to anticipate Jake's movements. If Jake got hold of him, it would be all over for Travis.

"Isn't anyone going to stop them?" he heard Shirley shriek, nearly frantic.

"They'll be done soon enough," Val said.

Travis chanced a look toward the porch. Mae and Claire stood on either side of his wife, holding her hands, keeping her from running out to get in the middle of things.

With a roar, Jake took advantage of Travis's distraction. He caught Travis in a flying tackle, driving his shoulder into Travis's stomach to knock the wind out of him.

Travis scrambled to get back to his feet, knowing that if he stayed on the ground, he was lost. He jabbed his knee upward, catching his brother's body, satisfied to hear a pained, guttural groan. He'd nearly gotten away when Jake's thick hands grabbed him by the leg and pulled him back down. His older brother landed a huge blow to Travis's face, even as Travis let loose with a desperate, wild uppercut that caught Jake in the mouth.

Jake fell on top of Travis, gasping for air. Travis endured his brother's vaguely-boozy breath, too weary to push Jake away.

"Give me a minute and I'll be good to go again." Jake replied, though he didn't budge.

Travis tried to move, but Jake's bulk held him fast. "I'm done. And if I'm done you're done, you got no stamina."

"Got more than you."

The cicadas buzzed, and the sun beat down, and neither of them moved.

"You get it all out?" Travis asked, rubbing his already-swelling knuckles.

Jake groaned as he rolled onto the grass. "Mostly. How about you? You say what you needed to say?"

Travis sat up, his entire body aching. "For now. Is this my blood or yours?"

Ten minutes later, Jake sat beside his brother on the edge of the porch. His breath caught every time he inhaled; he was fairly certain one or two of his ribs were cracked.

Shirley brought Travis a bag of ice, which he gingerly placed on the side of his already-swollen face. It looked like he was developing a remarkable black eye. Jake held a cold glass of iced tea to his fat lip while he licked the taste of blood from his mouth.

"Have they always been this stupid?" Jake heard Shirley's words clearly, even though she tried to be discreet.

"They've always been brothers," Mae responded.

Jake looked to Rita, who had not brought him anything but instead stood with Claire under the shade of the wisteria, hands on her hips, still shaking her head. He was definitely going to pay for this later. And probably for a long time to come.

Travis held his bag of ice out to Jake. "You need this more than I do."

"Thanks," Jake said as he placed the bag on his own face. "Dumbass."

"You're the dumbass," Travis mumbled. "And you punch like a girl."

"Then I hope you're comfortable telling people a girl beat the crap out of you."

Travis laughed, then groaned and clutched his ribs. He spat bright red onto the lawn. "Do you know what I've always envied about you?"

Jake grunted, shaking his head.

"You're so certain," Travis said. "You don't question yourself."

Jake laughed, but that hurt worse than grunting. Definitely a cracked rib.

"But it's your weakness too," Travis continued. Just like their father, he didn't know when to shut the hell up. "You can't put yourself in the shoes of someone with less confidence. You don't understand what it's like to be in a position where all your options suck, where there's no good way out."

Instantly Jake's mind was back at the Driskill, and he was looking into Carlisle's malicious eyes, wondering what was really going on. "You'd be surprised what I've come to understand lately."

Travis laid his hand gently on his brother's shoulder. "There was a third guy. At the construction site. Not just Sam and Roger."

"We know," Jake replied, around the ice he held to his lip.

"Got a name?" Travis asked.

Shaking his head hurt, so Jake merely shrugged. "We're trying hard."

"Mark Kidd."

Jake searched his brother's face, looking for any hint of insincerity, any sign that he was working an angle or making something up. He found nothing.

"Seriously? You're just giving up the name?"

"Yeah."

He handed the bag of ice back to Travis. "Don't think this makes the past ten years go away."

"Wouldn't dream of it," Travis replied. "Find Mark Kidd and we'll get the whole story."

"Do you want me to know the whole story?" Jake asked. "Are you positive Sam didn't kill Peter Carlisle?"

Travis hesitated. He gingerly pressed his fingers against the rising bubble of his black eye while he weighed his answer.

"Positive," he said at last.

18

TRAVIS SAT IN HUT'S, THE remains of his burger in front of him, the work papers he'd reviewed strewn across the rest of the table, and the flash drive burning a hole in his pocket. He hadn't told Jake what Marina had given him. He hadn't told the police either.

But he had watched the video.

Reilly Wayne Sutton was guilty of murder. The video was crystal clear, and Travis still felt sick to his stomach after watching it two days ago. The footage would be more than enough to put Sutton away, more than enough to make the death penalty stick.

Which was why Travis kept silent, even though doing so was itself a crime.

Without the video, the case against Sutton was circumstantial. Winnable, but circumstantial, which meant that the DA's office would likely not go for capital punishment. With the video, Sutton's fate was sealed. He would be sentenced to die. Travis didn't know if he could be the agent of that fate. He hadn't slept for days, his mind and heart a knotted mess.

A shadow fell on the table. It took Travis a moment to realize that someone was standing in front of him, expecting to be acknowledged. He looked up, but it wasn't the waitress.

A tall woman in a business suit stood before him, her hands wrapped around a small steno pad. She shifted awkwardly from foot to foot and brushed a strand of dark brown hair from her face. She pointed to the chair beside Travis, asking if she could sit.

"I'm sorry," Travis said, "do I know you?"

The woman blushed slightly and held her hand out. "My name is Chris Morton. You may have seen me on television? I'm a reporter."

"I don't have much time for television," Travis said. "I don't want to be rude, but I have a girlfriend."

Morton set her steno pad on the table, right on top of Travis's paperwork. "Well, I do think you're cute in a frat-boy kind of way, but I'm here to talk to a District Attorney."

"I'm not a DA," Travis replied. "I'm just a clerk."

"But you're Jake Lynch's clerk," Morton said. "He's the one working the Reilly Sutton assault case."

Travis froze. What did she know?

"I hope you don't mind," she said as she reached over to grab a few cold French fries, "but I haven't eaten all day."

Travis still had nothing to say. He resisted the urge to put his hand over the flash drive in his pocket.

Morton waved a waiter over as she helped herself to Travis's iced tea. "I'm trying to get an inside line on him. Sutton. See what makes him tick. From what I've found out, this guy's a real piece of shit."

Travis relaxed slightly. She was just looking for information, dropping a lure in an unfamiliar pond, hoping for a bite. "In the DA's office we can't put it that way, but, yes, he's a career criminal."

Pausing a moment to order her own hamburger, Morton made a few notes on her pad. "I've been asking around and I think there's a connection between Sutton and . . . Sayeed Homayanpour. Liquor store owner who was killed two weeks ago. I got no eyewitnesses and none of you bastards in the DA's office are talking. But for some reason Sutton's still in jail, charges pending. That's a pretty long time for a domestic abuse rap. Something else is up, right?"

"I can't comment on that," Travis said, only now realizing he was giving his first interview to a reporter. The DA's office had a pat answer, which he mumbled. "The investigation is ongoing, so I can't release any details."

"What do you think?" Morton pressed further, staring Travis in the eye. "Did he do it? Did Sutton finally cross the line? Did he kill that guy?"

Travis felt his jaw drop. She'd ambushed him, a hyena picking off the youngest lion cub. She might be new—Travis had certainly never heard of her—but she was good. She had a career ahead of her.

Finally he stood, hastily gathering his papers. "I have to go. Anything I said is off the record."

"Not until just now," Morton replied, a slight grin creasing her lips.

Travis fled, wondering how he was going to explain this to Jake.

"Did you hear a word I said?"

Travis stood in front of Sam Park, so angry he could hardly see straight. Infuriating, frustrating, insolent—Sam was like a middle school punk rebelling against a strict principal. Sam shrugged, his handcuffs rattling on the metal table, staring at Travis as if he were speaking another language.

"Do you want to go to prison?"

Sam shrugged again, and tried to shake his black hair out of his eyes. It fell right back. "What the fuck happened to your face, man?"

Travis's hand went to his still-swollen black eye and the bruise that took up half of the right side of his face. It had been two days since he and Jake "reunited," and he hurt more now than the prior days put together.

"I got in a fight."

"No shit," Sam scoffed as he scanned Travis's face. "If you need someone to teach the other guy a lesson, I know a few dudes."

"I asked you a question," Travis interrupted.

Sam nodded, pointing to Travis's eye. "Your big brother ... Jim?"

"Jake. Jake Lynch, the District Attorney, the man who's trying to stick a needle in your arm."

"Charlie used to beat the crap out of me, too," Sam said, a soft touch of sadness creeping into his voice. He scraped a fingernail across the table and looked away.

With a sigh, Travis finally sat. The tiny, squalid interview room seemed to press in on him. Layer upon layer of poorly applied paint rippled on the cinderblock walls and fluorescent lights cast a greenish glow and made harsh shadows. It seemed like everything Travis touched was either oily or sticky, and he was certain he didn't want to know why. The room smelled like cigarettes, urine, and B.O.—a truly deadly trifecta of odors.

"Seriously, Sam," Travis said wearily. "Are you trying to go to prison?"

Travis waited for a reaction but he didn't get one. Seconds ticked by and Sam just stared at his fingers, his chin down, his lank hair obscuring his face.

"Mark Kidd."

Sam's head jerked up, then just as quickly he looked down. Other than that one slip, he showed no emotion, but his hands clenched into fists and the knuckles turned white.

"Don't pretend you don't know the name," Travis said. "And don't keep up the charade that it was just you and Roger that night. There were three of you, three of them."

"How'd you find out?" His words were small, and Sam still refused to look up.

"I know some dudes myself. I told Jake."

"You did what?" Sam's voice was low and threatening, but still he made no eye contact.

"I couldn't find Mr. Kidd on my own." For the first time Travis began to feel uneasy. Sam's body was tensed, a coiled spring ready to release. "The District Attorney's office has the resources and the expertise to find him. Plus, they're obligated to disclose all evidence to me."

Sam nodded slowly, almost to himself. "Where did they find him?"

"They haven't yet," Travis replied. "But if I know my brother, they'll get him sooner or later. Sooner, most likely."

Silence. Sam said nothing, Travis said nothing. The clock ticked, accompanied by the buzzing of slowly-failing florescent bulbs and the metallic rattle of the air conditioning duct. A dark cloud seemed to have descended on Sam, who still sat curled into a comma, hands clenched and body so tense he almost vibrated.

"Do you want to come clean about what you were doing in that construction site at three in the morning?"

No reply. Sam didn't even look at Travis.

"I'm going to find out eventually. You might as well tell me the truth now."

Sam's mouth worked, as if he were talking to himself, having a conversation in his head. But he still didn't look up, he still didn't say a word.

"There were three of you and one gun," Travis pressed. "Which one of you shot those kids in the BMW?"

Sam shook his head.

"This is important, Sam. I need the truth."

Sam's hands worked, twisting at the cuffs as if he were trying to slip out of them right there. He glanced briefly at the door behind Travis, no longer sullen and defiant but enraged, then his chin touched his chest again and his hair obscured his features.

"No."

The word was so soft Travis might not have heard it at all. But Sam shook his head slightly.

"I'm sorry?" Travis said.

Sam's chin raised slightly, but not enough for Travis to see his eyes. "No, I'm not trying to go to prison."

"Then why did you lie to me about how many of you were there that night?"

He shrugged again, a multi-purpose answer. "Where I'm from, we take care of our own problems."

"Mark Kidd is a problem?"

Sam's mouth worked, like the words were trying to force their way out.

Travis leaned in, his forehead almost touching Sam's. "Who pulled the trigger?"

Another shrug.

"Dammit, Sam, you just don't get it," Travis sighed. "One of those dead kids was Dave Carlisle's son. You don't even know who that is, do you?"

"Like I give a fuck."

Reaching across the table, Travis grabbed Sam's chin and hoisted it up, forcing the young man to look him in the eye.

"You understand favors, don't you?" he snapped. "You understand a guy who makes things happen? Someone who greases the wheels? Someone who a lot of people owe something to, whether they like it or not?"

Sam's only reply was a fierce glare accompanied by a furious rattling of his handcuffs against the metal table.

"That's Dave Carlisle," Travis said. "That's the man whose son was murdered. That's how deep the shit you're in goes, Sam. So you'd better start taking this far more seriously. You'd better start telling me the truth."

Sam's eyes flashed. "Get your fucking hand off me."

Travis collapsed back into his chair. "I don't know how to make you understand."

Sullen again, almost pouting, Sam relaxed and sat back in his chair, his hair still obscuring his face. "So this Carlisle guy's a big deal, huh? He's kind of King Dick of Austin?"

"Not 'kind of,'" Travis mumbled. He glanced at his watch. Less than half an hour had passed and he was already exhausted. Maybe Shirley was right. Maybe he should give up and spend his time working for paying clients.

"What if I did pull the trigger?" Sam asked. "What if I did shoot that rich fuck in the back of the head? You gonna quit on me?"

Travis hesitated, just the briefest pause as his heart dropped into his stomach. "I wouldn't do that."

"So it doesn't matter if I did it or not," Sam said, spitting his words like a challenge.

Of course it does, it's the only thing that matters, Travis thought. He didn't look away, holding Sam's gaze steadily. "It doesn't affect the way I defend you."

Finally, Sam broke, lowering his chin again, letting his hair fall into his face. "I get it. This is your community service, like those church groups that come into my neighborhood to paint a fence or mow some old lady's lawn. You need me to make you feel better about yourself."

"Hardly," Travis scoffed. "If you saw my office, you'd know how wrong you are."

"Then why are you doing it?" Sam asked.

"Someone needs to get between you and the system," he said. "Someone has to care what happens to people."

"Why?" Sam mumbled. "Why do you care?"

"I just do."

Sam sat still, his lips moving as he talked to himself. He shook his head, he nodded, he considered first one point, then another, silently, the conversation all in his head.

"How many times have you done this?" Sam finally asked.

Travis cracked his knuckles, shaking his hands to relieve the tension. "Defended one of my clients in court?"

"No, defended a ... " Sam replied, his voice cracking, "...a death penalty case."

"Counting yours?" Travis replied. "One."

Sam's face paled. He sank lower in his chair, his unfocused eyes staring at nothing.

The District Attorney had a fat lip.

Jake sat at the front of the hotel conference room, a horrible lunch uneaten on the plate in front of him, catching sidelong glances from the main table. At him. When he made the long walk from the door to his seat, he could hear the silence follow as conversations stopped and people tried to look without seeming too obvious. He was in the center ring at a circus, with nothing to do but finish his performance as gracefully as he could.

There was no way to hide it, and Jake wasn't about to cancel his appearance at the symposium. So he gave the keynote address with a swollen lip—which probably needed a stitch or two, truth be told—and a cut above his eye and a hitch in his breath every time he inhaled.

No one asked him about it. Not the hotel staff, not the other attorneys, not the symposium organizers. It was as if the District Attorney always came to these things a little bruised, a little beaten-up. People wanted to ask: Jake could see it in their eyes, but everyone went about their business as if the keynote speaker didn't look like he'd taken a pounding in the boxing ring.

When the lunch mercifully ended, Jake took quick leave of the other attorneys, judges, and bar association members and asked the first hotel worker he found to lead him to the freight elevator. The entire proceeding had been embarrassing enough; there was no need to make it worse. In short order, he was standing on the scarred linoleum of the service corridor. He pressed the down button and heard the rattle of the large elevator as it slowly clambered up to his floor.

"What's the other guy look like?"

Jake sighed, and his head dropped. "How do you do it, Christine? Are you stalking me—or are you just that lucky?"

Morton stood beside him, hands on her hips, an entirely too-amused smile on her face. "When I first heard about it, I didn't believe it. But the proof's right in front of me. You got your ass kicked."

"I did not," Jake snapped, too quickly, too defensively.

"Who was it?" Morton's eyes sparkled, like she knew the answer already and was just waiting for the confirmation.

"No comment."

"Come on …" Morton cajoled.

"Don't you have better things to do than follow me?" Jake snapped.

"Believe it or not," Morton replied, "the world does not revolve around you, Jake Lynch. Nor do I. I'm working on many stories, and I just happened to be downtown. My lunch tray is full enough, metaphorically speaking. But I did absolutely have to take time for this. Seeing you after someone punched you in the mouth is just icing on my cake."

"If we were in my office, I'd have the deputies escort you to the street," Jake snarled.

"Funny how that works out," Morton replied. "But seriously, how are things going? You've been the DA for quite a while now, it must be getting stale. Routine. Just a little bit boring?"

Jake raised an eyebrow but said nothing.

"They say job satisfaction is at an all-time low nationwide," Morton continued. "Even the great Jake Lynch can't be immune to that. You ever think of what you'd do if you weren't Austin's District Attorney?"

Jake's pulse quickened, and he could feel his face flushing from his chin to his forehead. "I'm in no mood, Christine."

"You're like an oak tree," Morton continued. "It seems like you've always been there, and it seems like you always will be. But I remember Matt Caroll before you, and Lemire before him. You're not going to hold this office forever, Jake, no matter what you think."

Jake exhaled through clenched teeth, determined that Morton was not going to get the better of him. Not this time. "What's your point?"

"Word's on the street," Morton said. "You're moving up. Running for governor."

Jake paused for an instant, but that was long enough to telegraph every emotion coursing through his body. Morton watched him like a cat watches a mouse, toying with him before going in for the kill.

"I have a job," Jake said dismissively. He sounded unconvincing even to himself. "I'm going to continue to do that job. Anything else is just a rumor."

"So you're not denying?" Morton pressed.

How the hell did she do it? Who was her source? There were four people who knew about Jake and the Texas governorship, and Jake was positive neither he nor his father had talked. That left Davis, who was sharp enough to keep quiet until the official announcement, and Carlisle....

Son of a bitch.

"I am denying," Jake said. "I am not running for governor, and that's a fact."

"You're not now," Morton said. "Does that mean you won't tomorrow?"

With a ding and a rattle, the freight elevator arrived, saving Jake. He stepped inside, and of course Morton followed him. Jake pressed the button for the basement parking garage, trying to ignore her.

"Come on, Jake," Morton pressed, "for old times' sake. We've been through so much together. At least let me know you're announcing an hour before you officially do. Let me get it up on the air before anyone else."

"You are consistent," Jake muttered. "I'll give you that. Annoying, a pain in my ass, but consistent. I'll always know where I stand with you, Christine. That's worth something, I suppose."

The elevator door creaked shut and with an alarming shudder, the car descended. Morton stepped uncomfortably close.

"Carlisle's gunning for your brother," she whispered. "You did not hear this from me. Understand?"

It took Jake a few moments to process the words. Was she trying to help? Morton?

"Carlisle's going after the defense?" Jake replied, confused.

"No, after Travis. Personally."

The elevator jerked to a stop, and the doors groaned open to reveal the vast cement expanse of the basement parking garage.

Jake looked her in the eyes. "What's in this for you?"

"Everybody's got an axe to grind," Morton replied as she stepped out of the elevator. "Mine is plutocrats. Like Carlisle."

A knowing smile spread over Jake's face. "Ah, he screwed you over. You'll have to tell me the story."

"Someday, maybe," Morton called out she walked off.

19

VELASQUEZ HEARD THE SATISFYING CLICK of his car doors locking. He pressed the button on the key fob to lock the car again. Then he pressed the button one last time for good measure. This was a terrible neighborhood, the kind of place where they'd strip a car bare on a pleasant Sunday afternoon. Hopefully he could do the job and get out quickly.

He'd gotten a call from the office less than an hour ago, from a guy who owed him a favor. The name Mark Kidd had come to the investigators' desk, and the process had begun. In a few hours, once all the paperwork was filed and the judge was satisfied, two investigators and three or four officers would descend on this house and tear it up.

He needed to get a look inside before they did.

As he walked to the front door, he could feel the eyes on him, stares from the neighbors. He straightened his tie and smoothed the wrinkles on his suit before he pressed the doorbell, as if that would make a difference.

He could hear movement in the house, but no one answered. After a minute or so he pressed the doorbell again. The sound of several locks being undone filtered across the threshold, and in a moment the door opened a crack.

"I'm with the District Attorney's office." He showed his badge. "I'm here to talk with you about your son Mark."

The door opened wider, releasing a blast of stale cigarette-and-dirty-laundry vapor that blanketed Velasquez in an instant. A ragged, weaving, drunk man stared out suspiciously. "Unless you got a warrant, you can step the fuck off."

"I just need a few minutes of your time, Mr. Kidd. It's important." With a flick of his wrist he held out a crisp one-hundred-dollar bill. After a brief moment's hesitation, Mr. Kidd snatched the bill away.

Velasquez stepped inside.

Less than fifteen minutes later, Velasquez departed, a red-and-blue gym bag clutched in one hand. He tried to appear nonchalant, though his heart beat wildly as he dialed the phone.

"It's me," he said. "You are not going to believe what I have."

Velasquez took a sip of coffee, the mug warm in his hand. He tried not to show his impatience, but he hovered over the technician like a miser after gold.

"I'm telling you, sir," the tech, Tim, said, "it's going to be a while before this is done. You can come back."

"Absolutely not," Velasquez replied, anxious. "I'll stay as long as it takes."

"Where did you say you got this?" Tim asked as he dabbed a brush into graphite. A handgun rested on the table in front of him.

"I didn't," Velasquez replied.

Tim gestured at the red-and-blue gym bag sitting on another table. "I'm going to need you to write down everything you touched."

"I'll get it to you," Velasquez replied.

Bending low over his work, Tim continued to stroke the graphite over the pistol. Velasquez stepped closer, crowding the table and blocking the light.

"Look," Tim said, rolling his chair back, "I don't mind you barging in here, demanding I drop everything—"

"You shouldn't," Velasquez interrupted. "Taking care of a DWI isn't easy. Two is harder. But three? Tim, you need to learn your lesson."

Throwing his hands in the air, Tim walked away, his pale skin just a touch paler. "You don't own me, all right?"

With a sneer on his face, Velasquez straightened his tie and smoothed his suit coat. "I need to know whose fingerprints are on that pistol. How long?"

"A couple hours," Tim said. "Maybe longer. This doesn't work like on TV. You know that."

Taking long steps, Velasquez headed for the lab's door. "I'll be back after lunch. This is between us."

"Sure, sure," Tim replied, shooing him out of the office.

Velasquez took his time leaving, giving Tim a hard stare before he finally exited.

Tim went back to work, diligently processing the evidence he had no official paperwork for. After five minutes, when Velasquez hadn't invited himself back in, Tim reached for the office phone.

His eyes glued to the door, Tim dialed a number quickly. The four rings were an eternity, but finally someone picked up the other end.

"Mr. Lynch? It's Tim. There's a problem."

20

THIS IS NOT WHAT I *wanted to hear, Lynch."*

Matt Caroll frowned as he removed his thick glasses and rubbed the bridge of his nose. Travis sat next to his brother, but he knew which Lynch the DA was talking to.

"I wish I had better news, but we don't have enough for a capital conviction."

Caroll slid his glasses back on, blinking as he tried to focus. "I can see that. It's just that we're going through this effort, we'll get a murder conviction, but eventually Sutton's going to make parole. Then we're going to have another body."

"I'm sorry," Jake said. "Really, really sorry. But we just don't have what we need."

"How do you know he's going to commit another murder?"

For a moment, neither of the other men reacted, and Travis wondered if he might not have voiced his thought aloud. But then both Jake and the DA turned to regard him with concerned disbelief.

"I mean, what if he serves his time and just … stops?" Travis felt his face getting hot.

"Have you seen Sutton's rap sheet?" Caroll asked. "Shoplifting leads to petty larceny leads to auto theft leads to assault leads to robbery leads to felony assault leads to aggravated robbery. And now murder. It's like he's trying to earn merit badges or something."

"*Trav, the guy gets arrested so much, he knows some cops by their first names,*" *Jake said, barely hiding his exasperation.*

"*But you're just writing him off, like he's some kind of animal,*" *Travis protested to more incredulous stares. He felt like the one vegetarian at Thanksgiving.*

"*He is an animal,*" *Caroll responded bluntly. "I agree, murder is usually a crime of passion. You get in an argument, have too much to drink, whatever, you grab a gun to solve the problem. Sutton's crime wasn't passion. It was to get cash. That shopkeeper had what he wanted, and Sutton killed him to get it.*"

"*Have either of you thought about the larger implications?*" *Travis asked. He sounded timid to his own ears, uncertain. "I mean, of capital punishment. Like what we give up as a society if we allow the government to execute …*"

"*Christ, Trav,*" *Jake exploded, "I know this is Austin, but you don't need to turn all Greenpeace on us.*"

Caroll put his hand on Jake's arm, calming him. "He's just making sure we've covered all bases, aren't you son?"

Cowed into submission, Travis nodded and stared at the floor.

"*Any way you can keep an investigator on the case?*" *Jake asked his boss. "If I only had something tying him directly to the murder …*"

Travis bit the inside of his lip to keep quiet as his hand squeezed the flash drive.

Travis tugged nervously at his collar. He didn't set foot in the DA's office for 10 years, and now he was about to make his second visit in a month. As he walked from the elevator lobby to Jake's office, his knees wobbled, his mouth went dry, and he sweated like he'd just been mowing his lawn on a hundred-degree afternoon.

He marched past the assistant DAs and the paralegals, past the IT guys and everyone else, making a beeline for the largest office at the back. Susan saw him coming and stood to greet him.

"Thanks for making an appointment this time." She raised an eyebrow when she saw his black eye, then she scanned his face, frowning. "All right, I get it now. Who won?"

"I did." Jake stood in his doorway, jacket off and shirt sleeves rolled up. If he'd had more hair, he could have been the Jake Lynch of ten years ago. "I'll take it from here, Susan."

"I think you should leave your door open," Susan cautioned as she stood.

"Heard and understood," Jake said as he closed the door.

Susan put her foot in the way and pushed. "I *really* think you should leave your door open."

Travis saw the tiniest flush begin on Jake's neck, the warning sign of bad things to come. But his brother pursed his lips, thought for a moment, then let go. Susan pushed the door wide, and watched them both with her hands on her hips as Jake ushered his brother in.

"She's my second mother," Jake muttered. "Like the first one isn't enough."

"She's right, you know," Travis said. "I don't think you and I should be in a locked room together. Not yet."

Jake eased into his leather executive chair. "The worst part is, she's almost always right. And never lets me forget it."

Travis perched nervously on the edge of his seat while his brother leaned back in his, clasping his hands behind his head. For a moment, neither of them said a word, staring awkwardly at one another. Travis glanced out the open door behind him, where Susan sat at her desk, watching them both like a mother hen watching her chicks.

"Well …" Jake sighed. His voice trailed off and he shrugged.

"Yeah, uh …" Travis said. "Sorry about, you know." Travis gestured at Jake's face, at his still-swollen lip.

"Me too," Jake replied. "That's some shiner. And I know you have to appear in court from time to time."

"Shirley didn't want me to come here." Travis inched back, daring to become a little more comfortable.

"Rita's already called twice to make sure I don't do anything stupid," Jake said. "She's known me a very long time."

Travis slid a manila envelope across the desk. Jake left it where it stopped, eyeing it suspiciously.

"This is the report from a private detective I hired to find Mark Kidd," Travis said. "She didn't smoke him out, but I figured maybe your people could use her notes."

"Certainly couldn't hurt," Jake said. "As long as she didn't do anything illegal."

Jake hadn't moved, still reclined in his chair, hands still clasped behind his head.

"Don't you want to look at it?"

"I'll get someone to review it," Jake replied.

"She didn't come cheap," Travis continued, "and Shirley hit the roof when the bill came. That's part of the reason she didn't want me to come here. Her opinion is since we paid for it, it's ours."

Jake nodded slowly. "I'll have one of the investigative staff review it."

"Are you sure you don't want to take a quick look—"

"Travis!" Jake barked. "The sun does not rise and set at your whim. I told you I will have my staff review it, and you're going to have to trust me on that. Understood?"

Chastened, Travis glanced back at Susan, whose attention was riveted on him. "Okay. Sorry. It's just that the sooner we find Mark Kidd, the sooner we can prove Sam didn't kill those two."

Jake sighed deeply, and leaned forward to cradle his head in his hands. "Why the fuck are you doing this?"

Travis bristled. "Excuse me?"

"The Park kid," Jake said wearily. "You've seen his record, you've talked to him, and you've talked to the family. Hell, you defended his scumbag drug dealer brother. Sam Park's been working his way up to murder since he was twelve. Even if he didn't pull the trigger, he's clearly the ringleader. The entire expedition that night was his idea, he admits it."

"So?"

Jake's face was growing pinker. "So that makes him as culpable as if he had pulled the trigger. No difference under the law, Trav. None."

Travis wanted to fly into a rage. He wanted to leap to his feet and start the Sunday brunch battle all over again. But he held his temper. Barely. "I'm not going to give up on him."

"I know what this is really about," Jake replied. He jabbed a finger at his brother. "And so do you."

The butterflies that had been swarming in his stomach since he walked into the building all settled at once, and Travis felt ice running through his veins. He knew it was going to come down to this, but he didn't know it would be quite so soon.

"Why don't you enlighten me?"

Jake counted to five, then counted again for good measure. His little brother was doing everything he knew would drive Jake insane, and he was doing it on purpose, like they were kids on a family trip and Travis had nothing better to do than push Jake's buttons.

But Jake wasn't going to let him do it this time. He glanced past Travis, through the wide-open door that allowed the entire office to see what was going on. Susan was a smart one, that was for sure. With everyone watching, Jake had to behave himself, he had to show restraint. Travis waited for an answer, watching Jake with an almost dismissive sneer.

"Reilly Wayne Sutton."

Travis's face scrunched up and his lips pursed tight enough to make a thin white line around his mouth. Jake had scored a direct hit, and his little brother had no way to disguise it.

"This has nothing—"

"It has *everything* to do with Sutton, and you know it," Jake interrupted, his voice rising dangerously.

Travis glanced over his shoulder, taking a long, slow exhale. "I came here to share information, not to rehash something that's over and done with."

"It's not over, Trav."

"He's dead and buried," Travis replied. "It doesn't get more over than that."

Jake stared at his little brother, who stared right back, not backing off an inch.

"He was a murderer." Jake's pulse throbbed in his head.

"He was a human being."

This argument would circle the same track over and over again, just like it had then. Jake knew it, and he could see the same realization in his brother's eyes. The world had changed but they were stuck in the same place they'd been ten years ago.

"I still don't know why you did it," Jake growled.

"You know exactly why," Travis replied. "I'd do it again. In a heartbeat."

Travis sat straighter, throwing his shoulders back, so confident in his position, so condescending. It was almost as if he were proud of his betrayal.

A knock sounded at the door. Susan, wearing a concerned expression. "Can I get either of you something to drink?"

Jake relaxed, which allowed his brother to ease off, his shoulders dropping. "You know what? Don't bother. I got the thing right here."

He reached into the bottom left drawer and pulled out a new, unopened bottle of bourbon and two glasses.

"Mr. Lynch, it's barely one o'clock," Susan admonished.

Jake raised an eyebrow. "Yes. And?"

Shaking her head, Susan retreated to her desk. Jake cracked open the bottle and poured a strong two fingers in each glass. He pushed one across the desk to Travis.

"I don't know, Jake, it's a little early and I don't usually …"

"Take the fucking drink, Trav," Jake interrupted. "I'm trying to be nice. Rita made me promise."

Travis reached for the glass. "Shirley made me promise, too."

"To our wives," Jake said, raising his drink, "each of them is smarter than both of us put together."

"Our wives," Travis agreed. He downed the bourbon in one gulp and slammed the glass on Jake's desk so loudly it turned heads in the office.

"We're obviously going to have to take this slowly," Jake said, sipping his bourbon. "There's a lot of water under the bridge."

"It's good to talk shop again," Travis replied. "Even if you're an arrogant jackass."

"And you're a smug know-it-all," Jake replied.

"To the Lynch boys," Travis said, holding his empty glass up. "Together again. Kind of."

"To us," Jake agreed. He finished his drink and reached into the bourbon drawer to retrieve a folder which he pushed across the desk.

"What's that?" Travis asked.

"A look at your credit records, your bank statements," Jake replied. "Before you get defensive, I got word about Carlisle coming after you. He's not the kind to throw a punch or burn your house down, so I had our financial investigators look into it. In the past two weeks there have been nine credit checks run on you and your practice."

"What?" Travis grabbed the folder and flipped through the pages. "Too many of those will … the banks will cut me off."

"You need to watch that like a hawk," Jake advised. "Get Shirley on it. I got a feeling you're going to find a few of your recent clients might be reluctant to pay, too. I wouldn't be surprised if there's some sort of lien put on your property."

"Well, Goddamn," Travis hissed. "Thanks, Jake. I'll take care of it."

"I didn't hear you say that," Jake replied.

Travis turned and scanned the office beyond the open door. "Since we're doing each other favors … your guy Velasquez there?"

Jake frowned and rolled his eyes.

"He's talking to Morton," Travis said. "I saw him get into a car with her."

"I know."

The look of astonishment on his little brother's face was priceless. "And he still works here?"

"This was never your sort of place, was it, Trav?" Jake replied. "You never got the ins and outs of how to deal with office politics."

"Christine Morton," Travis hissed. "You hate her almost as much as I do."

"More," Jake corrected. "Sometimes, though, it's worthwhile to let things play out. Let people show you their endgame. Give them enough rope to hang themselves."

Travis slumped in his chair. "Seriously, Jake. Sometimes you sound so much like Mama it scares me."

21

THIS IS THE ABSOLUTE WORST," Jake sighed as he walked through the side gate.

Rita's fingernails dug into Jake's arm while she beamed her dazzling beauty-queen smile across the well-manicured and crowded yard. She leaned in close to whisper in her husband's ear. "It's part of the job, honey. Meet 'n greet, just ask their name, smile, nod, move on."

Mel Davis had set up his two-acre backyard for an afternoon barbecue, which was really an under-the-radar fundraiser for Jake's bid for governor. Since they hadn't officially announced—or filed any paperwork—Jake was simply collecting favors from people who owed Mel Davis favors. He and Rita had just arrived and turned the kids loose before they got their nametags.

As if anyone here didn't already know his name.

"This isn't my first time," Jake muttered. He tried to move toward the open bar but Rita refused to let him go.

"You were a little more enthusiastic before." She groomed him, adjusting his shirt, brushing off non-existent pieces of lint.

"Before, I actually wanted the job they were offering," Jake replied.

Rita held his gaze, deadly calm and deadly serious. Her bright white smile seemed more like a threat now, the tiger's grin before she pounced. "This is a step up. A big step up. You need to let these people know you're ready to be the governor."

"What if I'm not?"

Rita kissed him on the cheek and wiped away the rose-shaped residue of lipstick. "You are."

She let him go and called out across the yard, waving to friends of hers that Jake barely knew. He barely knew *any* of these people. Eric and Heather raced by, shoes already scuffed, playing with children they'd just met as if they'd been friends all their lives. Jake envied his kids the ease they had with others; they took after their mother in that respect.

"Shouldn't you be over there?"

A hand landed on his shoulder, and Jake found himself wrapped in a fatherly hug. Val Lynch pointed across the huge backyard where smoke billowed from the grill as the caterer's staff worked the crowd with trays of hors d'oeuvres and a band of maroon-clad mariachis tuned up.

"All these people want to see you in the governor's mansion," Val said. The people clapped as the mariachis launched into "El Rey."

"If a monkey promised to vote their way, they'd back him."

Val shrugged, but didn't disagree with Jake's assessment. "You gotta admit, son, these are good friends to have."

"They're not my friends," Jake replied, frowning across the lawn at the people. "They're your friends. And Mama's. And Davis's."

"Well, they're never going to be your friends if you don't go talk to them," Val said.

A black-and-white clad caterer walked by with a bucket of beers on ice and Jake helped himself to one. "I notice you're over here with me."

Val grinned broadly. "I'm trying to get you to press the flesh. Besides, I'm not the one they're here to see."

Jake sipped his beer, watching his wife work the crowd, smiling, nodding, laughing. Pretending she actually cared what these vapid, small people thought.

"I have a question," Jake announced. "Whose idea was it? For me to run for governor. Yours?"

"A little bit me," Val said, his eyes on the ground. "Like father, like son, right?"

"A little bit you," Jake replied, "and a little bit someone else. Who?"

"Davis, mostly," Val said, pointing across the lawn to the whip-thin, white-haired man greeting the crowd like a pro. "He said he thought it would be a good thing for you. Move you up."

"And if Davis thinks it, chances are good Carlisle thought it first." Jake waved at Rita, who was pointing at him and explaining something to a withered old woman, the kind who had nothing better to do than come to a covert fundraiser in the middle of a Saturday afternoon. "Usually I can spot a motive a mile away. Carlisle hates me, so why is he trying to reward me?"

Val sipped his drink, liquor so brown it had to be Southern Comfort, lost in thought. Jake knew the look; silent consideration was his father's habit when things didn't turn out quite like he expected. Jake had been on the receiving end of that stare when he lost the first Sutton case.

"Change is good sometimes," Val said.

"Sometimes," Jake agreed, "but not just to make a change. There should be a reason, and it should make sense. I'm not sure me being governor makes sense."

Jake hoped he was making his point, but when he looked for his father's reaction, he got nothing. Val was turned to the side, staring at the party they were avoiding. Across the yard, things carried on without father or son, the various political functionaries mixing with the people who funded them, a cotillion where influence and money blended with ambition and promises. It was an intricate waltz, one Jake had grown tired of dancing.

There was Jake's mother, Mae Kerr Lynch, laughing and joking, making her point with a raised eyebrow and a knowing nod. She had pigeonholed a tall, thin man with a salon-perfect haircut, the only person at the entire gathering who wore an expensive suit in the heat of a Texas afternoon.

"Who's the jackass in the three-piece?" Val asked, pointing to the man his wife interrogated.

"Roberto Velasquez," Jake said. "Did Mama invite him?"

"Not that she told me," Val replied. "So that's what Velasquez looks like. He sure works fast."

Velasquez took his leave of Mae Lynch and turned to a group of older couples eager to make his acquaintance. He talked and smiled for a few seconds, polite as could be, but he was rapidly working his way over to Mel Davis. He used each brief meeting as a slingshot into the next, a toad hopping from lily pad to lily pad, aiming for the bullfrog.

A thought popped into Jake's head then, as Velasquez reached Davis and pumped his hand, slapping the older man's shoulder in a patently false display of familiarity. Jake scanned the yard, examining every person, looking for one in particular.

"Where's Carlisle?" he wondered aloud.

His father wasn't paying attention, fully engaged in asking a caterer for another glass of Southern Comfort. Once the deal was done, he promptly turned around.

"I'm sorry, son. What were you saying?"

"Nothing important," Jake replied. He stiffened as someone pointed Velasquez toward Jake and his father. The fact that they had separated themselves from the crowd didn't seem to matter to Velasquez as he launched himself across the lawn. A wide politician's grin plastered to his face, he stopped in front of Jake, his hand extended.

"I heard the good news," Velasquez said. "Congratulations. I think you'll make a great governor."

It took every ounce of politeness and restraint Jake had to take Velasquez's soft hand.

"Let's not get too far ahead. I'm still DA, and I will be for quite a while."

Velasquez's grin broke for just an instant, and he blinked a few times like a deer caught in a spotlight. "You mean you're … I thought you'd jump at the chance."

"I haven't decided either way," Jake said. "Being governor would be nice, but being DA has a whole lot more to it. You can understand that, right?"

Val's hand landed on Jake's shoulder, squeezing hard the way he had when Jake was small. "I'll leave you two to talk business. See you at brunch tomorrow."

"That's your father, right?" Velasquez said, his voice small. "He looks a lot like—"

"My little brother, I know." Jake held Velasquez's gaze. "Where did you hear I might run for governor?"

"Around." Velasquez shifted self-consciously. "People talk."

"And people have names," Jake insisted.

"Do you think they're serving dinner yet?" Velasquez retreated hastily, his composure shot to hell.

Jake took a long draw off his beer and settled back against a table. He watched Velasquez work the crowd, now and again glancing nervously at Jake over his shoulder.

"Are you kidding me?" Rita appeared at Jake's side, a glass of wine on her breath. "You haven't moved from where I left you?"

"Talking to Dad," Jake said.

"I saw Velasquez over here." It was almost an accusation.

"Him too." Jake drained his bottle dry.

Rita sighed, but she caressed her husband's shoulder. "You really need to get out there and talk to people. You learn so much when people have been enjoying themselves."

He didn't say a word, just waited. With Rita it was best if he let her go, let her get to the point in her own time.

"I have a bit of news," Rita said, leaning in close, keeping her voice down. "When you run for governor, who do you think they're going to put up as your replacement for District Attorney?"

Jake stared across the yard. He knew the answer before Roberto Velasquez's name left Rita's lips. It was like a puzzle: When the very last piece fell into place, the picture was complete. Anger sparked in Jake's gut, not the usual quick flare that was his habit but a cold hard rage that sat heavy in his stomach.

If Roberto Velasquez thought Jake was just going to surrender the District Attorney's office to him, he needed to think again. And he needed to watch his back.

When the gate guard returned Travis's license, he couldn't help but stare at the black eye, yet he seemed genuinely apologetic.

"I am *so* sorry for the inconvenience, Mr. Lynch, it's just that we haven't seen you here in a very long time."

"No problem." Travis put his car in gear, "I haven't needed to be here in a very long time."

The guard waved him through the gates of the Austin Country Club, and Travis drove down tree-shaded lanes he thought he would never again travel. When the news broke ten years ago, when Travis's face was plastered across all local media, several senior members had made it very clear that he was no longer welcome at the club. Travis had been only too happy to oblige them. He prepared for a fight today, possibly even an escort off the property, but evidently his parents maintained him on their membership.

His beaten, battered car was absolutely the oldest and most out-of-place auto in the parking lot, and Travis took an empty spot right up front, where the pampered members could see it as they left the main club building. He took special pleasure in reminding these people that there were far more of the "others" than there were of them.

The sounds of the driving range off to his right brought back memories of old Saturday afternoons. There had been a time when Travis could walk the golf course blindfolded, he'd done it so often at his father's side. The thought now embarrassed him; remembering his younger self was like watching someone else's home movies. He felt no connection to the boy he had been. In fact, Travis would rather not have come back here ever again. But there were some problems a man had to solve in person.

Up the front steps and through the door, the sights and sounds brought Travis back ten years in an instant. It was the same, yet oddly different. It smelled like it always had, vaguely syrupy, with overtones of mowed grass, but the carpet was new and the walls were a different color.

A foursome heading out to the links paused, looking back at him. It was a reaction Travis had grown used to: They recognized him but couldn't put a name to the face. He ignored them and hoped they'd do the same to him.

The lounge—what other people called "the bar"—waited down a long hallway hung with photo after photo, some of them nearly one hundred years old. The sight brought Travis up short. He'd almost forgotten about this hallway, about the pictures. His family appeared in many of these photographs, even the earliest ones. He remembered the first time he saw the name plaque with "Lynch" carefully engraved beneath a black-and-white photograph of a smiling young couple who looked vaguely familiar. His father explained that they were Nana and Papa, Travis's great-grandparents, when they were much younger. Val went on to explain then about the long history Travis's family had, both in Texas and at the club, and how he should be proud to be part of such a long line of accomplished people.

Travis ran his finger along that same plaque as his great-grandparents smiled back at him. His great-grandfather had been an attorney, of course, as had his father and his father before that. They carved a place for themselves here, they lived and worked and played among the elite and established the Lynch family's place at the metaphorical head of the table.

Travis had given that up.

He walked slowly down the hall, remembering an eight-year-old boy stopping every few feet to look at another picture of his family. Each one told him a different story, brought him to another era in his history. And with each succeeding generation, the Lynch men seemed more and more unsatisfied. Travis's grandfather had a forced smile in most pictures, his father Val barely smiled in his own pictures, and when Travis found pictures of himself, close to the end of the hall, he seemed wistful, even sad.

Standing there, his finger on the last picture of him, taken eleven years ago with his brother at his side for a golf tournament, reaffirmed the fact that he didn't miss the country club at all. Staring at that picture of him with a frozen smile, his arm wrapped awkwardly around Jake's shoulder, he realized why.

This place wasn't his. The dream that made his grandparents and their grandparents work so hard to be here, that wasn't his, either. They'd done their best to build a legacy without considering whether their descendants would want one.

The Sutton case had been the catalyst, the last brick in the wall, but Travis now realized his desire to break ranks had been burning long before then. Probably for Jake, too, though he'd be the last to admit it. A man could walk in his ancestors' footsteps for only so long before he needed to blaze his own trail.

Travis looked back down the hall and knew that he'd made the right choice. Both with the Sutton case and with starting his own practice. Which made what he had to do next that much easier.

He rounded a familiar corner, coming upon the lounge with its dramatic, age-darkened oak bar. Many times he and Jake had sipped lemonade while his father had an "adult beverage" with past or potential clients. This room had not changed one bit; even the people looked exactly the same, mostly old and white, with a few kids and a few trophy wives. Travis paused at the entrance and scanned the faces, searching for one in particular.

There. The man Travis had only ever seen on TV stood at the far end of the bar, bottled water in one hand, chatting earnestly with another man. Dave Carlisle. Jake would have known who the other person was in a heartbeat, and Travis thought it was someone he should recognize, someone he'd been introduced to before, but he couldn't have cared less now. Carlisle was his target, and he approached like a heat-seeking missile.

"Of course not, he can't possibly win," Carlisle said as Travis came within earshot. "He's out, and our guy is in. Simple."

"Is that your opinion," the other man asked, "or do you have something to back that up?"

Travis stopped beside Carlisle and tapped him on the shoulder. "Excuse me, sir. I need to talk with you."

Carlisle turned around, his tired eyes narrowed and suspicious. It took him a moment, but he recoiled slightly when he made the connection. "You're Travis Lynch."

"I am," Travis replied, more a challenge than an affirmation. "Who the fuck do you think you are?"

"I couldn't care less about you or what you have to say," Carlisle spat. "I will call security, though."

"Someone's trying to screw with my practice's credit rating," Travis said. "Someone has called my bank, told them I'm a bad risk, and they've called a few of my clients and said the same thing."

"Don't know a thing about it." Carlisle turned his back.

Travis grabbed his shoulder and turned him around. "I have the paper trail back to you and your companies. This is the Internet age. Did you think you could try to ruin me without leaving any record?"

Carlisle knocked Travis's hand away. "So sue me."

"Already done." Travis slapped folded pages into Carlisle's hand. "David Carlisle, you've been served."

Carlisle raised an eyebrow at the pages then tossed them on the bar. "Good luck. I have my own attorneys, an army of them."

Travis jabbed a finger into Carlisle's chest. "When you fuck with my practice, you're not just fucking with me, you're fucking with my wife and my child. You do not want to do that."

Carlisle's face hardened, and some color came to his gray cheeks. His dull eyes flashed and his face contorted into a mask of anger and grief.

"You're defending the bastard who killed *my* son. You deserve every ounce of hell on Earth I can give you."

Travis saw red, actual color at the edges of his vision, a flash so strong he almost threw the first punch. Again. But he jammed his hands into his pockets to keep them from doing things he didn't want. Carlisle saw the rage on Travis's face and actually backed up a step.

"I'll argue the case in court," Travis spat through clenched teeth, "not here. This crap stops now, or I'll own everything you think is yours, and my brother will put you under the jail. Do you read me loud and clear, Mr. Carlisle?"

Carlisle paled. He nodded, defeated, an old dog put in his place. He turned away, his hands shaking so badly he had to rest his bottle of water on the bar.

Travis ignored the eyes on him. He backed up a few steps until he was well out of reach, then turned around and headed for the doorway, where two security guards waited discreetly. Before he could exit the room, one final, muted word reached Travis's ears.

"Traitor."

Travis stopped dead in his tracks. He turned around to find Carlisle staring murder at him.

"Traitor?" He stalked back, his fingers curling into fists.

"Your family has been …" Carlisle began, his voice choking off as his own anger rose. "How can someone like you defend someone like him?"

"What do you mean?" Travis pulled himself up to his full height, towering over Carlisle.

"Your family is one of the best in Austin," Carlisle said. "In Texas. You wasted your opportunities, threw away everything your parents fought to give you."

"You don't know anything about how I got where I am," Travis said. "What does my family have to do with a defendant's right to a fair trial?"

Carlisle's finger shot out, coming dangerously close to Travis's face. "Why would you agree to defend that beggar?"

Travis almost shook as fury swept through him, but somehow—*somehow*—he kept his voice low and even as he replied.

"I'm sorry for your loss," Travis said. "But taking that boy's life isn't going to bring your boy back."

Carlisle's lips quivered, he was barely holding himself together. His voice broke as he fought back tears. "He wanted to use my car. I tossed him the keys, didn't think anything of it."

"It's not your fault," Travis said.

"He was going to be with Shane," Carlisle sobbed, the tears flowing freely now. "The Ablin boy, the one in the magnet school at Westlake. I thought maybe some of his smarts would rub off on Peter." He brushed the tears away and grimaced as he tried to pull himself together. "Dammit, why did he *do* that?"

Great, heaving sobs wracked Carlisle's body, and he wept into his hands, his tall frame bent almost double.

Travis left the lounge, brushing past the security guards as if they weren't there. He ignored the whispering, the knowing glances, the people who now recognized him. He hurried through the club, making his retreat before the guards could catch him and throw him out.

In Travis's mind, Dave Carlisle blurred, becoming Min Park. Both grieving, both anguished, both trying to make sense of a horrible, senseless thing. Neither would find any solace until this was over with, until the matter was resolved—one way or another.

And maybe not even then.

22

A PLEA DEAL? YOU GOTTA BE *outta your fuckin' mind ... "*
Travis sat silently at Jake's side, letting Sutton's words fall over him and past him. Words didn't matter, not here and not now. He wanted to look into Sutton's eyes. What kind of man was he, really?

Blevins laid a hand on Sutton's pale arm. "We may want to think about this ... "

"You know what it means, don't you?" Sutton sneered. "They got nothing. Not a Goddamned thing. That's why they want me to plead, so they don't have to bother with a trial or proving anything."

Jake leaned forward, his face beet red. "We're trying to help you out, Reilly."

"Bullshit," Sutton countered, "you're trying to help yourself. So you got me for assault."

"Aggravated assault," Jake interrupted, "which is a felony."

"Big fuckin' deal," Sutton finished. "I'll be out in two years. Less, if nobody pisses me off."

The tête-à-tête continued, making no real progress, and Travis blocked the noise of the conversation. He watched Sutton intently, almost obsessively. For the first time in his life, Travis was prepared to say that someone was unredeemable. Sutton showed no remorse for anything he'd done, and even seemed proud of his criminal career, especially the things he'd gotten away with. As Jake and Blevins went back and forth, Travis knew Sutton was right; there was no reason for him to plead to anything. The DA's office lacked essential evidence. Though Sutton was undeniably vile, Travis couldn't bring himself to produce the proof of guilt he carried in his pocket.

A loud bang echoed in the tiny room, and Travis realized all eyes were on him.

"I asked you what you were looking at, Junior," Sutton snarled. He glared across the table, radiating hatred from every pore.

"You have a sister, don't you, Mr. Sutton?" Travis asked.

Sutton blinked, confused. "What?"

"And your mother's still alive, isn't she?"

"Trav … " Jake hissed.

"What do they think of all this? About you being in jail for murder?"

For a moment, a brief instant, Sutton's facade broke. His eyes dropped and his lower lip trembled. For an instant, he was an actual human being.

"Wouldn't your mother want you to come clean?" Travis prompted.

His vulnerability lasted for one moment longer, then Sutton went back behind his wall. "You don't know me or my family, you rich bastard. You got no idea who I am. You and your brother can go straight to hell."

Blevins closed his notebook and packed his things in his briefcase. "That's the answer, then. We're not taking the deal."

Jake shrugged and leaned back in his seat.

"I guess we'll see you at trial," Blevins continued. He shook Jake's hand and held it. "But seriously, Jake. Two failed convictions for the same defendant? That's a career-ending statistic."

"I'll keep that in mind, Ken," Jake said as the deputy escorted Sutton from the room.

A sharp rap at his office door demanded Jake's attention. Susan stood in the doorway, a stern, disapproving scowl on her face.

"You have a visitor, Mr. Lynch. Shall I send her away?"

Jake closed the folder on his desk; he couldn't be leaving things out where anyone could read them. "Of course not, let her in."

Susan raised an eyebrow, communicating her complete disdain for the situation. She jerked her head toward Jake's office as she returned to her own desk, and in a moment Christine Morton appeared on Jake's threshold.

"I never thought I'd be summoned to your office," Morton said. "Escorted out, maybe."

"Would you mind closing the door, Christine?"

A flash of surprise crossed her face before she could suppress it. "'Would I mind?' Are you okay, Jake? Hit your head? It's not like you to be polite."

He came around the desk as Morton eased the door closed, ushering her to a seat. "It's a good day in the DA's office, which means it's a good day for you, too."

Suspicious, Morton took her seat. "That's not usually the way it works."

Jake perched on the edge of his desk, clasping his hands together. "I've been watching the news, the papers, online, the whole thing. I haven't seen one detail of the Carlisle case that I didn't already know about."

"That was our deal," Morton muttered, annoyed. She produced a pad and pen.

"I'll be honest, I didn't think you could do it," Jake said. "A day or two, maybe a week at the outside and then something would slip. But you made it happen. And now I have to make good on my end."

Morton waited impassively, her pen at the ready.

"We got the third shooter in the Carlisle case." Jake couldn't help but raise his chin proudly. "A guy named Mark Kidd. The Texas Rangers are bringing him in as we speak."

"Rangers?" Morton replied. "Was he in Mexico or something?"

Jake nodded.

Morton held her hand up. "Before we go any further, we agree this is on the record?"

"I'll let you know when it's not," Jake replied. "Yes, he was in Mexico. Living off his winnings at online poker, of all things. He taught English a few hours each day to pretend he was respectable, but that doesn't pay the rent."

"Where?" Morton scribbled furiously.

"An apartment in Monterrey." Jake handed her a single sheet of paper. "Details are on there, if you have contacts in Mexico you want to check things out. I'd be interested to know if anyone understood who he really was."

"How'd the Rangers catch up with him?"

"It's always the stupid things, isn't it?" Jake explained. "He'd probably be there still, except for his habit."

Morton brushed the hair out of her eyes, letting Jake have his moment of suspense.

"He came across the border once a week to get a phone card and a cheeseburger. And that's where the Rangers got him. At the Whataburger in Hidalgo."

"You're kidding me," Morton said, even as she wrote it down.

"Hand to God," Jake replied. "He's supposed to arrive for booking in an hour."

Morton stood, suddenly radiating nervous energy. "When can I break the story?"

His hands held wide, Jake presented the image of a magnanimous benefactor. "Any time. But you and I aren't done yet."

Morton's huge, resigned sigh filled the room. "Let me guess, *now* we're off the record?"

Jake gestured at the chair and Morton returned to her seat. But she didn't put away the pad and the pen.

"You seem to know a lot about behind-the-scenes Austin politics," Jake began.

"It's my beat. One of them. You can't fault me for doing my job."

"But lately you're more informed than you ever were." Jake sat in his leather-upholstered monstrosity of a chair and put his feet on his desk. "Almost like you found someone on the inside."

Morton waved her note pad. "You mean like yourself? You're my best source in the DA's office."

"But not your only one."

Jake waited, staring at Morton, who refused to react, neither confirming nor denying what Jake already knew to be true.

"Is Velasquez your line in to Carlisle," Jake asked, "or do you have something on that old bastard too?"

She didn't flinch. "My sources are confidential. Always."

"Velasquez knew I was being considered for governor," Jake said. "He either heard it from Carlisle, or he heard it from you."

Up until this moment, Jake had remained remarkably calm, surprising even himself. Not even a trickle of sweat. But now, staring across the desk at Morton's smug face as she refused to admit the truth, Jake felt his temper rise.

"They're picking my replacement," Jake continued. "And guess who's at the top of Carlisle's short list? Your carpool buddy Velasquez."

"He's not my ... " Morton began.

"Don't bother, Christine," Jake interrupted. "I know he's your source. Or one of them. That fraud is being groomed for *my* job. I know it, and, more to the point, you know it."

Morton shrugged. "And?"

"Why didn't you tell me?"

A confused look came over Morton, and after a moment Jake realized it wasn't an act, and it wasn't stalling. His question truly puzzled her.

"You and I aren't friends, Jake," Morton replied carefully. "You've made that abundantly clear over the years. Matter of fact, we barely tolerate one another. What in our history leads you to believe that I have any obligation to divulge information like that?"

Jake swung his feet off the desk and leapt up. "It's the right thing to do, dammit."

"I don't know if that's arrogant or naive," Morton replied, "but nobody plays fair in this town, or at least, plays by the same rules you do. As DA, you should know that."

"This is my career!" Jake erupted. "My livelihood!"

Morton kept her infuriating cool. "If you heard the station was going to fire me, would you pick up the phone and let me know? Or would you pick up the phone to find out who was replacing me and try to get in good with them beforehand?"

Jake slumped in his seat. She was right. He hated it when she was right.

He was steamed, now, but not at Morton. Not really. She waited him out, calmly watching as every emotion he'd been bottling up the past few days raced through him. Finally, Jake threw his hands up, surrendering.

"I don't want to be governor."

"Of course you don't," Morton replied. "It's a crap job—especially after being DA."

"Who told you that? Being governor of Texas is like a two-year vacation."

Shaking her head, Morton laughed softly. "Is that really something you'd enjoy?"

Jake let the question hang for a long time.

"I don't know any more."

Morton stood again, finally putting away her pad and pen. "We done?"

Nodding, Jake waved her out. Defeated, deflated, he collapsed into his chair. Morton stopped at the door and he waited for it, for the triumphant dig, for the celebration of her win.

"Christ, Jake, self-pity doesn't suit you at all." She tugged at her blouse and plucked at her hair as if she were making herself presentable for broadcast. "Even if we hate each other's guts, we do go back a long way."

Why was she still here? Why wouldn't she just go? Jake let his impatience dissolve into indifference.

"My sources tell me the other side's putting up Adams. For governor. They won't announce it for months, but he's got it locked down."

Jake sat straighter. "Bill Adams? From Dallas? *That* Adams?"

"That's the guy."

"Adams has been Lieutenant Governor, Railroad Commissioner, Comptroller." Jake's mind whirled, putting together more bits and pieces of the puzzle. "That's the experience someone needs to be governor. I'm nowhere near that."

Morton shook her head, agreeing.

"If I get the nomination," Jake continued, thinking out loud, "and I have to give up the DA's office …"

"You're still not going to win the governorship," Morton finished.

A new fire stoked in Jake's stomach, a long-burning, strong blaze of righteous indignation and betrayal.

"Son of a bitch."

"There's the Jake Lynch everyone knows and hates," Morton said, reaching for the door. "Tear 'em up."

"Christine."

She turned back halfway.

"It kills me to say this," Jake said grudgingly, hating Morton's sly grin. "But I owe you one."

Her dazzling, *entirely* too pleased with herself smile lit up the room.

"You sure the fuck do."

23

I**'M SORRY, WHAT WAS YOUR** name again?" *Jake barked, less a question than a demand.*

The pretty, if somewhat mousy, woman blocking the sidewalk in front of Jake and Travis smiled and brushed her brown hair over her shoulder. "Chris Morton. Your brother and I spoke about a week ago."

Jake turned to Travis, who found something interesting in the pavement. He never said anything about speaking to a reporter.

"We don't give interviews outside the DA's office," Jake snapped as he dodged around Morton and continued down the sidewalk. It took Travis a moment longer to do the same.

Her footsteps followed closely. "If the only way I can get to you is to ambush you at lunch, I'll do it every day until you talk to me, Mr. Lynch."

Jake stopped, gathering every ounce of patience he had in his body. His face flushed, but he stayed composed and turned to her. "Mrs. Morton, I have a very short fuse. My brother will be the first to tell you that, and I'm old enough now that I'm not likely to change. I'll tell you once only: Leave me alone."

"It's 'Miss,'" Morton replied, with a wink to Travis, "and I know all about you and your temper, Mr. Lynch. I'll brave the wrath of the dragon to ask one question. A tiny one. Shouldn't take a second of your time."

Jake sighed. "Fine."

"What is the DA's office going to do with the surveillance video Mrs. Homayanpour handed over last week?"

Video? Jake had never heard of any video. He turned to Travis to find his brother pale as a ghost, his hands trembling.

"Oh? Did that not come to your attention?" Morton asked. She clearly knew the answer ahead of time. "Well, there is surveillance video of the liquor store the night of the murder. The widow Homayanpour provided a copy of it to the DA's office a few days ago. She gave it to 'the nice boy who came out to talk.'"

She was staring at Travis, who avoided her gaze and looked like he might break into a run at any moment.

"I suppose she's also provided a copy to you?" Jake replied.

Morton held her hands up and shook her head. "Heaven forbid, Mr. Lynch, that would be illegal, wouldn't it?"

"It would," Jake replied coldly. "The DA's office evaluates all evidence as soon as we have it. And we're currently evaluating this new footage as well. The press will get notification through the proper channels."

"As always, of course," Morton replied. "I just wanted to be able to reassure Mrs. Homayanpour that all measures were being taken."

"They are," Jake said, angry enough to chew nails. He didn't know who was more deserving of his fury: this reporter or his own brother.

"That's all I needed then," Morton said. Her lips parted in a smug, self-satisfied grin. She knew exactly what had happened, and she was letting Jake know he had a problem he needed to address. Which didn't make him like her one little bit.

"Chris? Do you spell your first name with a K or a C?" Jake asked as she turned away. "So I can tell the front desk who to keep out."

"It's Christine with a C-H, actually," she said. "Starting now, I'm going with Christine. It sounds a bit more professional, don't you think?"

The smell of the jail's interview room didn't bother Travis any longer; he only really noticed it when he first walked in and then when he left and was breathing clean air again. The clammy humidity didn't seem all that bad today either; he was barely perspiring. Shirley remarked that he was in jail more than some offenders, and Travis dismissed the notion outright. But he knew he'd spent far too much time there when he realized he was rearranging the chairs to make sure he got the only one that was remotely comfortable.

He pulled a bound stack of paper from his briefcase—a solid two hundred pages—and planted it conspicuously on the corner of the metal table, where no one could miss it. Once he knew where to look and what to look for and who to talk to, he'd managed to put all the disparate parts together into a whole case. In a few minutes, two people were going to walk through that door, and Travis would present the evidence. They would protest, certainly, but the facts were solid and they all pointed to one thing.

Mark Kidd killed Peter Carlisle and Shane Ablin.

Travis laid his hand on the paper, his road map for keeping Sam Park off death row. The sheets set out the case as plainly as he could present it: all the facts, all the coincidences, all the conclusions that any reasonable jury would draw about what happened that night. It would work. It had to.

The door opened and a deputy led in a thin, tanned young man, wearing an orange jail jumpsuit and handcuffed like Sam had been. His short dark hair had the crisp lines of a just-finished haircut, and the spots of dried blood on his face said he'd shaved minutes before. Huge, dark circles ringed his downcast eyes and he shuffled like a man resigned to his fate.

This was Mark Kidd, at last returned to face justice. He didn't look like much. This was the genius who ran to Mexico? This was the guy who made a living from online poker? He didn't look like he could punch his way out of a paper bag, let alone plot and plan and murder. Still, Travis knew looks could be deceiving. The deputy carefully locked Mark's hands to the table and then left.

The door closed and Travis glanced up at Mark's attorney, a tall, slender, severe woman who wore her long black hair gathered behind her head where it trickled down her back. Her large eyes locked onto Travis's from behind thin lenses and one side of her mouth curled up slightly. Contempt. Travis had seen it before, many times, but this time it hurt.

"Bonnie Wong," Travis said, extending his hand, "it's been a long time."

Reluctantly, she shook hands, but it was cursory and she broke contact quickly. "Where's your client?"

So that was the way she was playing this? Bonnie had been a year behind Travis in law school; he'd helped her with a contracts class. Evidently that counted for nothing.

"Sam doesn't need to be here," Travis explained. "And he had a bit of a misunderstanding in the day room yesterday."

"He's in the hole where he belongs." Mark had a surprisingly deep voice for such a slight person.

Bonnie sat and rifled through her briefcase. "Let's get this over with."

"I thought we could collaborate on a defense," Travis offered. "I mean, at least we could compare notes and coordinate strategies."

"I remember your 'collaboration' from the Sutton trial," Bonnie replied icily. "So you'll forgive me if I'm skeptical."

Mark watched the exchange closely, not missing a thing. Travis could feel the kid's eyes boring into him.

"I don't want to rehash a ten-year-old case," Travis said carefully. "Especially when it has no bearing on this one."

"No bearing?" her eyebrows went up. "Is that what you believe? Or is it something you say to ease your conscience?"

Travis held his tongue. He wanted so badly to blurt out his findings, but he'd have to approach it carefully. Bonnie was a superb trial lawyer; she could have a lot of influence over a jury.

"It's good to finally meet you, Mr. Kidd," Travis said. "I've been waiting weeks."

Mark scoffed and shook his head.

"You can talk," Travis offered. "This meeting isn't just for me and your attorney."

"He's been through a lot in the past few days," Bonnie replied. "He's had a few misunderstandings of his own."

"They tried to take my shoes," Mark blurted. He looked at Travis with haunted eyes. "I thought that kind of crap only happened in federal lockup. Or a playground."

"A jail's a jail," Travis replied. "I'm sorry to hear you're having problems."

Mark slumped further into his chair and shook his head as he muttered to himself. The bound stack of pages was within his easy reach but he ignored it.

Bonnie leaned back and crossed her arms over her chest. "What's your game, Lynch?"

"I don't have one," Travis lied. Why were neither of them interested in the papers?

"From what I hear, you've been telling anyone who'll listen that you're positive Sam Park didn't kill those two kids." Her eyes flashed anger. "That leaves two others."

"And Roger's a fucking moron, so that leaves me," Mark spat. Bonnie tapped him on the hand, shutting him up.

Bonnie locked eyes with Travis. "We have to keep together on this. Present a united front."

"That's going to be difficult," Travis replied, "since the state's going to prosecute all three defendants for a crime your client committed."

Travis expected anger, or surprise, or defiance, but Bonnie just glanced at her client.

"Fucking told you," Mark mumbled. "Sam's got him snowed."

"Excuse me?" Travis reached for the bound pages. "This is a timeline I've put together, with evidence gathered by the DA's office …"

Mark snapped straight, challenging Travis with his eyes. "So you think I bought that gun? You think I fired it?"

Folding open the pages, Travis pointed to one in particular. "This is a withdrawal record from an ATM the day of the murder, on your card's account. For sixty dollars."

"Can't buy a gun for sixty dollars," Mark snapped.

"Interesting that you know that," Travis replied. "You're right, a gun costs more than sixty dollars, but guess how much a box of bullets costs?"

"You're stretching, Lynch," Bonnie protested.

Travis flipped a page. "Guess what the detectives found in Sam's bedroom? A receipt, on that same day, about half an hour later, for a box of bullets. Fifty-five dollars."

Bonnie pushed the document away, refusing to look at it. "This is circumstantial. The receipt came from your client's place. Not Mark's."

"That's a pretty strong circumstance," Travis replied. "I say it proves that Mr. Kidd was not blameless in the murders. He bought the bullets, or paid for them at the very least, and knew what the money was for. That makes him an accessory."

"I didn't do it," Mark said. "I didn't shoot anyone."

Flipping another page, Travis continued. "A few days earlier, someone withdrew three hundred dollars from Mr. Kidd's account. Which is not, by itself, suspect. However, I was reviewing the information the DA's office provided, and something caught my eye."

Travis tapped on the page. "There's a fence on the east side, pretty well-known guy, and when the cops talked to him, he admitted he sold a pistol to someone roughly matching Mark's description. Guess how much a pistol goes for in his shop? About three hundred dollars. Pretty big coincidence, huh?"

Bonnie glanced at Mark, who shrugged. "'Roughly matching?' I hope you're not suggesting that this bogus paper trail means my client shot those kids."

Travis addressed Mark. "If I can connect the dots, a jury can too. Do you still want to claim you knew nothing about the gun, or do you want to come clean?"

Slumping, Mark let out a long, low breath. His lips moved as he said something under his breath, something neither his lawyer nor Travis could hear.

"I'm sorry, what was that?" Travis said. He remembered this feeling, this triumph, from his time with the DA's office. He got a bad guy.

"I didn't shoot anybody, and I didn't buy a gun," Mark said, his voice barely audible. "I swear to God. I owed Sam money. That's it, that's all. Three hundred and sixty dollars."

"What for?" Bonnie prompted.

"It's stupid," Mark said, blushing.

"No more so than buying bullets," Travis replied.

"Go to hell," Mark muttered.

"Tell him. We're all working on a defense here. Mr. Lynch understands that." She glared at Travis. "Don't you, Mr. Lynch?"

Mark pushed his shoulders back, trying to be tough. His lower lip quivered and a tear came to his eye, but he blinked it back. Travis waited impassively, putting on his best courtroom face.

"College applications," Mark said. "A few months ago I got the idea that I could go to college. Four-year, not the two-year craphole I'm at now. I mean, if some of the idiots I see going to the university can make it, I should have a chance, right? But the deck's stacked. They don't let you apply for free."

"There are ways to make money that didn't involve my client," Travis said. "Like, say, your job at the coffee shop. If you needed cash to apply for college, why did you borrow it from Sam?"

"Deadlines, man." Mark's eyes went out of focus as he remembered. "I wanted to start in the fall. Somewhere back east. Away from Austin. I had the applications filled out, I had the stupid essays written, the whole thing. Five of them. But I didn't have the cash when I needed it."

"Where did the money from your job go?" Travis asked skeptically.

Mark muttered something, and Bonnie laid her hand on his arm again.

"Rent on my old man's house," Mark said softly. "He hasn't had a decent job in, I don't know, ever. And our house isn't much, but it's better than living in the gutter."

"How long have you been paying the rent?" Bonnie asked, glaring at Travis.

Mark shrugged. "Since high school. Four, five years. I don't know. I tried to pick up extra shifts to pay for the applications, but it wasn't … extra shifts are hard to come by these days, you know? That's where Sam comes in."

"How did you make the money to pay Sam back?" Bonnie prodded. Mark mumbled his reply, looking at the floor. His attorney patted his hand reassuringly.

"Poker," Mark said, louder, "I taught myself how to play poker. Online. I know technically it's illegal, but I thought … " He broke off, shrugging helplessly.

Travis felt his detailed investigation falling apart around him. If Mark wasn't lying outright, if he actually did apply to schools, that was one-hundred percent traceable. And a story like his, true or not, was something a jury would eat up.

"I knew Sam, not that we were friends or anything," Mark continued. "But he always had a few bucks, you know? Not a lot, but enough to get by."

"Did Sam have a job that you know of?" Bonnie asked pointedly.

"I never saw him go to work, if that's what you mean. But he had a few jobs, the gray-market kind."

"Could you be clear?" Bonnie said.

"People he knew from his brother," Mark explained. "Sam didn't steal cars, but he knew people who did. He didn't grow pot, but he knew people who did that. Understand? He made introductions for a little piece of the action."

Bonnie pushed Travis's papers back across the table at him. "I'm sure you knew that, right, Lynch?"

"Sam's past … "

"He's lying to you," Mark interrupted. "That's what he does, it's *who he is*. If he told you he's lying to you, he'd be lying about that."

Travis's blood ran cold. Sam didn't pull that trigger. He couldn't have. Could he?

"Let's work on a few things," Bonnie suggested. "Since we're here together."

"Who pulled the trigger?" Travis stared at his hands.

"I don't think we're quite to that point in discussions yet," Bonnie replied.

Travis scooped the two hundred pages of "evidence" into his briefcase and headed for the door. "I'm wasting my time."

"So much for sticking together," Bonnie remarked dryly. "I hope your client's defense has a few more pegs than what you've shown me here. This is weak stuff, Lynch. Amateur hour."

"Whatever," Travis replied, trying to appear unconcerned even as he recognized the truth. "I'll leave that up to the DA."

"Wait." Mark's voice was strong, insistent.

His hand raised to knock for the bailiff, Travis paused.

"You're the DA's brother, right?"

"I am," he said. "Don't worry, we don't get along, so it's not like we have an arrangement or anything."

"But he's your brother," Mark pressed.

Travis came back around the table, looking into Mark's eyes. There was the smart kid, the guy Travis had heard about, the guy who impressed everyone he met with his intuitive grasp of things. This was the Mark Kidd who could organize a drug deal. Or plan a killing.

"Should that make a difference?"

"You're family," Mark said. "You talk. Even if you don't talk to each other, you talk to your wives, your cousins, your kids. People know things. Word gets around."

"And?"

"You get me a deal with the DA and I'll talk," Mark said. "Who did what, when we did it, how we set it up. The whole thing. Even … " his voice caught in his throat, "even who shot those rich kids in the back. All of it. But you have to get me a deal."

"I'm not your attorney," Travis said.

A thin smile showed on Mark's lips as he shrugged his shoulders. "Like you said, we're on the same side. And I can tell it's important to you. You need to know what Sam did."

The kid was right, and Travis hated him for it. To do his job, Travis didn't need Sam to be innocent, but he did need to know the truth. All of it. And if he had to crawl to Jake, if he had to ask for a deal for other defendants, that's what would happen.

"I'll see what I can do," Travis said.

"Thanks, Mr. Lynch," Mark said. "As soon as the DA gives the word to my lawyer, I'm spilling my guts."

Travis rapped on the door.

"Lynch," Bonnie called out sharply. "It's not ten years ago. You're licensed now."

The door opened and the bailiff stood aside for Travis, but Bonnie interrupted before he could walk out.

"You will not fuck me around like you did your brother. Are we clear?"

Travis turned and stiffly left the room without replying.

The "smoke-filled room" did still exist, and Jake sat smack in the middle of it, a political animal in his natural habitat. With the dark wood paneling and the fine taxidermy lining the walls, it was approaching a cliché, but this was where the real work got done.

Jake rubbed his eyes hard, the momentary discomfort and sharp white sparks in his vision snapping him out of his stupor. He stretched, feeling his lower back twinge, and he stood, kicking his legs to get the feeling back in them. Beside him, Mel Davis took a break, reaching for a cigar and a shot of tequila. The other four men at the table, Texas politicians all, did likewise, getting out the kinks, waking up their brains however they could. Davis was the only one he knew personally before he walked in, but the others he knew by reputation. Cut-throat sharks of Texas politics.

Jake had been in this room for hours, listening to the men drone on and on about strategy and positioning and the hearts and minds of their fellow Texans. It was all drivel, so much guesswork and "gut feeling" that none of them could put any rigor to the process. No matter what these men tried to anticipate, no matter what they decided, the next election would largely run the same course as every other; most of the incumbents would win again, with a few upsets that would keep the political analysts busy for the next two years.

"Did your daddy tell you about this part?" Mel Davis said, clapping Jake on the back. He blew his cigar smoke to the side, but Jake still got a lungful. "He used to fall asleep in his chair."

"It's not so bad," Jake said, wishing he were anywhere else, doing anything else. "Part of the process."

"I hate it, too," Davis said. "But it's gotta be done. And if you're gonna be governor, you gotta get used to making decisions."

I make decisions now, Jake thought. He wished his father were here; he needed a friendly face and some honest advice.

Jake refused Davis's offer of a cigar, but he accepted the shot of tequila. "How much longer is this going to last?"

"Only a few more hours."

Jake started to laugh until he realized it wasn't a joke. He downed the shot and felt the tequila's warm fire burning its way down his throat and into his stomach. He normally wasn't one for tequila, but here, now, he'd take all the help he could get.

"Tell you what," Davis offered, "why don't you take a break, get a bite to eat across the street or something, and come back in an hour?"

Jake shook his head. "In for a penny, in for a pound."

His head wreathed in thick cigar smoke, Davis looked Jake in the eye. "I don't think you get it, son. You're hungry. Go find yourself some food."

"Oh, I get it, Mel," Jake replied. "We've gone through the minor offices, now we're up to the major ones. You're going to talk about Austin's District Attorney."

Davis's chin raised, and he stroked his snow-white mustache as he regarded Jake. "You ready to be part of that conversation?"

The other four men had stopped talking and now watched intently as if they were in the front row at a boxing match.

"I don't see why not," Jake replied. "If I'm out, someone has to take my place."

Davis's head disappeared for a moment behind a huge plume of cigar smoke. When the vapors subsided, he looked at Jake skeptically. "You've been DA for quite a while, we were led to believe that you'd be resistant to change. Maybe not objective in regards to a new candidate."

Jake shook his head. "Who told you that? Carlisle? Maybe he's the one with objectivity problems."

Eyes wide, Davis turned to the other four, who seemed equally astonished at Jake's words. Did they think Jake was new to this game? He'd been elected DA twice, he knew which puppet-master pulled the strings.

"You know who would be good?" Jake offered. "Roberto Velasquez."

Davis nearly dropped his cigar. "Wh—why ... what makes you say that?"

"He's been in the department for a while," Jake replied, putting on a slight smile to mask his overt hostility. "He's been making the rounds, getting to know people."

Two of the men whispered to each other while the other two furiously took notes. Jake felt warm on the inside and it had nothing to do with the tequila; he loved stirring up the hornets' nest.

Davis's hard eyes stared at Jake. "What's your opinion of Velasquez as an attorney?"

"That hardly matters, right?" Jake answered. "He's got great hair. He'd look perfect on a yard sign."

"Is he qualified to be DA?" Davis pressed.

The room fell silent, with all eyes on Jake.

"I don't know. Am I qualified to be governor?"

This time no reaction betrayed Davis's thoughts. He took a long draw from his shot glass, draining it, and took a few more puffs on his cigar.

"You're sharper than your daddy."

"Not at all," Jake demurred. "My father's brilliant. Most of the time, he just can't be bothered. I'm more like my mother."

Davis nodded. "I'm beginning to see that. You're sure about Velasquez?"

"I've already given him more responsibility on the Carlisle case," Jake said. "What do you think about an even higher profile? It'll get him out in front of the public, under the bright lights. I think it would make Carlisle happy, too. Win-win-win all around, right?"

Another huge puff of cigar smoke escaped Davis's lips. One of his eyebrows stayed raised. "If you say so."

It was Jake's turn to clap Davis on the shoulder and flash his most sincere politician's smile. "I have every confidence Roberto Velasquez will show you and everyone else in the city the kind of man he is."

Judging by his frown, Davis did not like that answer one bit.

24

SAM SAT IN THE JAIL'S media room, the hard plastic bench uncomfortable and sticky. The men who shared the space kept at least an arm's length away, a generous allowance given the tight confines. It wasn't that Sam had proved himself especially dangerous—no desperate fights for supremacy—it was that the other inmates didn't want to be associated with a guy who faced a capital murder rap.

It had been this way for weeks, ever since the television news had broken the death penalty story. Sam didn't mind so much, it gave him a little more elbow room, but he hated the pitying glances, the sad shakes of the head the other inmates gave him from afar. They obviously counted him tried and convicted, just a long car ride away from the needle.

It wasn't supposed to be like that.

A kind of desperate prestige attached itself to convicts in Sam's neighborhood. Sam had romanticized prison when Charlie went, even though Charlie was the first one to tell him that it was a terrible place. To Sam, jail was a way out, out of the depressing neighborhood, out of the dead-end jobs, out of the cycle.

Now that Sam had a taste of prison, even if it was just the county lock-up, he realized he might have been mistaken. Going to prison did take you out of a bad situation, but it was only to put you in a worse one.

He heard the guards coming down the line, tapping their clubs on the bars. Free time was over, it was back to the cells for everyone. But something on the television caught his eye, a flash of a familiar image. There was a guy, someone he should have recognized, being led into a building, but it went by so fast he didn't catch it.

"Hey, turn that up," he called out.

No one responded. "Thanks for the help. Bastards."

Going to the TV, Sam turned up the volume himself. He saw the Justice Center, the outside of it anyway, and some blonde reporter standing in front of it.

" ... Was released minutes ago," the woman said, caught in mid-sentence. Sam saw "Christine Morton" at the bottom of the screen. "Once again, one of the three suspects in the Rich Kid Murders, Mark Kidd, has posted his bond."

"I'll be Goddamned," Sam muttered. He heard the guards getting closer, and the other inmates began to file toward the iron bars, ready to return to their tiny cells.

"There is no report as to why Mr. Kidd's bail was set so much lower than the other two suspects," Morton continued. "And there is no official word on whether Mr. Kidd has agreed to cooperate with the investigation."

"Let's go, Park," one of the guards called out. "TV time is over for today."

The camera moved in for a close-up on Morton. "There has been talk that Mr. Kidd may have made a deal with the DA, a deal that allows him immunity of some kind in exchange for testimony. But I have to stress that there is no confirmation of that, these are just rumors at this point."

"Mother fucker," Sam muttered.

The television clicked off, and a heavy, leather-gloved hand grabbed Sam's shoulder. Sam tensed then immediately relaxed, throwing his hands up. "Sorry, sorry," he said, allowing the officer to spin him around, "I was watching something interesting."

"I know what you mean," the deputy said, marching Sam to the door, "Christine Morton is somethin' else. But that doesn't mean you get to stay by yourself."

Sam got into line for the march back to his cell. It was done, nothing to be angry about. Mark had gotten himself out of jail after just a few days. Barely enough time to wear a groove in the mattress. But the more Sam thought about it, one thing became obvious.

The light of an idea sparked in Sam's head, a brainstorm coming on strong. He still had his contacts on the outside, Charlie's contacts really, but they owed him for a few things he'd made happen on his brother's behalf. They could get things done, they knew people who knew people. And they knew who Mark was. By the time Sam had shuffled back to his cell, he had it all worked out in his head, he knew what needed to happen.

It was time to call in a favor.

The sun had gone down hours before, but the heat of the day still lingered. Even in the darkness the air hung thick and heavy, a hot blanket hugging the low spots, making it difficult to sleep.

Red and blue lights flickered on and off, three patrol cars at the scene. This early in the morning, the police could block entire streets and only inconvenience a few people. It made crime scene investigation easier, but the lights drew bystanders. It seemed that everyone in Austin with no particular reason to be up this late meandered over to get a look.

Morton parked her car next to a police cruiser, nodding to the EMTs waiting patiently by their ambulance; the fact that they weren't feverishly working on a patient told Morton volumes about the condition of the victim.

She went to the line of yellow tape circling the police zone, scanning the scene for any familiar face. There, Officer Thorson, a barrel-chested veteran of fifteen years, who knew her and liked her.

"Any chance I can get a statement?" she asked.

Officer Thorson shrugged. His mustache had grown grayer since Morton first met him, and the lines on his face had gotten deeper.

"Looks like a hit and run," he said. "Poor guy's just walking along the street, minding his own business, and bam!" He shook his head sadly, at the loss of life, at the random cruelty. "The car that got him is long gone."

"Can I take a look?"

"I don't know," Officer Thorson said. "It's pretty gruesome. He lived long enough to crawl about ten feet. There's blood everywhere."

"I've seen some pretty bad stuff."

"All right …" Officer Thorson said, lifting the yellow tape to let her in. "But only for a second, and no pictures."

"No camera," Morton replied. If she needed pictures, she had a phone.

A mangled newspaper box lay halfway in the street, its last edition torn and scattered on the pavement. There was a dark spot on the sidewalk, but no skid marks that Morton could see. And there was a shoe. There was always a shoe.

The dark spot repeated, then became a trail, a wide, glistening patch painted on the sidewalk, leading to a congealing pool underneath a body. The hands and feet were twisted awkwardly, painfully, and Morton could only imagine the agony this man had suffered pulling himself along before his heart pumped all the blood out of his body.

"We don't officially know who he is yet," Officer Thorson said. "We're not supposed to touch the body until the coroner gets here."

"I recognize him," Morton said as she looked at the man's pale, broken face.

"We do too," Officer Thorson said. "Just not officially. Figured that's why you showed up. Bet you're not going to tell me who called you, either."

"Not a chance," Morton replied. She stared at the body, wondering how she could quantify the thing that was missing, the vitality a living person had that was absent from dead flesh. It was something mystical, and nothing she had ever been able to put a word to. It was the difference between Reilly Sutton before the first injection and after the third. Something had gone away, and that same something had fled from this body on the pavement.

"So what's the headline going to read?" Officer Thorson asked.

"I like to keep it simple," Morton replied. "'Mark Kidd Found Dead' pretty much tells the story, doesn't it?"

25

TRAVIS HAD EXPECTED HIS BROTHER to be a human volcano, rumbling with rage and moments from erupting. But Jake was calm. Eerie, sinister calm, his expression placid, his face as neutral as Travis had ever seen it.

Jake closed the conference room door and took a seat opposite Travis, looking him in the eyes. Seconds ticked off the clock in the room as the brothers locked gazes.

"I'd ask if you knew how serious what you've done is," Jake said at last, "but I think you understand already."

Travis swallowed, his mouth suddenly bone-dry, and nodded.

"I'd like to have whatever Mrs. Homayanpour gave you." Jake extended his hand, palm up.

Travis shook his head. "I can't do that."

Jake closed his eyes, resigned, but kept his hand stretched across the table. "No second chances."

"I can't be party to an execution, Jake," Travis protested. "If I give you that video, it's as good as putting the needle in Sutton's arm myself."

Jake pulled his hand back and sighed deeply. He looked into his brother's eyes again. "You concealed evidence. If Caroll knew about this, you'd be behind bars with bail set so high Dad could never get you out."

Travis broke out in a cold sweat. The flash drive was in his pocket. He could just hand it over and be done with this.

"Do what you think you have to."

For a moment—an instant—fury flashed across Jake's face. Then it was gone, and placid Jake was back. "You're putting me in a hell of a position. Damn you, Travis, I will not compromise myself or my job for you."

"I won't either," Travis replied, his voice stronger than his conviction. "I'm sorry, but you won't get to kill Reilly Sutton."

"I have investigators talking to Mrs. Homayanpour right now," Jake said sadly. "We're asking for a 'safety copy' from the original, telling her it's going to a special evidence locker. Total bullshit, but we can't let her know what really happened."

Travis's jaw dropped. "You're still going to do it? The death penalty?"

"Your Custer's Last Stand didn't make a bit of difference."

Though he had gone numb from head to toe, Travis stood, his knees threatening to buckle. "Then I quit."

"Only because it takes more paperwork for me to fire your ass," Jake replied. "Get your shit together and get out. We'll decide what to tell Mama later. Dad can get you a position at Lynch and Brockhurst."

"No." The numbness in Travis was slowly turning to anger, to driven purpose. "If I work there it's like … like still working for you. For the system. For a government that thinks it's okay to kill its citizens."

His face now pink, Jake slapped the table. "Trav, I'm keeping this quiet. For you. Don't be a martyr. You can have a conscience and still have a decent job."

"But I won't be a decent person," Travis replied. "I'd be just like you."

Jake breathed like a bellows, but for the first time in his life, Travis wasn't frightened.

"It might be better if I didn't see you for a week or so," Jake said through clenched teeth.

"I told you, Jake, I quit," Travis replied. "All of it. The DA's office, Lynch and Brockhurst, and you."

"Don't be an idiot," Jake said. "Think of what you're throwing away."

"I'd rather think of what I'm keeping," Travis replied as he walked out the door.

"Aren't you going to say anything?"

Travis's words echoed around the interview room, eventually dissipating against the cinderblock walls. He stood in a corner, facing the table where Sam sat, shackled. His client seemed more sullen than usual today, keeping his head down so his shaggy hair obscured his face. His eyes.

Finally, Sam shook his head. A slight movement, yet more than he'd done since he walked in.

"He was your friend."

Sam coughed but refused to look up.

Travis stared at Sam, trying to read the body language, straining to hear what remained unspoken. But Sam was a closed book. Or perhaps Travis was rattled enough that he couldn't focus. His breath was short, and his pulse throbbed in his ears. His fingers twitched with the overwhelming urge to shake Sam until the constables knocked down the door. Until something inside Sam broke. Until he looked Travis in the eye. Until the truth fell out.

"He was your friend," Travis continued, "and now he's dead."

Sam hid his eyes behind his hands. A huge sigh filtered from his lips. "Mark wasn't my friend."

"That's bullshit, Sam," Travis said, his voice calm and even. No sense getting upset. "You loaned him almost four hundred dollars."

Dark eyes shot toward Travis. "You know about that?"

"I know a lot of things," Travis replied. He walked from his corner to the barred window and ran his finger along the flaking, ancient paint. "More than you think I do."

"You don't know dick."

"I know you were friends with Mark Kidd. He was the third man in your crew that night. When one of you shot those two kids in the back."

"I barely knew him." Sam hadn't moved but he was so tense his knuckles were white. His arms had broken out in a thin sheen of sweat and his breath came in angry bursts, like a bull stuck in a rodeo cage. "And anyone who says otherwise can go to hell."

"Why don't you drop the tough guy act?" Travis tried not to seem annoyed. Or desperate. "Just for once, just for now, talk to me like a real human being. I'm on your side."

Sam muttered something under his breath, still with his head down, staring at the tabletop.

"If you have something to say," Travis responded, "be man enough to say it out loud."

"I said no one's on my side." Sam finally turned toward Travis, his face a mask of rage.

Travis held Sam's gaze, never flinching. He'd seen that kind of self-destructive fury before. In Reilly Sutton's eyes. Like with Sutton, Travis had never heard Sam apologize for inflicting his pain on others.

"Are you fucking kidding me?" Travis stared Sam down. "How long have I put up with this? With you?"

"I didn't ask for your help."

His fists clenched, and Travis bit the inside of his mouth to keep from exploding. Infuriating. He paced from the window to the corner and back again. Finally, he grabbed the chair across from Sam and fell into it.

"I didn't tell you," Travis said, leaning forward, "because I didn't want to get your hopes up. But I was going to work a deal with my brother. For Mark."

Sam's chin lifted and he eyed Travis suspiciously. "Fucker has his own lawyer."

"Doesn't need her now, does he?" Travis replied. "I wasn't representing him, I was trying to get a deal. Which would have included you."

Sam shook his head defiantly. "I don't need a deal."

Leaning in, Travis put his face inches from Sam's. "Hold your hands up."

"Fuck you."

Travis grabbed Sam's right hand and lifted. Sam's left hand rose with it and the silvered glint of handcuffs connected the two.

"If you keep this attitude," Travis said, "these aren't coming off. Ever. You don't need a deal? I haven't met a man who needed a deal more than you do right now."

Pulling his hands free, Sam turned in his chair, giving Travis as much of his back as he could.

"Mark was going to tell me what happened that night," Travis continued. "Everything. That's all anybody wants to know, even my brother. But now Mark's dead."

"He got what was coming to him," Sam muttered. "I just hope he knew what was about to happen, right before that truck took him out."

Could he really be that unfeeling? Was there that much busted glass inside this kid? Travis tried to meet Sam's eyes, tried to make a human connection, but Sam refused. His lips moved, barely, as if he were having a conversation with himself that Travis wasn't privy to.

Travis returned to the corner, his mind whirling as he tried to determine what Mark Kidd's death would do to his client's defense.

A sudden thought shook Travis. "How did you know that?"

Sam rattled his handcuffs, but said nothing. Travis rushed the table, slamming his hands down in front of his client.

"How did you know a truck hit Mark?" Travis demanded.

"I saw it on TV," Sam said.

"I saw the reports this morning, too. Nobody said 'truck.'"

"Then I read it in the newspaper, heard it on the radio. Whatever. Leave me the fuck alone."

"My brother told me all about it," Travis said. "No witnesses. The cops figure it was a truck, but they haven't told anyone. They kept that detail from the media."

Sam glared defiance at Travis. "I'm tired. I need to go back, get some rest. We're done."

With furious strength Travis grabbed Sam by the shoulders and shook him once. Hard. "You did it."

"Did what?" Sam said, the tiny flicker of a sinister smile playing on his lips. "I'm in jail, man."

Shocked, Travis collapsed into his chair. "Oh my God."

"God ain't got nothing to do with it."

Travis leaned back in his chair, breathing into his hands. It was almost too much to take in, almost too much to believe. But the truth was there, he could feel it in his soul.

"How did you do it? You know people. That's what Mark said. Did you make some calls?"

"One call," Sam said softly. "Is that what you want to hear?"

"I want the truth." Travis's fingers had gone cold, and his mouth was dry. "That's the only thing I want."

"Some guys owed me a favor," Sam said. "I called it in. Simple as that."

"You had Mark Kidd killed." Saying it out loud didn't make it any easier for Travis to take.

"I was afraid he was going to talk," Sam replied bitterly. "Only now you're telling me that was the plan all along. I really fucked it up. What else is new?"

"Oh, *Sam* ..." All the breath left Travis's body.

The room sat still and quiet, with nothing to break the silence. After what seemed like an eternity Sam leaned forward, his cuffs rattling on the metal table, and he looked Travis square in the eye, finally making direct, human contact with his attorney.

"I shot those kids."

The blood froze in Travis's veins. His hands quivered. He wanted to run from the room but his knees had turned to rubber. A satisfied smirk settled on Sam's lips.

"I pulled the trigger. Did you know I never fired a gun before? Turns out I'm a natural."

Travis tried to find the lie, tried to find the prison-born bravado in him, but there was none. For probably the first time in his life, Sam was telling the unvarnished truth.

"Why?" Travis managed to utter.

Sam shook his head. "Fucker was trying to drive off with five thousand dollars. I couldn't let him do that."

"They didn't have five thousand dollars," Travis said softly.

"I know that now," Sam said, shrugging. "That's okay. We didn't have any meth. Double-cross all around."

Travis's chest hurt like someone had dropped an anvil on his ribs. It was all so senseless. And *preventable.* So many things had to line up in precisely the wrong way to put Peter Carlisle and Shane Ablin on the wrong end of Sam's pistol. If either side had made even one— just *one*—good decision, none of this would have happened. Six lives would have continued on their trajectories uninterrupted. It all made Travis want to weep.

"At least I know," Travis sighed.

They fell into silence again.

"I'm a bad seed," Sam said at last. "Me and Charlie both, it's genetic or something. I belong in prison. Maybe I belong on death row."

"No one deserves to die," Travis said.

"You're out, right?" Sam said. "Done with me? It's okay, I understand."

Travis paused, not certain what words would come out of his mouth. "No, I'm still your attorney. This doesn't make any difference."

"Yeah, right," Sam scoffed. "You're fighting a different war, man. You're not in it for me."

Travis wanted to protest, he wanted to argue that Sam had it all wrong. But the man in prison orange proved eerily perceptive. And all too right.

"Jake, can you tell me why we're here?"

Velasquez stood at the end of the pool table, still with his suit coat on, watching as Jake lined up another shot.

"I spent a lot of time here when I was in college and law school," Jake said. He'd rolled up his cuffs and stuffed his tie into his jacket, which he'd draped over a bar stool. "I'd come shoot a few games when my mind needed a vacation."

"Okay," Velasquez replied. "But that doesn't answer my question."

Jake sunk the seven-ball, then stood straight. Smitty's hadn't changed much, still dark and humid, still row after row of pool tables and walls hung with failing neon beer signs, still the same disreputable clientele. This had been his haven. His sanctuary. Then the Sutton case came along and Smitty's changed for him. This was the first time he'd been in the place in ten years.

"I guess you can't smoke in here anymore," Jake muttered.

The air in the pool hall was surprisingly free of blue-tinged cigarette vapor. The absence robbed the place of its dingy ambiance, and a clear view across the room revealed just how shabby Smitty's really was.

"A guy named Buehl Smith used to own this place," Jake continued. "Smitty. I thought I knew him pretty well. Yesterday I tried to find him, and as far as I can tell he doesn't exist. He's not current on any state property records or driver's license. He hasn't paid the IRS in five years. So he's either dead with no death certificate on file anywhere, or he's cheating on his taxes. Guess I didn't know him at all."

Velasquez sighed with exaggerated patience. "Seriously, I have a lot of work to do. Why are we here?"

"We need to talk," Jake said, leaning against the pool table.

"Oh," Velasquez almost moaned. "That can't be good."

"No, no," Jake replied, "this is just something better done away from the office."

Velasquez paled, and it looked like he might throw up. Jake tried not to smile but couldn't help taking pleasure in his subordinate's discomfort.

Jake tossed the triangle onto the table and fished the balls out of the pockets. "I'll rack 'em, you break."

The waitress arrived with the two beers Jake had already ordered. Jake flipped her a twenty and then told Velasquez to take off his coat and grab a stick. With his distaste plain on his face, Velasquez reluctantly complied.

"Why did you want to find this Smith guy?" Velasquez asked.

Jake shrugged. "Old business. I'm pretty sure I owe him money. You know how to play nine-ball?"

Velasquez nodded noncommittally; clearly he had no idea. Jake racked the balls quickly, as if he had money riding on this game.

"So, ah, what is it you want to talk about?" Velasquez asked. As he inexpertly lined up the break he tried to appear nonchalant, but his hands shook. If he wanted to hold public office, the man was going to have to develop stronger nerves than that.

"Your future," Jake said.

Velasquez cleared his throat, took a deep breath, and smacked the cue ball. It was a decent break, a good beginning especially for someone who didn't know what he was doing. He looked to Jake, uncertain how to proceed.

"You didn't sink any balls," Jake explained. "My turn."

Velasquez took a sip of his beer, his hands still trembling. Jake lined up his first shot.

"You know, with all that's going on," Jake said, "I thought it would be best if we mapped out a few things. Maybe came to an agreement."

With a deft hit, he sunk the one-ball. The cue rolled to a stop, lined up perfectly for Jake to sink the two-ball.

"You know I'm going to run for DA," Velasquez said. Not a question.

Jake sank the two-ball and lined up on the three. He nodded.

"It's nothing personal," Velasquez said, too quickly. "I mean, I have to go for what I want, right? Just like you did."

"Don't worry," Jake said, easily sinking the three. "Like you said, you have to protect your interests. So do I."

Jake frowned. His shot on the four-ball wasn't the best. He could scratch. He lined it up slowly and carefully, getting the feel of the cue in his hands again. It also gave Velasquez time to stew.

"I've been doing a good job," Velasquez insisted. He was sweating even though Smitty's was cool and dry. "And I think it's time for me to move on. Move up."

Jake caromed the cue ball off two rails and sank the four-ball, leaving himself an excellent line on the five.

"Maybe so, but you're not going to be able to do that unless you have your name out in front of the public."

Jake paused his run on the table and took a draw off his beer, gratified to see the confusion on Velasquez's face.

"I'm sorry?"

"Nobody knows who you are," Jake explained as he bent back to the green felt and sank the five-ball with no effort.

"It's a little early for campaign signs," Velasquez said, leaning on his cue as if it were a walking stick. "I think I have a good strategist."

"Davis is one of the best," Jake agreed. "But that's not what I mean. No matter how many signs you have your name on, if the voting public doesn't know who you are, they won't vote for you. I had the Sutton case, my name and face were on TV for months. Love me or hate me, everyone in Austin heard my name. What have you done to make yourself known?"

Velasquez cradled his beer thoughtfully. His concerned expression said that until this moment, he had never really considered his lack of recognition. Jake used the lull in conversation to send the six-ball into a pocket.

"I guess you're right." Defeat colored Velasquez's words, and Jake almost felt sorry for him. Almost.

"You gotta think this stuff through, Bobby," Jake admonished as he lined up the seven-ball. "Don't rely on the behind-the-scenes guys to make your career for you. You're the one in the driver's seat. Take the wheel."

"This was supposed to just … fall into place," Velasquez said finally. "You're going to run for governor, I'm going for DA. It's all part of the cycle."

Jake tapped the seven-ball in. "This isn't kindergarten, it's not 'my turn, your turn.' Your opposition is just as dedicated to winning as you are. Maybe more."

Velasquez began to pace. His hands worked to loosen his tie as beads of sweat formed on his forehead just at his hairline.

Jake ignored his dithering subordinate, losing himself in the geometry of the table. Billiard balls were like people: Push this one into that one and they would both go off in different directions. They were all related to one another, and sometimes the least likely one could change the entire complexion of the table. Or you could nudge one just enough to put it into a corner, where it would see no action for the rest of the game.

"I'm not sure what you're telling me," Velasquez said, his voice shaky.

"If you're going to run for DA," Jake replied, "expect a fight. Even if you have Davis on your side."

With a deft tap, Jake spun the cue ball just enough to nudge the eight-ball. The ball teetered on the lip of the pocket, then rolled in. He grinned broadly; he hadn't lost his touch.

"It's just that … " Velasquez sputtered. "Governor is such an opportunity, I thought—"

"I want you to prosecute the Carlisle case," Jake interrupted.

"Pardon?" Velasquez said.

Jake lined up on the nine, the last ball sitting all alone, a simple shot. He had run the table, and Velasquez didn't seem to have noticed. "You've been working hard during pre-trial. I don't see why you shouldn't get the glory."

"I don't know what to say," Velasquez gasped.

"It's the only way to get you out there," Jake replied. "A high profile prosecution gets your name in the papers for free. Front page. All over the TV news too. Your opponent can't buy that kind of advertising."

Velasquez stared at Jake, waiting for the punch line, but there wasn't one. "You mean I'm the lead?"

"First chair," Jake said. He pointed his stick at the far side of the table. "Nine-ball, corner pocket."

A broad smile spread over Velasquez's face as he collapsed onto a bar stool. "Thanks, Jake. I won't let you down."

Jake tapped the cue ball solidly, driving the nine-ball into the pocket with authoritative finality.

"That's game," Jake said softly, almost under his breath. "I win."

26

DON'T LEAVE TOWN, OKAY? IF we need you again, we'll call you back to the stand," Ken Blevins said as he shook Travis's hand.

"I'm ready," Travis replied. Testifying had been nerve-wracking and he absolutely did not want to be up there again where he couldn't hide from accusing eyes. But he'd do it if he had to.

Blevins clapped him gently, almost sadly, on the shoulder. "I know what this cost you. I thank you, and Sutton thanks you."

Travis smiled wanly and took his leave. The idea of someone like Reilly Wayne Sutton grateful to him for anything was nauseating, but there were higher principles at stake. Which was what Travis told himself at night when he couldn't sleep.

He turned and headed for the back entrance, the one away from the press. He stopped short when his brother emerged from the court room. Jake stomped over, fists clenched.

"What the fuck, Trav?"

"You knew they were calling me."

"I knew they might call you," Jake snapped, "I never thought you'd go through with it."

"I had to testify, Jake, there was no other choice."

Higher principles. Travis testified for Sutton and against the DA's office to serve a greater purpose. And there was still one more thing he had to do.

"You're my brother," Jake began.

"You probably will get a capital conviction," Travis interrupted. "Slam dunk, right? But on the day they kill Reilly Sutton, I want you to remember that his death is your responsibility. His clock runs out because of you, Jake. No one else."

"You stupid … " Jake sighed. "Now that you're a witness, you're open for cross-examination. And this will be all over the news. That reporter woman is already sniffing around, asking tough questions. It's going to come out, Trav. The video. I won't be able to help. You're looking at obstruction of justice. At best."

Travis shrugged. *Higher purpose.* "If you want to charge me with something, then do it. That's the only way you're ever going to see my face again."

"What?" Confusion drained a little of the color from Jake's face.

"I told you, I quit," Travis replied. "The DA's office. Lynch and Brockhurst. You."

For nearly a minute, sixty precious seconds, Jake had nothing to say. Travis relished the confusion and consternation on his brother's face. Until it slowly transformed back into Jake's regular anger.

"You'd do that to your family? To Mama?" Jake snarled. "What kind of selfish—"

"I'm still part of the family," Travis replied. "But I don't ever want to see you again. I'm certain Shirley will send an invitation to the wedding. Don't bother with an RSVP."

The shocked outrage on Jake's face quickly hardened into granite resolve. "If that's the way you want it—"

"That's the way it has to be." Travis turned his back on Jake and headed for the exit.

Behind him, his brother's muttered cursing filled the hallway. Travis half expected Jake to tackle him, but with each shaking-knee step he took toward the exit, he got farther and farther away. As the tears welled up in his eyes, Travis prayed that no one would see.

Travis had shaved so close his face felt raw.

Shirley batted his fumbling hands away from his necktie and quickly knotted it for him. She pulled it too tight, then loosened it up again. She tugged down on his shirt and up on his pants and brushed his shoulders.

The first day of Sam's trial was making them both nervous.

Travis had been up late, going over his notes and practicing his arguments with Shirley sitting in for the judge. It had been like last-minute cramming for an exam, down to the blind panic. The time for preparations was over, and in less than two hours he would be standing before the judge and jury to argue against the death penalty for Sam Park.

The situation was not promising.

Even Shirley, his most ardent supporter, his *wife,* had not been easily swayed by his argument. Travis would be fighting an uphill battle to convince twelve strangers and a judge to come to his side. But it had to be done. There was no one else willing or able.

Shirley stroked his hair and kissed him on his stinging cheek.

"You're going to do great."

He hugged her and kissed her back, running a hand along her growing belly. He was nervous about becoming a father, and concerned for his wife's health and safety, but there was a corner of Travis's lawyer mind wondering how he might use that to his advantage. What judge could turn down a continuance based on the arrival of defending counsel's firstborn? Travis hated himself for thinking like Jake, but he had to do what he could to win for Sam.

With a shiver, he put the thought out of his mind. He didn't need tricks, he was prepared. He'd thought about nothing else but this trial for weeks, neglecting his paying clients without alienating them. He knew his own arguments and he'd prepared against every conceivable argument from the other side; there was no way he was going to lose the legal battle.

The jury was the wild card.

Travis knew that juries could reverse the best-laid, best-reasoned plans of the finest lawyers. There was no telling what they'd listen to, there was no telling whose side they were on until it was all said and done.

"I just wish it was Jake across the aisle," Travis replied. "I'd destroy him."

"Be nice, honey, he's your brother."

Travis shrugged on his suit coat. "It kills me that I can't figure out his angle. Velasquez is a decent attorney, but there are ten people in that office who could do a better job. A much better job. Why that guy?"

Shirley squeezed his hand reassuringly. "Don't worry about what you can't control."

"I know Jake," Travis muttered. "He's up to something."

"You need to eat before you go," Shirley commanded as she pulled him down the hallway. "And toast doesn't count."

Ten minutes later, and under his wife's watchful eye, Travis ate the last bit of his apple and finished his glass of orange juice. He went through his briefcase—again—making sure he wasn't forgetting anything. He walked Shirley to the front door, holding her hand tightly. Leaning down, he kissed her softly, lingering for just a moment.

"Go get 'em," Shirley said.

Opening the door, Travis saw something fall inward, landing at his feet. He reached down and picked up a long, clasped envelope, the kind he would have mailed legal documents in. On the front, in neat, black, handwritten letters were the words "For Sam Park's attorney."

"I'll throw that away," Shirley said, gently taking the envelope from her husband's hand. They never opened unaddressed mail, especially not random packages left on their porch.

"Hold on a second," Travis said. He knew that handwriting. "I think we need to see what's in here."

Shirley raised an eyebrow, but she handed the envelope over.

In a moment Travis had torn open the envelope and removed two pieces of paper—a printed e-mail message and a record of what looked like a police evidence receipt. He read them both closely, and his heart began to beat faster.

"I knew he was up to something."

At the courthouse, Travis threaded his way through the gauntlet of reporters waiting for him. Austin's television stations had sent their people, but teams from San Antonio, Houston, and Dallas crowded for space as well. News trucks were parked on the sidewalks, satellite uplinks extended, cables strung everywhere, each of the on-air personalities eager to get a word or two from the defense attorney. Travis passed them all by with a terse "No comment."

In the forest of media, Travis searched for one tree in particular, but Morton, of all people, was nowhere to be seen. With each step Travis took, he expected her to appear at his side, an unwelcome genie released from her bottle. She remained a ghost.

Through the security checkpoint, past the deputies and into the courtroom, Travis tried to keep his thoughts centered. All his carefully crafted arguments fled him, and he could only think of the envelope he carried, and how he was going to use what it contained.

Sitting at the defense table, Travis felt awkward, alone. The table could have seated four people comfortably, but Travis perched on one side by himself, like the unpopular kid in the school lunch room. In a few minutes the deputies would lead in Sam, who had no idea what Travis was about to do. No one did. Well, almost no one.

The prosecution arrived, four of them, with Velasquez in the lead. They took the table as if they were Marines taking a beachhead, each of them knowing exactly what to do and when to do it. The three junior DAs didn't look at Travis, but Velasquez's smug acknowledgement—a slight lift of the chin—conveyed the contempt they all had for their opposition.

"I think you and I should talk about a deal," Travis offered.

Velasquez glanced at his three subordinates, who all chuckled softly. "I'll pass. But thanks for giving me one last chance."

"You can't say I didn't put it on the table," Travis replied. "Remember that."

He didn't say anything, but the smirk on Velasquez's lips spoke for him. He and the other attorneys huddled together, whispering. Travis remembered those times, sitting at Jake's side; they were probably talking about where they would have lunch. One of the attorneys glanced behind the table, and stood sharply.

Travis turned, as the whole prosecution team did, to find Jake Lynch easing himself into a gallery seat. The DA was here after all, but only as an observer. Jake motioned his team to sit down, waving them off as they prepared to approach him. He turned to Travis, giving his brother a short nod.

The side door opened and the deputies led Sam Park in. He and Roger Laubach were being tried separately, Velasquez's choice to attempt a double-play on the death penalty. Handcuffed and shackled, Sam shuffled to his chair, his hair mostly hiding his face as he stared at the floor.

There was commotion in the gallery, and a word carried to Travis's ear, repeated over and over in mournful tones. "Soon. Soon."

Sam barely turned his head, but Travis scanned the faces until he saw them, Sam's parents, small and frail and courageous, watching their son with tears in their eyes. Sam coughed, burying his face in his hands.

The jury filed in, twelve citizens prepared to hear the evidence and hand down a death penalty conviction if one was warranted. A few of them made eye contact with Travis, most of them avoided it. Not an auspicious beginning, but Travis kept a brave face, more for Sam's parents than for Sam.

"All rise for Judge Esquivel," the bailiff called out.

The entire room stood, and the judge entered, a stern authority with white hair and black robes and a deadly serious demeanor. As the bailiff read the opening proceedings, Travis's fingers drummed nervously on his briefcase. He was going to have to break protocol, and that was not going to go over well in this court.

"All right," Judge Esquivel said, tapping his gavel, "let's get this started. Counsel knows how this goes, but for the jury I'm going to need to explain a few things—"

"Excuse me, your honor?" Travis said, rising.

"Already?" Judge Esquivel snapped, taking off his reading glasses. "I expected interruptions, but not from your side, Mr. Lynch. Not so soon, anyway."

"Your Honor, I have this morning received … " Travis paused, resisting the urge to glance back at Jake. "May I approach the bench?"

The judge shook his head. "I'm not playing that. Spit it out, Mr. Lynch."

"I received documents that indicate the DA's office is suppressing evidence," Travis said.

The court erupted, everyone talking and exclaiming at once. The judge tapped his gavel three times, restoring order, though some people continued to whisper.

"Your Honor, this is ridiculous," Velasquez protested. "We haven't even started yet, and he's trying these crazy tricks."

"Mr. Lynch," the judge said, "I assume you actually *do* have documents. Otherwise you'd be wasting this court's time, and you know that's a very, very bad idea."

"Yes, sir," Travis said. He took the pages from his briefcase. "I have e-mails and property records, obtained just this morning, from Tim Machajewski. He works in the police evidence lab, and Mr. Velasquez has coerced him into hiding evidence."

"What?" Velasquez cried out, as the court erupted again. The junior DAs sat stunned, and Velasquez went white. He turned, searching for someone in the back of the room. Travis followed his eyes, and saw … Dave Carlisle? who he quickly lost again in the bustle and commotion.

The judge pounded his gavel again and again, finally gaining control of the courtroom. "I need to see both counsels in my chambers. Right now."

Judge Esquivel put the pages down and took off his reading glasses. With a heavy sigh he leaned back in his chair, shaking his head.

"If what this man says is true," he tapped the papers, "you're in a lot of trouble, Mr. Velasquez."

The Assistant DA stood beside Travis, both of them in front of the judge's desk. Velasquez shook from head to toe, all traces of his old bravado and self-assurance vanished like morning fog in sunshine.

"He found the gym bag in Mark Kidd's house," Travis said, his temper rising. "He didn't log it as evidence, and he brought it to the police forensics lab anyway, completely violating the chain of custody."

"Sir," Velasquez pleaded with the judge, "I believe Mr. Machajewski's analysis—"

"That evidence is completely contaminated!" Travis exploded.

Judge Esquivel held a hand up. "I understand your passion, Travis, but you of all people need to rein it in a little."

A knock on the door sounded, and the bailiff ushered Jake into the judge's chambers. The DA didn't acknowledge his brother and kept a stone-chiseled face, the aggrieved parent called to account for his errant child's behavior.

The judge turned to Velasquez. "I'm going to find the truth sooner or later, so it might as well be sooner."

Still trembling, Velasquez nodded. "The pistol did come from a gym bag found in Mark Kidd's home. But the fingerprint analysis—"

"Seems pretty conclusive," the judge interrupted. "One set. Only. Matching Mr. Park's fingerprints exactly. On the bullets, too. I would think the prosecutor would want this piece of evidence smack front and center, not discarded and suppressed."

"What the fuck, Bobby?" Jake said. "Whose side are you on?"

Velasquez had gone from pale to gray in a matter of seconds. Sweat beaded on his forehead and he swayed slightly. Travis edged closer, ready to catch him in case he passed out.

"What's your explanation, Mr. Velasquez?" the judge stared him down.

"It's pretty clear what he was—" Travis began.

"Mr. Velasquez is the only voice I want to hear right now," the judge interrupted.

"Dave Carlisle," Velasquez replied slowly, struggling to maintain his composure, "he didn't want his son's name … he wanted things kept quiet, out of the news. No more publicity. We thought opposing counsel would file a motion to dismiss, and with no murder weapon, we wouldn't have any reason to object."

"You concealed evidence?" Jake snarled. "To keep Carlisle's drug-dealing son out of the news?"

Jake had missed his calling; he should have been an actor. The judge and Velasquez seemed convinced his outrage was real.

"Sir, you can't let this prejudice the proceedings," Velasquez pleaded to the judge. "We can regroup, review everything, make sure discovery has been…"

"Dammit, Bobby!" Judge Esquivel barked. "You can't recover from this! It's over! You're over!"

Jake took Velasquez by the arm and pushed him into a chair. "You need to sit. Take some deep breaths."

The judge settled back in his chair. "I'm going to need to talk to Mr. Machajewski."

"I have officers escorting him here as we speak," Jake said.

"When he confirms what the defense is saying," the judge continued, "I'll have to declare a mistrial."

"Then we'll just re-try him," Velasquez said, glancing back at Jake. "Right?"

"*You* won't," Jake said. "And we don't dare go for the death penalty again. Not after this fiasco."

Travis caught Jake's eye just then, the briefest moment. He saw relief, not anguish; poise and not worry. The DA should have been enraged. The brother Travis knew would have been angry enough to chew leather. But he wasn't.

"You may want to take a few days," the judge said, "get your thoughts together. I'm going to have you up on charges, Mr. Velasquez. And anybody else who helped you do this stupid thing, up to and including David Carlisle. Now get the hell out of my office."

Travis flinched as he stepped into the hall. Down at the end, a crowd of reporters had formed behind an intimidating mass of microphones, cameras, and lights, with the bailiffs the only obstacle that prevented them swarming down the hall like the locusts they were. Travis turned the other way.

Jake stood there, hands on his hips, wearing a solemn expression.

"Very slick," Travis said. "I don't know whether to shake your hand or punch you."

Jake shrugged. "I have no idea what you're talking about."

"Using me to do your dirty work," Travis replied.

A slight smile played on Jake's lips but he said nothing.

"You left that envelope on my doorstep."

Jake's grin never faded. "What envelope?"

"I was your clerk for almost a year," Travis continued. "I recognize your handwriting. I didn't realize you know where I live."

"I'm the DA. I know lots of things people think I don't."

"Like who's concealing evidence?"

"Ah, you help a guy in the evidence lab with his divorce for free, and he owes you a favor or two," Jake said. "You're not the only one who does pro bono work from time to time."

"What did this Velasquez guy do to piss you off?" Travis asked.

Jake shrugged. "Doesn't matter. He was looking for a new job anyway. And now there's no way we can charge Sam Park with a capital crime; the evidence against him is compromised. He'll never be on death row. You got what you wanted."

"Are you sure that's not what you wanted, too?"

Jake looked away and cleared his throat but said nothing.

Travis pointed down the hall, where the media crowd lurked. "Are you going to talk to them?"

"It's part of the job," Jake sighed.

"Not mine, thank God," Travis said.

They shook hands, and the brothers parted ways—Jake going to meet the reporters, Travis ducking out the back door.

"Hey, Trav," Jake called.

Travis turned around.

"See you at brunch Sunday."

27

TRAVIS SAT ON A BENCH *in the courthouse all by himself as people came and went. No one talked to him, no one even acknowledged him. The corridor might as well have been empty except for him.*

He knew it was going to be bad. But it was the kind of knowing he kept in his head, not the kind he knew in his heart. Now that it had happened it felt like his insides were hollow, like someone had torn them out and left him a shell.

"Here's another one, courtesy of Christine Morton."

A newspaper landed in Travis's lap, with the headline screaming "Brother Betrayal" with his picture centered underneath. Travis looked up to find Jake at his side, the only person willing to admit he existed.

Travis looked away.

"Still with the silent treatment?" Jake asked. "You can be pissed at me, but you know it's your own fault."

Travis refused to look up. If he was alone, so be it. If following his principles made him a pariah, that was a price he was willing to pay.

"I told you this would happen," Jake continued. "You need to stay out of sight."

"I can't," Travis muttered as he stared at his shoes, "I have to see this through to the end."

"You're only making it worse," Jake snapped. "Do you look at the jury when you're in there? They hate Sutton. And they hate you."

"They don't need to like me," Travis said.

"Of course they do," Jake said. "They won't listen otherwise. Same thing with these reporters. You need them on your side, not against you. For God's sake, Morton's making her career out of destroying yours."

Travis shook his head.

Jake sighed. "You can't do it by yourself."

"I will if I have to," Travis replied.

"You're just determined, aren't you?" Jake said. "Life's lonely without your family."

"It's lonelier without your conscience."

Jake didn't say another word, just walked away, leaving Travis alone in the crowd.

"You know this isn't over," Travis said. He leaned against the far wall of the interview room, where dim sunlight filtered through the filthy glass. "Your bail is still half a million dollars."

"It ain't so bad," Sam said with a shrug. "They put me in my own cell. I get to exercise alone. Working on my lay-up."

"I don't think you understand," Travis said. "The DA is going to try you for murder."

"But not the death penalty, right?"

Now it was Travis's turn to shrug. He'd been in virtual seclusion for the past week, filing motions and following the judicial process. Despite the rebukes from the DA's office and restraining orders from Judge Esquivel, the media circus still had not folded up its tents. Every day Travis received a stack of new requests for comment, and the reporters camped out in their vans up and down his street.

"As far as I know, the DA's office will not pursue a capital indictment."

"Cool," Sam replied. "I can handle a murder rap."

Travis wanted to jump out of his skin. "No, you can't. You're looking at life in prison."

"Better than dying on a table."

Travis kept his cool. Barely. "Prison is not the county lock-up. You might think you're tough, but you're not. Not like those guys. Prison breaks you, Sam. I've seen it, with a guy ten times tougher than you think you are. You have to take this seriously."

Leaning back in his chair, Sam looked at Travis as if seeing him for the first time. "You're for real, aren't you?"

"Excuse me?" Travis replied, confused.

"I thought you were full of shit," Sam said. "You know, a poser, like those Westlake fucks."

Travis raised an eyebrow.

"I can smell the money coming off you, man," Sam explained. "I thought you were a trust-fund kid. Build houses for Habitat for Humanity, a member of Greenpeace, give to public radio. Like that."

"Guilty," Travis said.

"But you're on the level. You really do care."

Travis nodded.

"Then you're a moron," Sam sneered.

"You're probably right," Travis admitted. "A smart man would have given up on you weeks ago. A brilliant man would never have taken your case in the first place."

"See? In the yard, I'd get punched for insulting you. Here you just agree with me. Idiot."

Travis shook his head at his client's desperate swagger.

"You think you're on your own," Travis said. "For everything. Whatever you want, you're going to have to make it happen by yourself. Am I right?"

Sam shrugged and nodded.

"Well, you didn't do this by yourself," Travis said. "You needed help, and you got it."

"What do you want?" Sam muttered. "A ribbon? You did your job, big fuckin' deal."

So guarded, so cautious. Travis wondered if that was what he'd been like ten years ago.

"Tell me something," Travis said. He took the seat across from Sam. "That night, when you went to the construction site? Why did you take a gun?"

"For protection, man," Sam blurted. "Jeez, you really are stupid."

"You didn't think those guys were a threat. Not really. Three high school punks facing off against three tough guys from the wrong side of town? What kind of contest is that?"

Sam's posture changed, and he lost the boastful pride he'd been taking in his misdeeds. "They could have had a gun, too."

"Those guys?" Travis replied. "Hardly. You didn't bring the gun for them, did you? You didn't need it for high school kids. You needed it for someone you couldn't handle on your own. Who was it? Mark? Roger? Both of them?"

Sam stared at Travis with big eyes. He clearly hadn't expected anyone to figure that out. His lips moved as if someone else were working them. "Mark. Only Mark."

Travis's heart fell. He wanted so badly to believe that Sam was a victim of circumstance, that everything he'd done had been a series of tragic errors, fateful missteps.

"Why?" Travis desperately wanted to know. He needed to know.

For a long time, Sam said nothing. He stared at the table, tracing patterns with his fingers.

"That bastard deserved it."

Travis said nothing, holding Sam's icy gaze.

"He thought he was better than me. Than us. He tried to make himself into … into you."

"Are you saying it was because Mark wanted to go to college?"

"You are what you are!" Sam exploded.

An officer appeared at the door, and Travis waved him back.

"Even though you pretend you're not, you're just some rich fuck from the right side of the tracks. I'm trash from the wrong side. So was Mark. He thought he was going to break out, thought he was going to be like you someday, get an office job, live in a nice place instead of the rat hole he was born into."

Despite his suspicions, Travis was still astonished to hear Sam admit his motive. "You wanted to kill Mark because he was trying to better himself?"

Sam leaned back in his chair as far as the shackles would allow. "I told you, I belong in prison. This is where I deserve to be."

Travis wanted to tell Sam that it wasn't true. But he didn't really know. His mind was changing, slowly, on certain things. Maybe someone like Sam didn't have a place in regular society.

"I think I understand," Travis said, rising.

"Let me guess," Sam said. "I'm going to have to find another lawyer."

"That's probably for the best," Travis replied.

"'That's probably for the best,'" Sam mocked. "Listen to yourself."

Travis went to the door, motioning the deputy to let him out. "Maybe I should."

Standing in the upper lobby of the Driskill Hotel, Mel Davis clasped Jake's hand and slapped him collegially on the back. "Too bad it didn't work out."

"We'll get 'em next time," Val Lynch added, unenthusiastically.

Davis brushed his thick white mustache thoughtfully as he regarded Jake. "Velasquez was a huge bust, and we don't have anyone to replace him. Looks like you're stuck running for District Attorney again. You okay with that?"

More than okay, Jake thought, though he kept the words inside. "It just wasn't meant to be. Besides, I think I'm better suited for DA. Governor Lynch doesn't sound right."

"What about Dave Carlisle?" Val asked, making Jake cringe. Sometimes his father was like a steamroller when it came to sensitive subjects.

Downing the last of his drink gave Davis a pause to reflect. He seemed genuinely sad. "Well, Dave's got some troubles of his own now. I think we're going to give him time to work those out."

"So you got an open spot?" Val asked. Jake blushed, embarrassed for his father.

Davis nodded. "Looks like."

"I can pull up a chair to help out if you need," Val volunteered. "I still keep in touch, I keep my hand in."

"You know, that's not the worst idea I ever heard," Davis replied. He clapped Val on the back with a resounding thud. "Come by the house tonight, we'll talk it over."

With a hearty handshake and a wave, Davis took his leave, making his way slowly out of the lobby and down the stairs, stopping to greet people along the way.

"He didn't pay for his drink," Val remarked.

"I'll cover it," Jake replied. "I guess I owe him that much. I kind of screwed him over."

Jake's father opened his mouth to speak but thought better of it. He mulled it over for another moment while Jake waited patiently.

"You're better at this than I was," Val finally said. "Both the politics and the lawyering."

"No, Dad …"

"You know it and I know it," Val interrupted. "Mel probably knows it, too. I used to wonder about you, Jake. Whether you were living up to your potential. Whether you were happy with what you were doing. I don't wonder any more. You're right where you need to be. I can't imagine you doing anything else."

"Me neither," Jake said. "But I know the ride's gotta end sometime. This past month made that clear."

"You should figure out your next move," Val said. "Before somebody makes it for you."

He drained his bottle of beer and hugged Jake tight.

"Say hi to Mama for me," Jake called out as his father ambled away.

Jake eased down into one of the lobby's thick, overstuffed leather chairs. For once in his life, he was going to ignore the schedule and pretend there were no clocks. He sipped slowly from the tumbler of bourbon in his hand, letting the alcohol trickle down his throat to warm his stomach.

"Anybody ever say you can take a flop like a pro?"

Morton appeared at Jake's elbow, her own glass in hand. Jake hadn't seen her come up the stairs; she must have already been lurking in the shadows.

He ignored her.

"Seriously, Jake," Morton continued, "that was pure genius in that court room. And you didn't even lift a finger."

"I have no idea what you're talking about," Jake replied.

With his acknowledgement, Morton took a seat beside him.

"Don't take this the wrong way, but you don't come across as … *astute* as you really are."

"You saying I'm not as dumb as I look?" Jake replied.

Morton waved over a waiter and ordered another drink. "That's not what I said. But, yes, that's an accurate restatement."

"Sometimes it pays to have people underestimate you."

"I'll bet," Morton said. "I assume you're running for DA again next year?"

"Best to stick to what you know," Jake said. "I don't know how to be governor."

"Oh, your wife—Rita?—she's got to be super pissed." Morton put a foot up on the coffee table between them. "It's hard to give up the governor's mansion when it was so close."

Jake shook his head. "It was never close."

They sat together in silence, listening to the conversations around them, just another two faces in the crowd. The waiter returned with Morton's drink, deferentially setting it in front of her.

"What do you want, Christine?" Jake asked.

Morton took her whiskey, three fingers of turpentine fire water Jake could smell from where he sat. With one gulp she downed the whole glass, asking the waiter for another before he could move away.

"I've had a few conversations since this 'Rich Kid Murders' thing started. Ones that made me reconsider the way I do my job. I haven't approached people as people, you know? I see them as obstacles. Or sources. I think I could do my job better if I changed my approach."

Jake searched her face for any trace of sarcasm or insincerity, but there was none. Maybe she was drunk, but she seemed truly remorseful.

"Thank you. Apology accepted."

Morton scoffed. "You wish. I'm just trying to explain myself."

"Is that all you wanted?" Jake prodded.

Morton brushed her blonde hair off her forehead and locked eyes with him. "Almost. There's one thing that's puzzled me for years. I never could figure this out, and I hate things I can't figure out."

"How far back are we going?"

"The Sutton case," Morton replied. "Your brother. Why did he change sides?"

"You didn't wonder that when you were using him for target practice every day?"

Morton sighed. "I told you I've been rethinking my approach, and what I did to Travis is maybe the start of that. Why did he turn on you?"

Jake held his arms helplessly wide. "Your guess is as good as mine."

The waiter returned with Morton's next drink. She sipped this one carefully, watching Jake closely.

"You're sandbagging."

A tiny smile crossed Jake's lips. "Not at all."

"Goddamn it, Lynch," Morton blurted, "you wouldn't be DA if it weren't for me putting your picture in every newspaper and on every TV screen. You owe me."

"Not long ago, you reminded me we weren't friends," Jake countered. "I don't think I owe you anything."

Morton grimaced her frustration. "Tell me the truth at least. You do know why he testified for the defense."

Jake nodded.

"But you're not going to share that information with me."

Jake shook his head.

Glowering into her drink, Morton sank back into the deep leather cushion. "God, I hate you."

28

WHEN SHIRLEY ASKED HIM IF it would make him uncomfortable, Travis said no. But now that Jake was here, on the back porch with a bottle of cold beer in hand, Travis had to reassess. While this technically wasn't Jake's first time on the property, it was the first time he'd been invited, and Travis just wasn't used to seeing his big brother anywhere, let alone in his home and office. For his part, Jake seemed a little put off as well, but perhaps not for the same reasons as Travis.

"Is this a new barbecue?" Jake ran his hand along the shiny stainless steel.

Travis tossed more burgers onto the grill. "We got it a week ago."

"You lock it up at night, right?"

Travis looked to see if his brother were kidding, which he wasn't. "Jake, this is a perfectly safe neighborhood."

Jake frowned. "Sure. These things usually come with a way you can chain them down."

"No one's going to steal my barbecue," Travis replied, exasperated. "Besides, we stick it in the garage when we're not using it."

Travis pointed at the slowly-sliding-downhill shed across the back yard, a building that looked like it might collapse at the slightest touch.

"That ought to scare anybody off," Jake muttered.

Eric and Heather raced past, shooting each other with squirt guns.

"They're going to have a new cousin before long," Travis said. "I think it would be good for them to get to know her."

"You saying you want me around more often?" Jake asked.

"Well, your kids at least," Travis replied. "If you're not afraid they're going to get tetanus from a rusty nail or catch poverty or something."

Jake had no reply, he just watched the children as they tore around the backyard, soaking each other.

"When're the burgers going to be ready?" Rita asked as she carried a bowl of sliced watermelon to the table.

"Ten minutes," Jake replied before Travis could open his mouth.

Rita disappeared back inside and Travis leaned in close to his brother. "How's she dealing with it?"

"Day by day," Jake replied. "I think she was already picking out curtains for the governor's mansion. How's Shirley?"

Travis flipped a burger. "Getting tired. Her legs hurt. At least we're past the morning sickness."

Jake laid a hand on Travis's shoulder. "How about you? You ready to be a father?"

Travis paled. "Hell no. Scares the crap out of me."

"It did me too, twice," Jake replied. "But then you get this little pink, helpless thing and you love it more than you loved anything ever and you get your shit together and act like a father. You'll be fine."

Eric and Heather ran past them going the other way, yelling about refilling their squirt guns.

"Jake, look, ten years … " Travis stuttered, "that was too long to hold a grudge. Too long to shut you out. It was childish."

Jake took the spatula from Travis and rolled the hot dogs back and forth on the grill. "Yeah, well, I didn't call you, either. It takes two of us to be that stupid."

"I was thinking," Travis continued, "about kids and family and, you know. Business."

"Oh?" Jake replied. "Headed for a corner office at Lynch and Brockhurst?"

"God no," Travis laughed. "At least not right now. Claire is doing fine and doesn't need me getting in her way. But I was thinking, maybe, one day, when you're finished being DA or governor or whatever you end up doing …"

Jake's eyebrows raised. "You and me? The Lynch boys, together again?"

"Think about it. It's a long-term option. The Lynch boys and girl. You, me, Claire. It could work."

"Or it could explode," Jake laughed. "Claire's more stubborn than both of us put together."

"Why are you dumbasses talking about me?" Claire had come around the side of the house, carrying a pink cardboard bakery box. Eric and Heather ran to hug her and to peer into the box.

"No reason," Travis replied. "You're just in time, we're almost ready to eat."

The back door opened and Mae and Val Lynch emerged onto the now-crowded back porch.

"Whose idea was it to have Sunday brunch over here?" Mae called out. "I want to shake their hand."

"That would be Shirley," Travis answered. "She figured you could use a break."

"Amen to that," Mae said as she hugged both her boys tight. "It's good to see you boys together and not throwing punches. Let's keep it that way, understand?"

Travis and Jake exchanged a glance, the kind of shared glance only brothers understood.

"I'm not sure we can guarantee that, Mama," Travis replied. "But we'll try."

A NOTE ABOUT THE BOOK

WHILE I DON'T HAVE ANY special expertise (and I'm not an attorney), I do have a reason for writing this novel. A friend of mine—a prosecuting attorney from Dallas—inspired it before he died. He worked for the Texas Fourteenth Court of Appeals, which hears the majority of death penalty cases in the state. He used to tell me that death penalty cases often seem murky and ambiguous from a layman's point of view, even though the facts are usually very cut-and-dried. He wanted to do a television show that explored that hazy area, where the facts might not be all *strictly* factual. He died before we could start any project together, so I created this story to try to accomplish his vision. It's taken me a few years to get the story to a quality I feel does justice to him and his career, and it's a work I'm proud of.

ABOUT THE AUTHOR

DON HARTSHORN is an author, freelance editor, volunteer mediator, and globetrotter, and he draws inspiration for his stories both from man's highest aspirations and from his petty, grimy motivations. After traveling the world for the US government and doing time as a prisoner of Corporate America's well-oiled machine, this Texas native has come home to roost at last in San Antonio. And there he'll stay—until the next big adventure comes calling.

CONNECT WITH DON

Sign up for Don's newsletter at

www.donhartshorn.com/free

To find out more information visit his website:

www.donhartshorn.com

Facebook

www.facebook.com/groups/2103015970026616

Twitter

@donhartshorn

GET BOOK DISCOUNTS AND DEALS

Get discounts and special deals on our bestselling books at

www.TCKpublishing.com/bookdeals

ONE LAST THING …

Thank you for reading! If you enjoyed this book, I'd be very grateful if you'd post a short review on Amazon. I read every comment personally and am always learning how to make this book even better. Your support really does make a difference.

Search for *The Guilty Die Twice* by Don Hartshorn to leave your review.

Thanks again for your support!

www.ingramcontent.com/pod-product-compliance
Lightning Source LLC
Chambersburg PA
CBHW031957120726
47898CB00002BA/557